Passage
ON THE
TITANIC

Passage
ON THE
TITANIC

a novel

ANITA STANSFIELD

Covenant Communications, Inc.

Cover image credit line *Retro Woman* © Peter Zelei, iStockphotography.com; *The Titanic on the Eve of Departure* (oil on canvas), Crossley, Harley (Contemporary Artist) / Private Collection / The Bridgeman Art Library International.

Cover design copyright © 2012 by Covenant Communications, Inc.

Published by Covenant Communications, Inc.
American Fork, Utah

Printed in the United States of America
First Printing: February 2012

18 17 16 15 14 13 12   10 9 8 7 6 5 4 3 2 1

ISBN-13: 978-1-60861-856-9

For Irene.
And to all of the passengers and crew of the *Titanic*:
the more than fifteen hundred who died with her that night
and the seven hundred and five survivors, who suffered most.
May you all rest in peace.

And a special thank you to Gary Cook,
who made this story happen.

AUTHOR'S NOTE

When I was told the story of Irene Colvin Corbett, a quiet stirring awakened in me, and in time I knew that I needed to tell her story. I have come to believe that it was something I had agreed to do in another time and place. It is my deepest wish that Irene and her family have made peace over the tragedy that took her life in 1912.

This is the first time that I have attempted to weave real people into the lives of fictional characters. I humbly petition my readers to be patient with me in any way that I may have fallen short in this endeavor. Allow me to clarify where those lines are crossed in order to avoid any confusion. Irene's story is true, and I have done my best, based on the information available, to accurately portray the kind of woman I believe her to be. William Thomas Stead is also a real person, and I have also tried to portray him accurately. Reading his documented interviews with young women in Ella's situation prompted me to make that a part of the story. He actually did write two pieces of fiction that seemed to have some foreboding implications about what happened to the *Titanic*. The story of the Mormon elders who were supposed to be on the *Titanic* is also true. I invite my readers to take advantage of the rich resources on the Internet and find out more about these great people, since I have only scratched the surface in honoring them and the part they played in the *Titanic* drama.

Beyond this, all of the characters portrayed in this book are fictional, although I hope that seeing the story unfold through their eyes offers an accurate scope of how it must have been to experience the tragedy firsthand. All of the information portrayed about the *Titanic* and the events surrounding it have been written about in an accurate way to the best of my ability. I hope that in reading this book you might acquire a greater understanding about the event, information that you might not have known before; but there is so much more to be learned. Pardon the pun, but I was only able to portray the tip of the iceberg in regard to all that I discovered through my research.

The very name *Titanic* implies the enormity of undertaking an attempt to tell the story and add this book to the many books and films and other forms of media that have endeavored to tell other views of the same tale. For my own storytelling style and purposes, it was not so much the technicalities and facts of the event that I felt were important to relate, but I chose rather to focus on the human element, the emotional and psychological impact on the lives affected by this monumental disaster. And we are affected still today. I believe our human fascination with the event—one hundred years later—is greatly tied into the way it forces us to face our own views of mortality. The *Titanic's* tragic demise stands as a vivid metaphor of man's pride and the need for God in our lives. Whether the disasters we face in life are personal or global, our connection to God is the only path to finding peace. I hope this book offers that message to all who read it.

PROLOGUE

The Atlantic Ocean — April 15, 1912

Ella could hardly breathe as the shock of icy water grabbed hold of her feet and ankles. She looked down as if her eyes might convince her of what seemed impossible for her mind to believe. Lifting the hem of her skirts out of the water, she watched the fabric dripping and heard the sound of the drips intermittently hitting the water, like the span of time between the flash of distant lightning and the ensuing echo of thunder. It seemed to take several heartbeats for her mind to absorb the message. It was true! The *Titanic* really was sinking! It could no longer be denied as a possibility too horrible to consider. The life belt she wore seemed inconsequential in light of the temperature of the water in which she stood. What point might there be to floating in such water, when its icy fingers promised to strangle the warmth out of any blood flowing through human veins? Ella gasped as a familiar hand took hold of her arm with an unfamiliar force, startling her back to the moment.

"Don't just stand there," Irene ordered and turned Ella around on the stairs. "We've got to get out of here. Getting on one of those lifeboats is our only hope of surviving this."

"What about the children?" Ella demanded, resisting Irene's firm tugging. "What about—"

"You mustn't think about that now," Irene said, exerting more effort in moving Ella along quickly.

Ella's feet felt bitterly cold as she dragged them up the stairs, but her heart froze in her chest at Irene's implication. She stopped in her tracks and stubbornly resisted Irene's efforts to budge her. "What on earth do you mean?" she asked, as if Irene might actually have a sensible response to such a question.

Irene came back down two steps to face Ella directly. The chill in Ella's feet rushed all the way up her body and back down again as this woman she'd come to call her dearest friend in all the world looked into her eyes with a gaze so intense and foreboding that Ella found it difficult to breathe. "Listen to me well, my friend," Irene said in a voice that matched the intensity of her eyes. "I don't know how all of this will end, but I know what I have to do, and I know what *you* have to do."

"How could you possibly know *that*?" Ella insisted.

"I've explained to you more than once how such a thing is possible, but now is not the time to quibble over details." Tears appeared suddenly in Irene's eyes, tears so hot that Ella almost expected steam to rise off of them. Ella wanted to know if they were tears of fear or of some kind of resolve. She suspected the latter but didn't have a chance to ask before Irene headed up the stairs again, dragging Ella along. "We must hurry," was all she said.

Conversation became difficult in their earnest trek toward the lifeboats that were stretched out along the massive deck of the ship. Chaos and noise threatened to swallow them, but Irene pressed forward as if she were a torpedo aimed at a very specific target. By some miraculous means that Ella could not account for while her brain was in shock and her surroundings were in pandemonium, she found herself scrambling into a lifeboat, aided by the capable hand of a uniformed member of the crew. She had to squeeze herself in but still eased over as far as she could to allow room for Irene, certain her friend was right behind her. She was barely seated when the lifeboat jolted into movement, and she realized it was being lowered. Sitting next to her was a young woman, crying and waving good-bye to a man near her age standing on the deck.

"No!" Ella shouted and tried to stand but could not find the balance to do so. "No!" she shouted louder and tried again, gripping the edge of the boat as if she might leap out of it to reunite herself with her beloved Irene.

"You've got t' sit down, miss," she heard a male voice say, and a firm hand on her shoulder made it impossible to ignore the command. But Ella's eyes were connected to Irene's. In a matter of a few seconds, all they had shared through these months of friendship raced through Ella's mind. Irene had given hope to the hopeless and life to the doomed. Ella had been both. How could they possibly be separated by whatever this terrifying disaster might entail?

Ella convinced herself in the next few seconds that Irene would get into another lifeboat and they would soon be reunited. She shouted toward her, hoping to be heard above the din. "I'll see you soon. Go and find yourself a seat and—"

"Whatever happens," Irene called back, and even from the distance Ella could see those steamy tears once again glimmering in her eyes, "you must live your life to its fullest. Promise me."

Ella hesitated, refusing to accept the implication that they might *not* see each other again. "Promise me!" Irene shouted.

"I promise!" Ella called back. After all that Irene had done for her, how could she refuse *anything* this great woman might ask of her?

Irene's countenance softened and she actually smiled. "All will be well," Irene called back, her voice becoming more difficult to hear, and her face more difficult to see, as the lifeboat was lowered farther toward the frigid, black ocean below. "I know what I have to do," Irene shouted, as if she desperately needed Ella to know. "Whatever happens, never forget . . . that I know what I have to do, and all will be well."

While Ella was trying to think of appropriate words to say in return, something that could be shouted with the hope of being heard amidst the chaos, the lifeboat jolted as the ropes on one side slid a little more quickly than on the other. The frightened voices of the women and children in the boat with Ella distracted her from her conversation. When Ella looked up again at the deck of the mighty ship, becoming ever farther away, Irene was no longer there.

CHAPTER ONE
Moment of Decision

London, England — One Year Earlier

ELLA BROWN WALKED AT AN unusually hurried pace through the dirty streets that had become so distastefully familiar to her. She shut out the sounds of crying babies and begging children, unable to consider the possibility that her own child might one day be among them. She refused to take in the smells of rotting garbage, and carefully avoided the sewage running in the streets. This was the part of London that her parents had taught her to forever shun. Liquor and brothels were in ample abundance. Good food and any sense of safety or security were brutally absent.

Not so many months ago, Ella had lived in a lovely house with comfortable beds and elegant decor. There had been ample to eat, and even a couple of servants who took care of any task too distasteful for Ella's parents. Ella had been protected from the fact that her parents had been spending themselves into enormous debt, apparently with no thought of the consequences to themselves or their daughter. Everything had seemed to fall apart in a day. Ella knew now that her security had been crumbling slowly for a long while, but she didn't have even a slight suspicion of it until the grim reaper of debt had come calling to collect. They lost everything! The servants were off to stay with relatives until other employment could be found, but Ella *had* no relatives. Her parents had deliberately alienated themselves from every family member, and their estrangements had been carved in stone for too many years to ever be reversed. Ella had never once even *met* a relative. The true shock for Ella had been hearing her mother's screams when she'd found her husband dead—by his own hand. Ella's mother had immediately reverted into some kind of mentally detached state that kept her completely oblivious to the incomprehensible horror that her life had become. In her mind she was still attending extravagant parties and wearing lavish clothes and jewels, apparently not recalling that her husband was dead, her house and belongings had been taken by those to whom she owed money, and her daughter was out on the streets—quite literally. For the first time in her life, Ella had been glad to be an only child, if only because that meant she would not need to care for and protect any younger siblings. Taking care of herself was challenging enough. How would she have ever kept anyone else from starving? She'd managed to get away with her own jewelry hidden in the two pieces of luggage she'd carried out of the house that fateful night when her world had crashed down around her. But work had been impossible to find, and her resources had disintegrated quickly in just trying to pay rent on the sparse and pathetic room where she'd been living and in keeping enough food in her stomach to stay alive. Her attempts to find a suitable job had all fallen short because she had no training or experience in *anything*, no skill whatsoever that would warrant anyone wanting to pay her for her services.

When her situation had become desperate, Ella had taken the advice of a woman who lived in the same building. Laetitia had been very friendly to Ella. She had been the only person to show any kindness whatsoever to Ella since she had been plummeted into a world that surely resembled hell on earth. Therefore, Ella had naturally felt drawn to her, and had mistakenly trusted her. *You'll make a lot of money,* her friend had told her. *Supposed* friend. No true friend would have ever lured an unsuspecting young woman into such a horrifying and degrading situation! No friend of any kind would have suggested such a thing without some kind of forewarning or explanation! Ella had been entirely innocent; young and naive and utterly gullible. She'd been raised by good parents—in spite of their penchant for spending more money than they'd had. She'd gone to church every Sunday, always holding in her heart the fear of God and a desire to please Him rather than do anything to incur His wrath. Now she had no doubt that she had disappointed Him in the worst possible way. What she had done was unforgivable, even if she'd had no idea *what* she was doing until it was too late. Ella felt certain she was now on a cursed path that could never be reversed. Her life had been ruined—surely and irrevocably. She had indeed been given a great deal of money, and Laetitia had laughed off Ella's traumatized reactions with that reminder—as if money might make everything all right; as if money might buy back what Ella had lost. In Laetitia's defense, Ella had spent enough time among the barely surviving souls of the earth to know that desperation drove people to do unspeakable things, and Laetitia had spent a great many more years living in that world than Ella had. She'd been hardened by it, no doubt. But Ella still wanted to believe that no amount of hardness or suffering could justify the deceptive methods Laetitia had resorted to in order to get Ella into that situation. And since Laetitia had taken a cut of the money for closing the deal, she'd certainly had ulterior motives. Ella now believed that Laetitia had never truly had any personal interest in being a friend to Ella. She'd simply been luring her into a trap all along. A horrible, inescapable trap. And now! Now . . . the unthinkable had come to pass. It had only happened once, and Laetitia had assured her that pregnancy was not a possibility after just once. Again Ella cursed herself for trusting such a woman and believing that *anything* she'd said was true.

Following the initial trauma, Ella had wanted to die, and she'd seriously considered—more than once—following her father's example of leaving this world by choice. But she couldn't bring herself to do it, not certain if that made her a coward or abstractly more courageous. Now as she walked blindly through the streets, trying to take in the reality of what she'd realized just this morning, she considered that choice once again. But now there wasn't only her own life to consider, but that of a child. Could she be responsible for taking the life of a child as well as her own? On the other hand, how could she be responsible for raising a child, for keeping it fed and safe in such a world? The clear memory of a terrifying sermon on the prospect of endless fire and torment tilted the scale in her mind more toward choosing to remain alive. But she couldn't completely rule out the possibility that she was already doomed to endless fire, unwed and pregnant as she was; and one more bad choice might not make any difference.

That night Ella lay curled up on her poor excuse of a bed in her poor excuse of a barely livable room and wept herself into shock. What on earth was she going to do? How could she ever care for herself and a child when she was barely surviving as it was? The very fact that she had a fair amount of money currently in her possession felt like a sick kind of taunting when she thought of what she'd suffered in order to get it. Her rent was paid for some months in advance, and if she used the remainder of it very carefully in acquiring sufficient food for herself, she could perhaps manage to get by for a while yet. If she had any hope of surviving, she had to find the means to earn some money—if it were even possible to do such a thing and remain respectable. Perhaps that was no longer an issue. But even if she managed to hold everything together until she could give birth to this baby, then what? She couldn't even begin to imagine!

Ella forced herself beyond her shock and fear in order to reach into the deepest part of her soul enough to do the only thing she knew how to do under such desperate circumstances. She prayed. She prayed with all the energy of her heart and mind. She prayed like she never in her life prayed before. While a part of her wondered if the prayers of such a woman might even be heard—let alone answered—she had to hope for the tiniest chance that God would have mercy on her and give her the strength and means to survive. Although she'd been oblivious to the passing of time, she had been conscious of the bells of a distant church tower ringing enough times to mark more than two hours while she continued to pray in the midst of contemplating the nightmare her life had become. An unpremeditated thought occurred to her that increased her hope just a bit. She recalled clearly a sermon she'd once heard about how compassionate and forgiving Jesus had been while He'd lived on the earth. He'd even offered forgiveness to a woman taken in the very act of adultery. Maybe, just maybe, if that were true, Ella too could be forgiven for the grievous sin she'd committed. As she allowed the idea to settle into her spirit, she felt her hope increase even further. Like a light in a dark room, the warmth began to tangibly fill her, starting in the center of her chest and filtering outward. By the time her every nerve became permeated with warmth, her desire to live and make a new life for herself had far surpassed any idea she'd ever had to leave this world and its misery behind. Contrary to every bit of logical assessment in regard to her present circumstances, she found it possible to believe that somehow, some way, someday, her life could be better than this. She was determined to find a new path and do whatever it took to travel that path with courage and enough strength to sustain herself and her child through whatever the future might bring.

* * * * *

Utah Valley, America

IRENE CORBETT SAT DOWN HARD on the steps of the back porch, forcing herself to take a deep breath and reach somewhere deep inside herself where she might be able to take hold of the belief that she was not crazy, and perhaps more importantly, that she was not somehow wicked or rebellious for wanting to pursue the course before her. She knew well enough that being a devoted wife and mother was her most important calling in this world. It was not only strongly taught as part of her religious beliefs, but she knew it for herself, from within her own spirit. She loved her husband and children, and she wanted to do right by them. But she also knew that women had been created to do great things. The Relief Society organization for the women of the Church had taught these principles from its very beginnings, nearly seventy years earlier. Women were created to make a difference in the world! Prophets had said so, and there were many shining examples of women in the scriptures and throughout the history of the Church that proved to Irene she wasn't alone in her thinking. Then why did she *feel* alone?

The frustration she felt grew to such a force that it hurtled her right off the porch and into a briskly paced walk about the yard. She was glad the children were sleeping, and grateful for the pleasant air of a summer evening. The sun had recently sunk beneath the western horizon, and had taken with it the intense heat of the day. She pondered the conversation she'd just had with her husband, and wondered why she had expected the outcome to be any different. Perhaps because she'd hoped and believed that he would be able to understand her reasons for wanting to take this step in her life. But she should have known better. Walter was a good man, and she loved him. But she knew well enough that he'd be more happy and content with a wife who was happy and content to simply care for her home and family. For all the countless conversations she'd had with Walter about the fire that burned inside of her, spurring her to the belief that she needed to do more, he simply couldn't seem to grasp it; he simply didn't understand.

Irene was an educated woman. She'd thoroughly enjoyed acquiring her education at Brigham Young Academy, and she'd immensely enjoyed teaching school following her graduation. But as soon as she'd become engaged to be married, she'd had no choice but to forfeit her teaching job. Married women weren't allowed to teach, a concept that Irene could *not* understand—and to this day, if she let herself think about it too much, she could become rather riled. She had gone into nursing in search of an alternate route of opportunity for making a difference in the world. She'd found a great deal of fulfillment and satisfaction in the way her knowledge and skills—and even her personality—had contributed to aiding people through times of suffering and pain. The doctors she worked with were impressed by her abilities, and more than one had encouraged her to continue her training so that her influence could be broadened. The first time Irene had heard the suggestion that she might travel to London and be trained in obstetrics, she had trouble not laughing out loud. *London?* The very possibility seemed absurd and too far out of reach. But the suggestion had come up again and again, and it had begun to grow in Irene's heart until it had filled her spirit so fully she could not deny that she was being guided to pursue this course.

Irene had grown up with the blessings of the gospel of Jesus Christ in her life. It had always been her guiding star, her deepest love, her most ardent affection. She had learned through much practice and experience how to hear the still, small voice of the Spirit, and she had actively applied Its guidance in every aspect of her life. When she unequivocally knew the source of that voice, and what it was telling her, how could she possibly deny it simply because there were people around her who could not capture the same vision or understand the urgency she felt? The very fact that the path before her was lacking in logic and practicality seemed all the more evidence to her that God's hand was in it. The desire was so strong in her that she almost felt as if she might die if she didn't do it. It wasn't that she believed she would physically lose her life, but she felt certain a part of her spirit would shrivel up if she could not go to London and be trained in all of the state-of-the-art procedures of midwifery. The area in which she lived was in great need of trained professionals who could help women through the process of safely delivering their children into the world. And Irene wanted to be able to do that. She wanted it every bit as much as she wanted to be a good mother to her children. A nagging voice in the back of her mind tempted her to believe that she could *not* be a good midwife and a good mother at the same time. But Irene knew the source of *that* voice as well, and she knew better than to listen to it. God had created women to do great things, and Irene was determined to heed His call, wherever it might take her!

It was completely dark when Irene finally went inside to find Walter sound asleep. She sat in the parlor near a lamp to read from the Book of Mormon, according to a lifelong habit. The book was undoubtedly her most priceless possession. It had been the source of peace and answers for her more times than she could count. She didn't read long, but set the book aside feeling more determined than ever to follow her heart. As she quietly got ready for bed, trying not to disturb Walter, she kept hearing in her mind the words of Nephi—a great prophet and an amazing man—echoing through her mind. *I will go and do the things which the Lord hath commanded, for I know that the Lord giveth no commandments unto the children of men, save he shall prepare a way for them that they may accomplish the thing which he commandeth them.*

Irene knelt to pray and silently poured out her heart to her Father in Heaven, speaking to Him as candidly as if He were there at her side, listening with perfect compassion to her pleas. She expressed a sincere desire to do His will, whatever it might be, and she asked for guidance in being able to know beyond any doubt the correct course for her life. She prayed for the hearts of her loved ones to be softened, and she concluded her prayer with the knowledge that if it was meant to be it would work out. At this point she couldn't even imagine how she would come up with the money to go, or how she would possibly arrange for the care of her children in her absence. She only knew that the need to go felt all consuming and it couldn't be denied.

Irene slept well in spite of her churning thoughts. The exhaustion of a busy life overruled her busy mind. She woke early, got dressed, and smoothed her dark, wavy hair. She had breakfast nearly ready before Walter and the children were up and about. Irene found great joy in helping the children get dressed, intermixing some play and teasing with the necessary tasks. Little Walter was getting old enough to start dressing himself with only a little occasional assistance. Roene was beginning to say some words here and there, but she was still in diapers, as was the littlest, Mack, who was crawling everywhere and quickly figuring out how to get into everything.

At breakfast Walter was polite but subtly aloof, and Irene knew only too well that his mood was focused on their conversation of the previous night and his resistance to her leaving the family in order to receive medical training. She could understand his reluctance, and she'd told him so. But she also needed him to understand how strongly she believed this was right for her. For all her efforts to communicate her feelings to him, he *didn't* understand. And that was the problem. Irene was praying very hard for his heart to be softened, but a part of her knew that she couldn't take away his agency any more than he could take away hers. He was entitled to his opinions, and as his wife she needed to prayerfully consider his wishes. But she had been taught all her life that her most important relationship was between herself and God. She had to honor God's will for *her* above all else if she wanted to be at peace with herself.

By the time breakfast was over, Irene had become decidedly discouraged. She wondered if she'd been overtaken by some kind of insanity to believe that such an endeavor might be possible. Needing some sound advice and a listening ear, she gathered up the children and paid a visit to her parents' home. She'd been hoping to have a good conversation with her mother, but considered it a great blessing to find her father at home as well. Now she could speak with them both, and if she was indeed losing her mind, they would kindly put her straight.

Levi and Alice Colvin were some of the finest people that Irene knew, and she counted herself very blessed to be their oldest daughter. Her father had served as a bishop for nearly two decades. In fact, it was difficult to remember when he *hadn't* been a bishop. He was kind and wise, as was his wife, and Irene knew she could speak candidly to them about the deepest feelings of her heart.

"Oh, how good to see you, dear," Alice said when Irene came through the back door with Mack in her arms and Roene and little Walter running in ahead of her.

"Hello, Mother," Irene said, and they exchanged a tight hug, with Mack getting caught in the middle. As the hug ended, Irene transferred Mack to his grandmother's arms, and Alice laughed as she kissed her little grandson.

"Oh, he gets cuter every day," Alice said.

"He does indeed," Irene said and turned to receive an embrace from her father.

"What brings you out for a visit?" Levi asked with a smile. "Not that I'm complaining, but I know how busy you are."

"I confess that I could use a listening ear," Irene said. Her tone must have come across more gravely than she'd intended by the way her parents' expressions both clouded over at the same time.

"Is something wrong?" Alice asked.

"No, everything is fine," Irene assured them. "I just . . . need some advice."

Alice said she just needed a few minutes to finish up something in the kitchen, and then she could sit to visit. Levi helped find some toys to occupy the children, then the adults all sat down around the kitchen table, where they could keep an eye on the children as they played nearby. Irene dove right into the conversation with words she'd been memorizing through the last hour. She got to the point very quickly, and wasn't surprised to hear her father say, "London?"

"As far as that?" Alice asked. "It's most of a continent and an entire ocean away."

"Yes, I know," Irene said, "but the General Lying-In Hospital in London is absolutely the best place at this time to learn midwifery. They are pioneering the way in using antiseptic techniques that lower the risks of infection related to childbirth. Think of all the good I could do with such training!"

Irene could see that her parents were a little startled with her idea, or perhaps with the intensity of her enthusiasm. They only stared at her, eyes and mouths wide for a long moment, so she went on with the details she had learned.

"They have nurses' housing adjacent to the hospital, and I would be able to live right there while I receive my training, which would take about six months. I would leave in the fall and return in the spring. It's not so very long when you think about the span of a lifetime and all the good that I could do with such training!" She realized she'd said that twice now, but it was the most prominent thought on her mind.

"How would you afford it?" Levi asked.

"I have no idea," Irene said, feeling a deep chagrin settle into her heart.

"What would you do with the children?" Alice asked. "Walter could never care for them if you were gone."

"Again, I have no idea," Irene said and looked down at where she was wringing her hands on her lap. She looked up again, attempting to convey in her expression the conviction she felt. "I only know that it feels like I'm *supposed* to do it. I feel like I *must* do it!" She put a fist to her heart. "I don't know how it's possible, or how to go about it, but I have to at least try."

"I shouldn't have to ask if you've prayed about this," Levi said, "but I need to anyway."

"I *have* prayed about it," Irene said. "I've prayed very much. At first I felt sure that praying about it would quickly bring the answer that it was out of the question, and that I would find peace with letting it go. But the opposite has happened. I *can't* let it go—even though Walter is opposed to it. I know I need to honor my husband, but I also need to honor my heart, and he has trouble understanding that."

"You *do* need to honor your husband," Levi said, "but it's not news to any of us that Walter has difficulty with the idea of women doing anything outside of caring for the family."

"Yes, and so does his mother," Alice pointed out in a tone that expressed what Irene also knew. Her mother-in-law would be outraged by such a decision, but Irene had learned long ago that it was more important to be right with God than it was to concern herself with anyone else's opinion—*especially* that of her mother-in-law. Mrs. Corbett was a good woman who meant well. She simply had a very different personality from Irene, and she had been raised with very differing views. For all that they shared the same religion and its corresponding values, their different interpretations of *a woman's place* and *a woman's purpose* had come between them many times. Since Walter had been raised by this woman, his views naturally leaned toward her beliefs on the topic. But Irene had been raised to follow her heart and honor her God-given gifts. Her beliefs were being put to the test, but she had to regularly remind herself that her desires were not wicked or rebellious. In fact, her desires were entirely righteous, even if people around her couldn't see or understand that. She wanted to serve God with the gifts and talents He'd given her. She wanted to help build His kingdom and aid His children in their suffering.

"But you shouldn't mind that," Levi said. "You must follow your heart, so long as it's in alignment with God's will."

"Yes, I know," Irene said, feeling so deeply validated that she wanted to cry.

"It's a mighty big undertaking you're talking about," Levi added in his most fatherly tone.

"I don't know if I can make it work," Irene said, "but I feel like I have to try. I've not only prayed, I've fasted as well. I pondered it a great deal before I even brought it up with Walter, but . . ."

"I take it he's not pleased with the idea," Alice said.

"Is that a surprise?" Irene asked. "I can't blame him for wishing his wife would be more conventional, but he *did* choose to marry *me*. I'm afraid if he loves me, he's going to have to love me the way I am. I certainly love *him* the way he is, even though I don't necessarily agree with all of *his* attitudes on certain topics."

"Marriage is full of give and take," Alice said. "If this is truly the right course, you'll know what to do."

"Maybe I'm just dreaming," Irene said.

"No harm in that," Levi commented with a warm smile toward his daughter, "as long as you don't have your head in the clouds." He glanced toward the children. "You're a good mother, and you do a great deal of good elsewhere too." He looked back at Irene. "I couldn't be more proud of my daughter. Just take care that you don't get too headstrong. Be considerate of your husband and continue to be prayerful. If it's right, it'll work out."

They talked a long while about the possibilities of how such an endeavor might come together, and Irene and the children stayed for lunch. When she left to take the children home so that the younger ones could take a nap, Irene felt validated and comforted by her parents' advice and support, but she also felt discouraged. Perhaps this was just some kind of test, and in the end it would simply not come to pass.

Over the next few days, Irene didn't bring the topic up again with Walter. She kept pondering and praying, and she fasted again with the same question prominent in her mind and heart. Her feelings didn't change, but she knew that Walter was likely hoping that the idea had been forgotten, and she dreaded bringing it up again. She finally *did* bring it up, and wasn't surprised by his aversion to talking about it at all. She assured him that her desire to do this was not a reflection of her feelings for him or her place with him as his wife and the mother of his children. But she wasn't certain he believed her.

"What will people think?" he asked. "If you run off to a foreign country to do something . . . so rash, people are sure to believe that there's something wrong between us."

"It shouldn't matter at all what people think as long as we know in our hearts—and between us—what the truth is."

Walter just shook his head. "I just don't see how it's possible. Even if it's what you want to do, there's no way we could ever afford it." He left the room as if that should conclude the conversation—and the very idea. Irene cried once she was alone, but she couldn't let go of the belief that somehow this would work out.

Several more days passed while Irene tried not to think about her dilemma, but it preoccupied her thoughts continually, nevertheless. She continued to pray that it would either work out or that she could feel peace over letting it go. But her feelings didn't change, and she knew that Walter was likely praying that she would let go of this ridiculous notion and just be content with the life she had. She sincerely wished that she could be more the wife that Walter wanted, but she couldn't deny who and what she was—who God had created her to be.

The following Sunday, early in the evening, Irene was pleasantly surprised to have her parents stop by for a visit. She realized within a few minutes that while they were glad to see Walter and Irene and the children, they had come with something specific in mind.

"Might we sit down and talk?" Levi asked Walter, then he glanced at Irene. "The four of us?"

"Of course," Irene said. Walter didn't comment. He just took a seat and waited.

Irene's heart pounded as she waited for what she believed would be some gentle guidance from her parents in believing that she should let go of the idea of traveling thousands of miles to engage in something that was full of uncertainty and so utterly impractical. She saw her father reach for her mother's hand, which implied that they were completely united in whatever they had to say. But it had always been that way. Even when they had disagreed, eventually they would come to an agreeable compromise, because they were both willing to go to the Lord, and that meant they would be able to know the Lord's will when it came to important matters. She wished that Walter could understand the true source of her desires, but looking into her parents' faces, she felt certain that her dream of going to England was about to come to an end.

"We've been thinking about what you came to talk to us about," Levi said.

"What would that be?" Walter asked.

"About going to England to study medicine," Irene said.

Walter let out an annoyed sigh and turned his attention back to his in-laws.

"We've both prayed about this," Levi continued, "and we've discussed it a great deal, if you must know. We didn't want to support you in something if it wasn't right. On the other hand, we didn't want to *not* support you if it *is* right. The thing is . . . we're both in strong agreement that you should do this, and we want to help make it happen."

Irene sucked in her breath and couldn't let it out. She felt sure she had heard them wrong. She'd wanted so badly to hear the words that they would be supportive that she had surely misconstrued her father's meaning. Or perhaps he'd transposed words and he'd said it differently than he'd meant it. She was still holding her breath when Levi said, "We've made the decision to mortgage our home to give you the necessary funds to pay for the trip and whatever you'll need to get your training and care for yourself while you're away."

Irene's breath came out in a sharp gasp that turned to a sob before she slapped her hand over her mouth. Alice smiled at her daughter with a sparkle of tears in her eyes, as if she fully understood how Irene was feeling. She then said, "We would also like to care for the children while you're away. That way Walter won't be burdened with having to concern himself with them, and he can come to see them as much as he'd like. Knowing how much we love them, you'll be able to focus on your studies and not worry."

Irene was only vaguely aware of Walter's silence that implied his displeasure. She was more focused on the reality that all of her prayer and fasting and pondering and desires had just come neatly together in a beautifully wrapped package, a gift from God as surely as if it had come wrapped in shiny paper with a big red bow. She sprang out of her chair and hugged her parents ferociously, laughing and crying at the same time, muttering her gratitude over and over. Alice and Levi both laughed as well, sharing in their daughter's joy. Walter just sat there, his aura of displeasure growing more visible by the moment.

When Irene had calmed down and returned to her chair, she saw her father lean his forearms on his thighs and look firmly at Walter. "I know this is hard for you, Walter," Levi said. "As your father-in-law I have no right to meddle, and I would never do so. But as a father to both of you, I would ask that you make an effort to understand Irene's need to do this. I know she loves you, and she needs your support. I earnestly believe that her desires are righteous, and her purpose in this is to honor God's will in regard to her mission in this world. If I didn't believe that, I wouldn't be offering my support in this way."

"I guess it's all settled, then," Walter said in a tone that sounded more like his pride had been wounded than anything else. He got up and left the room.

A wake of silence followed his departure, until Alice said gently, "You must be patient with him. Your disagreeing with him does not merit discord in the marriage."

"I understand, Mother. I've truly tried to help him understand why this is so important to me."

"A year from now," Alice said, "this will all be behind you, and you can work on putting things right."

"In the meantime," Levi said, "I would say you've got to take this to the Lord once again and be absolutely certain you're making the right choice. If you can know with confidence that you're right with Him, then you have to leave Walter in His hands and go forward."

"Yes, of course," Irene said and hugged her parents again, so grateful and happy she felt as if she would burst.

That evening Irene tried again to talk to Walter about her feelings regarding this endeavor, but he was too focused on being without his wife and children for several months, and he kept bringing up the problem of what people would think. For all of Irene's efforts to reason with him, she had to accept that he was never going to be happy about this. She assured him that she loved him, and that she would follow her father's advice to pray about it again and be absolutely certain it was the right thing. He made no comment on that, and once he'd gone to sleep Irene cried silent tears. She felt torn in wondering how she could honor her relationship with God and follow her heart, and at the same time have it come between her and her husband. She simply had to remind herself that for all that Walter was a good man in many ways, he was human and fallible. As she was. She couldn't stand up for her own feelings on the matter without respecting his. All she could do was continue to reassure him and move forward.

Following more prayer and fasting, Irene knew what she had to do. Once she had made her decision, she put her focus on making all of the arrangements, grateful for the modern means of travel available to her that made it possible to get to London within a couple of weeks. She thought of her pioneer ancestors, just a few generations back, who had come by wagon train to this valley, enduring great hardship to establish new communities and create the way of life they now enjoyed. A decade into the twentieth century, Irene had the luxury of riding in an automobile to the train station, and then going by rail to the East Coast, where she would board a steamer in order to cross the Atlantic. A part of her felt deeply nervous to be going so far on her own, but in her innermost self she knew it was the right thing to do. She'd made her decision for all of the right reasons, and she was prepared to stand by it.

CHAPTER TWO
Far from Home

IRENE FOUND IT EVEN MORE difficult than she'd expected to say good-bye to her loved ones. She assured Walter of her love for him, and that it would always be true. He told her that he loved her and he would miss her dreadfully, but his displeasure over her going at all came through very clearly. Irene reminded herself of what her mother had said: in a year this would all be behind them, and they could sort things out.

It was difficult saying good-bye to her parents and her other family members, but it was hardest of all to leave her babies. They would change so much in the months of her absence, and she thought of all the little pleasures of motherhood she would miss. But once she was on the train headed east, Irene focused on the path ahead, knowing that her journey was in God's hands and she needed to trust Him. She didn't know the long-range plan for her life, but *He* knew it, and she knew she could rely on the voice of His Spirit to guide her through whatever lay ahead. Her children were in good hands, her husband would manage, and she was embarking on the opportunity of a lifetime.

The rail journey was long and tiring, but when Irene came face-to-face with the Atlantic Ocean, she felt a sharp thrill that took her breath away; its vastness was impossible to comprehend. Knowing she would cross it to find her path in life, she felt resolved and firm in embarking on the next step.

The crossing from America to England turned out to be one of the worst experiences of Irene's life. She became rather ill, and practically every minute at sea was miserable. Alone and preoccupied with her own misery, Irene desperately missed her loved ones—most especially her three precious babies—and she began to wonder if she'd made the right decision after all.

But once Irene stepped onto English soil, her confidence returned. She knew this was where she needed to be, and that whatever adventures she might encounter would serve her well in becoming the person that God wanted her to become.

London proved to be an overwhelming city! She never could have found her way around on her own, and was grateful to be able to hire a cab to take her to the General Lying-In Hospital—a place that would become her home away from home for the next six months. She was glad to find the nurses' housing to be nicely adequate, and she was even more glad to find there were other nurses there who were friendly and kind. Sharing her living space and working hours with decent people would make a tremendous difference.

Irene was able to locate the meeting place for the local branch of the Church. On the Sundays when she didn't have to cover a shift at the hospital, she was able to take a cab to attend church. She quickly got to know some of the local members, and also some missionaries from America who were serving in the area. Being among people who shared her faith was a sweet reprieve and made her feel less homesick. But nothing could keep her from missing her loved ones. She was glad she would be in England for only six months, as opposed to the years the missionaries were required to be away from home.

Irene quickly found London to be a dirty and depressing city—at least most of the parts of it that she saw. She knew it was a city with great historical significance, and she was fascinated by the unique character and mood of the city. But it was entirely different from the new and blossoming communities of Utah that had been in existence for only a handful of decades. She missed her home and family, but she was determined to look for the good in her opportunities here and to make the most of each day.

Much of Irene's training was meant to take place in conjunction with practical experience. She was expected to visit the homes of impoverished women and children to help see to their medical needs. The living conditions that confronted her were difficult to face; being accosted by fleas and other unwanted pests nearly did her in. But her heart was drawn to these people in need, and she couldn't help pondering the stories of the New Testament, and how Jesus had walked and lived among the poor and the lame. She felt, in a very real way, that she was doing His work and His will more than she ever had. Even as exposed to wretched circumstances and conditions as she was, she believed she was making a difference. She wished every day that she might be in a position to do more, but she did what she could and felt gratitude to think of her own children, safe and clean and well fed in her parents' care. She hoped their father was taking time to visit them often, and that he was not too terribly upset with her. She wrote letters to everyone back home as often as time would allow, and she anxiously looked forward to receiving letters in return.

On a cold, foggy day that threatened the impending approach of winter, Irene was taken aback by how *different* London cold could be from Utah cold. The moisture from the river and the sea were so thick in the air that it was impossible to see more than a few steps ahead of herself as she made her way carefully back to the hospital after checking on a family with two ill children that had been assigned to her care. Every particle of moisture in the air seemed on the verge of freezing, and it bit at her face as she pressed her way through the thick cloud clinging to every brick and cobblestone of the ancient city.

Irene felt relieved to arrive at the door to the hospital, partly because she had actually found her way there in spite of the thick fog. Still, before stepping through the door, she took a long moment to look over her shoulder and soak in the strange, mystical effect of the fog she was leaving behind. There was something strangely wonderful about it, as if the fog itself had been a silent witness to all the years of life that had been lived by the human race in this city.

Irene drew herself away from her fanciful thoughts and hurried inside. She'd barely turned a corner before she came face-to-face with a doctor she worked with frequently.

"Good, you're here," he said. "We have a new patient. She came in because her water broke, but it's too early. Labor is just beginning and it could be a long one, from what I can tell. She's rather upset and not in very good condition. I think you can help her get through this better than anyone else around here."

The doctor rushed away, not allowing Irene time to determine whether that was meant to be a compliment. She'd like to think so. He called a name and room number over his shoulder as he rushed on to other business. Irene hurried to wash up and change her apron before she went to the specified room, feeling some trepidation regarding how she might help this young woman. If her water had broken, there was no stopping the labor, and if the labor had come on too soon, the chances of saving a premature baby were diminished by every week of pregnancy that had not been accomplished.

Irene entered the room to see a young woman with a gaunt face and hollow eyes who stared toward the window. She wondered what had happened to this woman to precipitate such darkness in her countenance. The other beds in the room were empty, but Irene knew that wouldn't last long. She took a deep breath and approached the young woman's bedside, wearing a smile that she hoped would help ease whatever anxiety the expectant mother might be experiencing.

"Hello," she said, "my name is Irene, and I'm going to be taking care of you." She brushed back straying strands of dirty brown hair from the girl's dirty face, noting that she made a hurried attempt to disguise the darkness that Irene had seen in her eyes. "You're Ella?"

"That's right," Ella said, and Irene was surprised by the evidence of refinement and education in her speech. Even from those two words it was undeniable.

Rather than focusing too much on her circumstances or the present situation, Irene said, "Why don't I help you get cleaned up before the labor progresses, and then you'll feel better."

Ella didn't comment but seemed agreeable. Irene worked quickly to help Ella clean her body and wash her hair, imagining as she did so that it might clean away some of the grime of the city and the obvious state of her life that was *not* good. The evidence of contractions came with minutes in between, but they were not terribly painful yet. Irene hoped that meant they would have some time to talk before the situation became too intense. She had a feeling this person really needed someone to talk to, and Irene prayed silently that she might be able to make a positive difference in Ella's life, for whatever time they might be able to spend together. When she sensed Ella relaxing as she was helped into a clean hospital gown, Irene asked quietly, "Do you have a place to live, Ella?" She considered that to be more polite than saying what she knew from the evidence, which was that this woman had likely been sleeping in alleys and had nowhere to clean herself, and she likely hadn't eaten a decent meal in days.

"Not anymore," Ella admitted. "My rent ran out last week."

"And do you have money for food?" Irene asked.

"Not anymore," she repeated and looked away.

"There's no need to feel ashamed, Ella," Irene said. "Not with me." Ella met her eyes, and Irene smiled. "It doesn't matter to me what your circumstances might be. I'll treat you no differently than any queen or princess who might need help today." Ella let out a skeptical noise, and Irene added, "You *are* a princess, Ella, and you must never forget it."

"A princess? Not likely."

"Perhaps not in the way that you might think, but the fact is that we are all children of a Heavenly Father, and He is a great king. While we are here on this earth, we are simply separated from Him. Just imagine your life like a very big story in which you've been separated from your Father, the King. People might not believe your true identity, but you know in your heart that you are a princess, and eventually you will find your way back home. In the end, you *will* be reunited with your Heavenly Parents, and you will live happily ever after."

"You have a vivid imagination, Irene," Ella said with continued skepticism.

"I know it to be true," Irene said. "I would be happy to talk to you about all of that as much as you'd like, but right now I think we should get you a little something to eat to give you some strength to get through this. I'll be right back."

Ella nodded, and Irene left to get Ella some broth. She prayed on Ella's behalf with each step she took, wondering why she felt unusually drawn to this woman. She'd encountered many women in appalling and atrocious circumstances; she'd felt a natural desire to help, and had wished over and over that she could do more. But she'd never felt this sure and sudden magnetism that could not be ignored. She had a feeling that Ella would become significant in her life—and the other way around.

Irene returned with the broth and sat on the edge of Ella's bed. "You shouldn't eat too much right now. We don't want your stomach to be upset. Some women get nausea along with the labor. But perhaps this will be adequate for now."

Irene watched Ella take to the broth eagerly, and she cautioned her to go slowly, assuring her that she could have more in a while if it settled all right. By the time she'd finished, the contractions were coming a little closer together and hinting at pain rather than just discomfort.

"Is my baby going to die?" Ella asked.

Irene took Ella's hand. "I don't know, dear. I'll not be untruthful with you. The labor has started very early, and premature babies have less chance of survival than those that go full term."

Ella nodded and said, "Is it going to be very painful?"

"I can't lie about that, either. Labor can be *very* painful, but it's my job to help you get through the experience as calmly as possible, and with the least amount of pain. We have things we can do to help ease the pain, especially near the end when it becomes the worst. But remember, the transition of birth—of bringing a child from one world into another—is completely natural, and it works the same for every woman."

"Even queens and princesses," Ella said with the slightest hint of a smile.

"That's right," Irene said. "When it comes to what it takes to give birth, all women are equal."

Ella endured a contraction that made her grimace. Irene held her hand and offered assurance that she would not leave her alone until it was over. When the pain had eased, Ella said, "You're very far from home."

"Did the accent give me away?" Irene asked with a little laugh.

"That and . . . just a way about you. I would guess that you miss someone very much."

Irene paused in her task to look directly at Ella. "You would guess correctly. My family is in America; my husband . . . and three children. I miss them very much. The children are staying with my parents, whom I miss very much as well."

"Why did you come here?"

"I'd heard this was the best possible place to learn midwifery." Again she laughed softly. "There are many babies being born where I live. I want to be able to help bring those babies safely into the world, and perhaps ease the suffering of the mothers as they go through that process."

"I'm very glad that you're here," Ella said with a hint of tears in her eyes. "You've been so very kind."

Irene put her hands over Ella's. "I'm very glad that I'm here too." She was quiet a moment, then asked, "Are you also far from home?"

"Yes," Ella said, her eyes distant, "very far from home." She focused more on Irene and added ruefully, "According to you I'm a lost princess."

"So you are," Irene said with a smile, wanting to be able to convince her of that principle. "Besides being separated from the Heavenly King, where are you from?"

"London," Ella said, not surprised by Irene's confused expression. In a sad voice she clarified, "But I grew up in an entirely different London. I had everything. Now I have nothing."

Irene sensed that this sweet young woman had a need to unburden herself. The possibility gave Irene hope that she might be able to make some kind of positive difference for her, as she believed she was meant to do. The Spirit had alerted her to pay attention and remain open to inspiration. If Ella was willing to be candid with her, assessing how she might help would be much easier. "Would you mind telling me?" she asked gently.

"It's a very pathetic tale," Ella said, "and it ends with my being here . . . giving birth to an illegitimate child."

Irene wasn't surprised by that last admission, but she wondered how it had come about. Ella didn't seem like the kind of girl to willfully get herself into trouble. That haunted look in Ella's eyes provided a clue that she had not ended up in this situation by choice. Once again Irene felt deeply impressed that Ella needed her in ways far more than every other woman she'd encountered in her work here. For a moment it was as if she could see a glimpse of the future. It wasn't that she actually *saw* anything, but she was overcome with the feeling that without a helping hand to guide her past this experience, this beautiful young woman would be utterly lost. Irene didn't know if that meant she would actually die, or if it meant being overtaken by circumstances in life that could be worse than death. Irene had witnessed many things in this city that had brought home to her indelibly that there were many things worse than death.

"Labor is bound to progress slowly," Irene said, "and I'm not leaving you in anyone else's care until it's over—no matter how long it takes. We've got a lot of time for you to tell me your story, and since we don't really know each other, you don't have to worry about my breaking any confidences. But I hope you can trust that I would never judge you or think badly of you for whatever you have done or not done to bring you to this day." Irene squeezed her hand gently. "I really would be glad to hear your tale, Ella, however pathetic you think it might be."

She offered a sad smile. "I confess I've heard some fairly pathetic tales working in this part of London."

"I daresay you have," Ella said and endured a contraction before she went on. "I grew up very comfortably. We were not rich by some people's standards, but my father was a very successful barrister, and my mother had received a plump inheritance. I was an only child and therefore somewhat spoiled. My parents were good people and I never felt unloved, even though they were very wrapped up in many social activities. I had an excellent nanny when I was young, and then an excellent governess who was a very good teacher and gave me quality education in every aspect that respectable young ladies are given."

Ella sighed, and Irene knew the story was about to take a turn for the worse. She looked down and said, "I had no idea there were financial challenges until it all came apart. Seemingly overnight we lost everything. To just . . . get to the point: we lost *everything*, and then . . ." she took a deep breath, "my father . . . committed suicide, and . . ."

"Oh, you poor dear," Irene said, tightening her hold on Ella's hand. "I cannot even imagine how horrible that must have been for you. And for your mother as well."

"She completely lost her mind—quite literally. She was put into a dreadful asylum, and died there."

"Oh my!" Irene said, feeling such heartache on behalf of this young woman that it was difficult not to burst into tears.

Between enduring the pains that were getting more intense and closer together, Ella shared with Irene the details of her struggle to survive on her own, and the unspeakable deception of a supposed friend that had lured Ella into the situation that had resulted in this pregnancy. Irene *did* cry when Ella shared the worst of it. She couldn't believe the wretchedness and evil of some people. She'd come to understand how desperate people could become, and she could never judge that kind of desperation because she'd never felt it. But if the people of this world could share a common decency and a desire to help each other, rather than ensnare victims or act with evil intent, the world would be so much a better place. If the rich could only be more generous in caring for the poor, if those in need could only have a place to turn for help, and be given a fair chance to care for themselves! Irene had to stop her thoughts from rampaging through her own vehemence concerning the injustices of the world, and to focus instead on the heartwrenching plight of this poor girl.

As the process of childbirth became intense for Ella, Irene was grateful for the things she had been learning, but she felt a desire to learn more, to grow in confidence in her skills, and to be able to ease the suffering of mothers and babies through this transition as much as it might be humanly possible. Her own experiences of bearing children, some harder than others, gave her empathy for the pain, but she still felt helpless in her desire to be able to ease it. Near the very end, Irene administered ether as she had been trained to do in order to spare the mother from the very worst. Irene drew in a deep breath of relief on Ella's behalf to see her drift into a slumber that was a blessed reprieve from the hours of difficult labor. The baby was successfully delivered with no trauma or damage to the mother, but Irene knew immediately that this tiny boy's chances for survival were slim. He wasn't breathing well, and his color was not good. By the time Ella regained consciousness, her baby was already close to death. Irene put the baby into Ella's arms and gently explained the situation, while at the same time trying to detach herself emotionally from the expected grief of this new mother. Irene put a hand on Ella's shoulder while she held her baby and wept uncontrollably. The training she'd received about appropriately delivering difficult news to patients could never adequately prepare her for how it would feel—especially given the stronger-than-usual connection Irene had felt with this woman.

After the baby took his final, strained breath, Ella wept harder. Irene whispered to her that her son was in a better place, and that he would be well cared for by angels until she could be with him again.

"I want to be with him now," Ella cried. Irene could only try to reassure her that she had much to live for and that she would be able to get past this, but Ella was in no mood to be convinced, and Irene couldn't blame her.

Irene stayed with Ella until long after she had calmed down into a quiet shock. She insisted that Ella eat something, and painstakingly guided her through taking bites of her food, like a mother would with her child. She then encouraged Ella to get some rest and was glad to be able to give her some medicine that would ease the pain and help her relax.

As soon as she had given Ella the medicine, Irene helped her get comfortable, then sat on the edge of the bed and held her hand. Ella was curled up on her side, looking toward the window with eyes that were even more hollow than when Irene had first seen her earlier that day.

While Irene was wondering what she might say, and praying silently for comfort to be given to this sweet young woman, Ella said, "I take it from what you said that you believe in heaven."

"Oh, I do!" Irene said. "In fact, I don't just believe, I know in my heart that it's true."

"Do you think then that my baby has gone to heaven? He won't be judged for his mother's sins, will he?"

"Oh, my dear," Irene said with compassion. "Let me tell you what I know to be true. Babies and little children are perfect and have no accountability for *anything*. Those who die so young are spared from the trials and suffering of this world, and they go directly to the best place in heaven to live with our Father in Heaven and our Savior. You have nothing to fear on that account, I can assure you."

Tears filled Ella's eyes and leaked onto her pillow, some of them crossing over the bridge of her nose to get there. "Oh, I'm so glad to hear it," she muttered. "And you say you *know* it to be true."

"I *do* know it!" Irene said. "In time I can teach you how it's possible for *you* to know it, but for now you can trust me."

"I *do* trust you," Ella said and became more emotional. Irene waited patiently for her to regain her composure enough to go on. "And what about me, Irene? Please tell me the truth. Will I be banished to hell for what I've done?"

"Oh, Ella. You had no control over what happened to you."

"But I *did*!" she insisted with a sob and a new rush of tears. "I shouldn't have been so stupid, so naive. I was . . ."

"That's just it, darling. You were naive, but you did not make the decision to do this. As I see it, sin is when a person makes a decision to do something that takes them farther away from God. Our Heavenly Father is merciful in regard to our weaknesses and our difficult circumstances, Ella. He understands the desperate situation you were in, and He also understands how you were deceived and taken advantage of. The marvelous thing is that even when we *do* commit sin—even grievous sin—there is always the opportunity for repentance and redemption. *Always!* But in your case, my dear, there is no need to repent when you did not choose for this to happen. You can choose now to put it behind you and make a good life for yourself."

"How would I do that?" Ella cried. "Where would I begin?"

"We can talk about that," Irene said. "I don't know how much I can help, but I can be your friend."

"Why would you do that?"

"Oh, dear, sweet Ella," Irene said with a warm laugh. "I would consider it a privilege to be your friend. Before you leave the hospital, we will come up with a plan, and I will do everything I can to help you. For right now, you need to get your rest. You've been through a terrible ordeal. I'm going to the nurses' home to get some sleep myself, but there are other nurses here who will take care of you, and I will come to see you just as soon as I can."

Ella squeezed Irene's hand tightly. "Thank you, Irene. There surely must be a God, for you are surely an angel."

"You are too kind," Irene said and pressed a kiss to Ella's forehead before she stood up. "Sleep well, and I will see you soon."

Irene slipped out of the room and hurried to where she could crawl into her own bed, physically and emotionally drained to the core. She cried on behalf of Ella, and prayed fervently to be guided in how she might help this young woman who had suffered so much. Irene didn't have the means to offer this girl any financial support, and she wasn't in a position to offer her a job. She didn't even have a home where she could allow Ella to stay. Not in this country, at least. But there had to be a way to help her. There just had to be! And God willing, she would be guided to the answers on how she might truly make a difference in this young woman's life. How could she just see her turned out onto the streets again, penniless and worn down so thoroughly by life?

Irene was lured into sleep by her body's desperation for rest. She awoke with Ella most prominent on her mind. As she habitually began her day with prayer, an idea came to her that gave her some peace and hope on Ella's behalf. She needed to ponder it—and acquire more information—before she would dare tell Ella. She didn't want to raise false hope or make matters more difficult. But she believed the Spirit was guiding her, and therefore she had to believe that something good would come to pass on Ella's behalf.

Irene found Ella looking better physically, and not experiencing too much pain from her childbirth experience. But her spirits were very low, indeed. While Irene had plenty of work to accomplish and was expected to remain very busy, she took advantage of every opportunity to check in on Ella and chat for a few minutes here and there. At the end of Irene's shift, she sat with Ella and asked intently, "Tell me how you're feeling. I mean . . . how you're *really* feeling."

Ella sighed, thought about it, then sighed again. "I hope you won't think too badly of me if I admit to the truth."

"I wouldn't have asked if I didn't want to hear the truth, Ella. Of course I would never think badly of you. Please tell me."

"I can't think of a single reason to want to be alive. I must confess that I've more than once considered taking my father's path, but . . ."

At Ella's hesitation, Irene had to bite her tongue hard to keep from trying to talk Ella out of such desperate feelings. She would never want this sweet, tender woman to do such a horrible thing. But who was Irene to judge such feelings? She couldn't begin to comprehend what Ella had been through, and she could never understand being in a situation that promised no tangible hope in any direction. So she just resigned herself to listening and trying to be compassionate.

"I think I'm too much of a coward to actually take my own life."

"Or perhaps it takes a great deal of courage to stay alive," Irene suggested, but Ella showed no response.

"A part of me feels glad that the baby didn't live; glad for him, at least. I've worried so very much over how I would take care of a child when I can't even take care of myself." Tears came with her confession. "I miss him, and I feel like . . . a part of me is gone . . . but I will never have to look him in the face and tell him why I don't know who his father is, and I will never have to see him go hungry. And yet . . . I feel guilty for feeling relief that he's dead."

"Oh, my dear," Irene said. "You mustn't feel guilty. Your feelings are understandable. God is merciful, and He knows your heart."

"If He is merciful, then I wonder why He didn't take me, too. Women die in childbirth all the time. Why not me?"

"There must be a very good reason that you're still alive, Ella. If you seek to understand God's purpose for you, I'm certain He will let you know; He will show you the way."

Ella's eyes responded with a glimmer of intrigue as she focused on Irene's face. "You talk about God as if you know Him personally; as if . . . the two of you are friends, or something."

"It feels that way, I suppose," Irene said. "He's just always been a part of my life, and I know He's there. I see Him quite literally as my Father; He is the Father of our spirits. I feel like I can go to Him just as I would an earthly Father that I trust completely and on whom I can rely. He's compassionate and merciful, and His love for His children is unconditional."

"And yet there is so much suffering in the world."

"He must allow His children to have their agency, Ella. Our purpose for coming to this world is to be tried and tested. There would be no purpose at all if we did not have our agency."

"You must be the smartest woman I've ever met," Ella said. "How can a woman know so much about delivering babies, and also know so much about life? And about religion?"

Irene shrugged and smiled. "I'm just . . . always trying to learn and better myself. And if you do the same, God will guide your path. I'm sure of it, Ella."

"How can you be sure?"

"I have faith," she said.

Ella became thoughtful, and Irene declared that she needed to leave so they could both get some rest. She promised to check back tomorrow, when they would find the time to talk some more.

When Irene left the hospital, she didn't go to the nurses' home. Instead she took a cab to the home of a charming older couple who were members of the Church. Irene had gotten to know them through her church attendance, and she'd once been invited to dinner in their home. They had asked her more than once if she had all she needed, and if there was anything they could do for her. She knew they were not necessarily well off, but they were comfortable, and they had extra space in their home since their youngest son had left home to attend college in Scotland. During the cab ride, Irene said a silent prayer that they would be receptive to the favor she wanted to ask of them.

Brother and Sister Pack were both pleased to see Irene, and she was graciously guided to the kitchen where they sat around the table to visit. She couldn't deny being grateful for the scones and butter and milk they offered her when she'd completely forgotten about eating any supper. They asked about news she'd heard from home, and how her work at the hospital was going.

"I confess that's the biggest reason I've come to see you," Irene said. "I wish to ask you a very big favor. I've prayed about it and felt that I should ask, but if you don't feel comfortable doing it, I would completely understand."

"Well, what is it, dear?" Sister Pack insisted. "Out with it."

"There is a young woman who will be released from the hospital in a few days, and she has nowhere to go. She's been through a terrible ordeal. I've seen a great deal of hardship and suffering, even in the short time I've been here, but . . . this poor, dear girl."

"Tell us about her," Brother Pack said, and Irene felt some hope to see that both of their faces expressed a keen interest.

Irene told them Ella's sad tale, omitting certain details that Ella might prefer to keep confidential—especially if she might be staying with these people. Brother and Sister Pack were astonished and very compassionate to Ella's situation. They insisted mutually and without hesitation that she should come and stay with them.

"Only for a short time," Irene said. "Just until she can get feeling better and find some kind of decent work to support herself."

"I'm certain if we spread word among the members that she's looking for work," Brother Pack said, "someone will hear of something."

"Oh, that would be wonderful," Irene said, unable to conceal her enthusiasm. She felt inexpressibly grateful to know that she could offer Ella some hope and comfort, rather than seeing her have to go back into the streets with nothing. She expressed her gratitude to the Packs, and they assured her that they were glad for the opportunity to serve one of God's children in need.

On her way back to the hospital, Irene considered the possible fate of a woman like Ella if someone didn't intervene. A woman in poor health with no decent clothes to wear or a place to rest and get clean had no hope of ever finding any respectable work. And Irene knew there was no government help available for people in need. She'd heard talk that attempts were being made to put something in place, but at the present time, it just wasn't there.

Irene fell asleep with less anxiety and more peace, seeing the evidence of God's hand in Ella's life. There had been many moments since she'd arrived in England when she'd felt grateful to be here, and many times she'd felt like she'd made a difference. But thinking of what might happen to Ella if she'd not been here to intervene made her want to shout out her gratitude to her Heavenly Father for guiding her and for giving her this opportunity. She imagined what it might be like when she could return home and share with Walter, and her parents, and other members of her family, such stories of fulfillment of hope. Surely then, Walter would feel that this endeavor had been the right thing for her to do. She'd barely thought it however, before she was reminded in her heart that she knew for herself this endeavor was right. She was where she was supposed to be, and she could never deny it. Whether or not Walter—or his mother—could *ever* accept that, she felt complete peace over it, and that was all that mattered.

CHAPTER THREE
Transition

THE FOLLOWING MORNING IRENE STARTED her day with great excitement, looking forward to her conversation with Ella. But the morning was chaotic, with many assignments in regard to her work and the rigorous training she was receiving. She was able to pop into Ella's room for just a moment with the hope of telling her that she'd be by later to talk, but she found Ella sleeping and didn't disturb her. She watched her resting for a long moment, however, glad to see that she had some color in her face. Irene felt an added excitement to think of how Ella might respond to the news she had to share. She felt privileged indeed to be the one who could extend to Ella the generous offering that Brother and Sister Pack were willing to give.

Irene wasn't able to find time for a visit with Ella until much later that day. She found her new friend leaning back against some pillows, looking toward the wall with that hollow look in her eyes. Irene considered for a moment what she might be thinking. Fearful thoughts of the unknown? Wondering how she would survive? Grief for her lost baby? Her parents' tragic deaths? Any one of those things would be enough to undo some people. Irene couldn't imagine how she was holding herself together at all. It was certainly time that someone gave this girl a chance.

"Hello," Irene said, and Ella turned and showed a wan smile.

"Oh, hello," Ella said.

"I came in earlier but you were sleeping." Irene sat on the edge of the bed. "How are you feeling?"

"Better, I think," Ella said.

Irene wondered how to begin the conversation, then glanced over to realize the other beds in the room were occupied with patients, and the woman closest was showing a curious interest in them. Irene nodded and smiled at the woman, who smiled in return, then she said to Ella, "I'll be right back."

She returned a minute later with a wheelchair, and Ella's eyes brightened when she said, "Let's take a little evening walk, shall we?"

"I'd love to," Ella said and was mostly able to get out of the bed and into the chair on her own. Since they'd hardly let her out of bed since the birth of the baby, she was weak and sore as well as stiff.

Irene engaged Ella in small talk as she pushed her up one hall and down another until they found a place where they could speak privately. Irene situated the wheelchair so they could sit to face each other.

"I have a confession to make," Irene said. "I've been praying for you, Ella. I've been very concerned about what you would do when you leave here, and—"

"I confess that I've been very concerned about that myself," Ella said. "It's very kind of you to pray for me, but you mustn't worry about me. I'm certain I'll be all right."

Irene admired her courage, but she felt sure that Ella's bravado came more from not wanting anyone to make a fuss rather than from feeling any confidence as to how she would manage.

"I'm certain you would figure something out," Irene said, wanting to express her own confidence in Ella. "Although . . . I'm hoping that I might be able to help in that regard."

Ella's eyes widened with hope, then narrowed with expectant cynicism. Nothing in life had worked out for this woman in a very long time, and it was understandable that she might have trouble trusting in the possibility of something good on her horizon. Irene hurried to explain.

"I've made some friends here through the church that I belong to. You see, there's a branch of the Church here, and so I've attended when I could. There are some very kind people I've met there. Brother and Sister Pack—that's how we refer to members of our church—have offered to let you stay in their home until you can find a way to support yourself."

Ella looked at Irene dubiously. She turned her head slightly to the side, but kept her eyes focused on Irene's. "I don't understand."

"It's not complicated. These are very kind people who have offered help to me more than once. They have no children left at home, and would be happy to let you use one of their spare bedrooms until you're feeling better and can find a respectable job. They also believe that if we ask around through other members of the Church, we might be able to help you find work."

Ella opened her mouth to speak, then closed it. She opened it again, hesitated, then muttered, "I don't know what to say."

"You don't need to say *anything*, Ella. Just . . . let us help you turn your life around. I know you're capable of working to provide for yourself, and I know you're not the kind of woman to take unfair advantage of the charity of others, so it's simply a matter of—"

"How do you know *that*?" Ella asked. "You hardly know me, in truth."

"I just . . . know," Irene said. "I had a good feeling about you from the moment we met. I want to help you. That's all."

"I . . . don't know what to say," Ella muttered again, but this time the words were accompanied by tears. She reached for Irene's hand. "I won't let you down."

"I'm not worried about that."

"Whether or not you are, I won't. I promise. I *will* find a job, and I'll work hard." She wrapped her arms around Irene's neck. "Thank you!" She drew back to look at her. "What a dear, dear friend you are! I've never had such a friend!"

Irene considered the short amount of time they'd known each other, and the very few conversations they'd shared. Had Ella truly been so deprived of friendship in her life that this was the dearest friendship she'd ever known? Whether or not that was the case, Irene was glad to be her friend, and she prayed that this would all work out well.

A few days later, Brother and Sister Pack came to the hospital to meet Ella and take her home with them. Irene had given Ella some of her own clothes, which didn't fit perfectly, but they were far better than the clothes she'd worn to the hospital, which had now been disposed of. Irene had reassured Ella that there was no reason to be nervous, but it was evident that Ella felt awkward with the situation and came across as very shy with these good people. But Sister Pack put a loving arm around Ella and assured her that they would take very good care of her. Irene hugged her new friend and promised firmly, "I shall see you as often as I can, and you know where to find me if you need me. All will be well. I promise!"

"Then I shall take your word for it," Ella said with a smile that wasn't completely forced. She then left with Brother and Sister Pack, and Irene didn't have even a minute to ponder the situation before she had to get back to work. But she kept a prayer in her heart that Ella's life would be changed for the better, and that this transition would not be too difficult or painful for her. She also expressed gratitude to her Father in Heaven for the promptings that had guided her, and for the generosity of good people like Brother and Sister Pack. Seeing evidence of the gospel in action warmed her heart and renewed her hope that her own presence here in London might make a tiny bit of impact on the world.

* * * * *

Ella was glad for the ongoing conversation Brother and Sister Pack engaged in during the drive to their home, mostly because it prevented her from having to say much. The mild awkwardness she felt over the situation was greatly compensated for by the fact that she was not homeless and left to her own resources—which amounted to absolutely nothing.

In the short time that Ella had known Irene, she had found a shift in her own thinking—if only a little. Perhaps it was more accurate to say she could think about making a change in her thinking. Irene had introduced many new ideas to Ella, but the most prevalent was her attitude about God. Ella had grown up in a home where there was a general belief in God, but it was a vague, abstract kind of thing. Beyond her family actually attending church on Sundays, religion had never been practiced actively except for a brief expression of gratitude before eating a meal. Ella had never thought to consider that God might actually be aware of her personally, or that His hand might be in the lives of His children. In fact, she'd never thought to consider the possibility that the people in this world actually might *be* His children. She'd indulged in desperate prayer a few times during her encounters with misery and desperation, but she'd had no reason to believe that God had heard her pleas; therefore, she'd not tried it again. She'd felt utterly abandoned and alone. But now she felt just the opposite, and she couldn't help wondering if there was something to Irene's beliefs. Given the gratitude she felt over the present situation—as opposed to what *could* have been—she felt certain that she should express that gratitude to God. She suspected that Irene would like her to, or that she would at least be pleased if Ella chose to do so. If only to please Irene, Ella determined that she *would* thank God at some appropriate moment. Even though she couldn't be sure if He would hear her, or even care, she felt that she had to at least try. But she had to think about how to go about it exactly.

In the meantime, she listened to the amiable chatter of Brother and Sister Pack. They were a pleasant couple, both a little shorter than average, and also pleasingly plump. They both wore glasses, and both had sparkling eyes and smiles that seemed permanent. Even when they weren't smiling, they appeared to be. She wondered if they'd led pleasant and happy lives that had gradually etched a smile into their faces. She wondered if it might be possible to turn her life around to the point that she could be in such a place in her older years. It was a nice thought, but seemed as fantastic as being given a magic wand. Even now, with the security of being in the care of these good people, she couldn't convince herself that it wasn't temporary. She would do her best to earn her keep and find work for herself, as she had promised she would, but she couldn't imagine being able to find work that would be of any significance. And she couldn't imagine anything in life taking her very far from what had become her reality since her father's debts and self-inflicted death had thrown her into a den of evil and wretchedness.

Ella tried not to think about that, but to focus instead on what she chose to see as an adventure—even if it was a temporary one. The skies were in rare sunny form when she stood before the home of the Packs and took it in as a place where she might find some safety and security. It was sandwiched between two similar houses of two stories each. It had no yard, but sported a quaint porch that had a wrought-iron rail. There were flower pots on the porch and window boxes in every window, where the winter residue of summer's flowers was lingering. Ella liked imagining how they might have looked in full bloom.

Brother Pack unlocked the door, and Ella was led inside and given a brief tour of the parlor, the kitchen, the dining room, and the bathroom before she was shown the room she would be allowed to use during her stay. It was up one flight of stairs and had a window that looked out over the street below. The bed not only looked warm and comfortable, but it was arrayed with a pink flowered quilt that made Ella just want to curl up in it and cry because of the depth of gratitude she felt. After appraising the room and the view out the window, Ella turned to the smiling Brother and Sister Pack and said with a tremor in her voice, "It's so lovely; so wonderful. I don't know what to say except that . . . I'm very grateful."

"A pleasure, dear," Sister Pack said at the same time Brother Pack said, "Glad to help; glad to have you here."

"You must let me know how I can earn my keep until I can—"

"We'll have no talk about that," Sister Pack said.

"Just give the matter some time," her husband added.

"I've got some lovely roast lamb left over from last night," Sister Pack added. "I'll just go put out the makings for a fine sandwich and we'll have a bite of lunch. Then perhaps you should rest, my dear."

"You're very kind," Ella said and turned again to look out the window, trying to comprehend how it felt to be looking *out* instead of *in*.

Even though her days of actually living on the streets had not been many compared to some others even less fortunate than herself, she had a deeply etched memory of how it had felt to pass by the windows of homes and shops and know that she could not go inside and find any shelter or reprieve. The very fact that she was looking out of the window of a lovely, comfortable room, knowing that a meal was about to be put before her, provoked tears that slid down her cheeks. She kept her back to her hosts, not wanting them to see, but she suspected they knew when Sister Pack gracefully shooed her husband out of the room and scooted out after him, saying, "Come down to the kitchen in a few minutes, my dear. And please do let us know if you need anything; anything at all."

By the end of the day Ella was becoming more comfortable with her surroundings, and with these people and their genuine kindness. Once she was ready for bed, wearing a nightgown that Irene had given her, Ella knelt by the bed and felt nervous as she considered how to go about saying a prayer that might express her gratitude. She finally just forced the words out of her mouth, even though Irene had told her she could pray silently and it would be heard. She simply thanked God for the blessings in her life, recounting them in a list, then she said amen and crawled into the bed where she cried into the soft, clean pillow— partly in gratitude for such comforts and security that she would never take for granted again, and partly from her churning emotions over the loss of her baby. She still had trouble reconciling her grief over losing the baby with her relief that he had not lived to face the only kind of life she had to offer him. She finally slept with the memory of Irene assuring her that her baby was in heaven and he was safe and happy. That comforting thought, combined with being safe and secure in this heavenly bed, enabled Ella to sleep well, and she woke feeling a sense of hope, in spite of rain drizzling down the outside of the window.

Ella went to church with Brother and Sister Pack. She was disappointed not to see Irene there, but knew that sometimes she had shifts at the hospital that prevented her from attending. People were very kind, and she didn't feel as uncomfortable as she thought she might when Brother and Sister Pack mentioned to nearly everyone they spoke to that Ella was looking for some kind of suitable work. She enjoyed singing the hymns, and was intrigued by the spiritual messages she heard, even though much of it didn't fully make sense to her.

Sunday dinner with Brother and Sister Pack was the best meal Ella had eaten since the servants had left her parents' home when they no longer had jobs. She couldn't stop talking about how good everything tasted, to the point that she almost felt silly. But these good people seemed to find joy in her pleasure, and their time together was pleasant. Ella helped clean the dishes, then she went along with them to visit their daughter who lived on the outskirts of the city with her husband and two children. It was a pleasant visit, and Ella liked these people, but she felt especially tired by the time they returned home, and she was glad for the comfortable bed waiting for her. She cried less that night than she had the night before, and she hoped that was a good sign.

Throughout the next few weeks, Ella settled comfortably into the Packs' home. She felt herself getting stronger in her recovery from giving birth, even though her tears over the loss of her baby still came without warning at times and overtook her. Sister Pack was especially compassionate about Ella's grief, and Ella was glad to know that Irene had told these people about her situation, so that she didn't have to do it. Irene came to visit a couple of times, and Ella was so glad to see her that she nearly burst. Hugging her friend tightly initiated tangible warmth in Ella that radiated out from her heart. Irene was keeping very busy, but found her work and all that she was learning to be very fulfilling. She shared news she'd received from home that everyone was well and missed her. Irene missed her family, but she spoke of how quickly the weeks were turning into months, and before she knew it she would be returning home again.

Irene was able to attend church two Sundays in a row, and Ella loved sitting next to her. She joined the Packs for Sunday dinner, and they all had a lovely visit. Ella asked Irene a few questions about the things she'd heard in church, for some reason finding it more comfortable to talk to Irene about such things than she did Brother and Sister Pack. Irene answered her questions in a straightforward way, and she shared some of her best-loved passages of scripture from what she called her favorite book, a volume entitled the Book of Mormon. Ella was most intrigued with the concept that Jesus Christ was real, and that He had somehow—by means Ella couldn't begin to understand—suffered for every mistake and sin that every human being might make, and He'd also suffered for all of the pain and grief of the world as well. Irene spoke strongly of the peace she had found through the Atonement of the Savior, and of how the Holy Ghost guided her in her decisions, and gave her peace and comfort. Ella was intrigued by the ideas, but it all felt very strange and foreign to her. In keeping with the vague and obscure teachings of her youth, she had always thought of Jesus as something of a myth or a legend, but had never considered seeing Him the way that Irene and other members of her church saw him.

Brother and Sister Pack gave Ella a copy of the Book of Mormon. Ella read from it a little here and there, but she found it difficult to concentrate on much of anything for too long when she felt preoccupied with the need to find a job and be able to support herself. Brother and Sister Pack were very gracious, but Ella knew she could not take unfair advantage of their hospitality, and more than anything she feared the prospect of ending up homeless and hungry. She wasn't certain she could ever survive such an experience again—emotionally *or* physically.

Ella graciously accepted the offering of some second-hand clothing from a very kind lady she'd met at church. She brought by a box of things that she said had belonged to her daughter who was near Ella's size, but they were things that hadn't been worn in a long time and they were destined to just collect dust.

"I'm afraid they're not very stylish," the woman said with mild apology, but Ella was thrilled to have them.

"Oh, I think they're lovely," Ella said, finding them to be of rather fine quality. "I shall get a great deal of good out of them. Thank you so much!"

Later, when she was alone in her room, Ella tried the clothes on and found them to fit rather nicely. There was a navy blue and white striped dress, and a few dark skirts with contrasting blouses, one white, one with a floral print, and one with tiny cream-colored stripes. For all that they'd been declared to be *not very stylish,* the hemlines were shorter as most women were wearing these days, and the fabrics looked practically new. There was also a lightweight black coat that Ella liked immensely. It was fine enough to wear to church over any of the other clothes, and hung about three-quarters of the way down over her skirts. In addition, there was a flat-brimmed black hat that Ella liked very much, and when she pinned it into the bun on the top of her head, she found it rather flattering. It went very well with the coat, which looked quite elegant—however simple in style—over the skirt she was wearing. The only real problem was that with shorter hemlines, Ella's shoes were quite visible and they looked terribly worn, but there was nothing to be done about that for the time being. She was grateful for what she had, and she got down on her knees that night and told God so. She still didn't know if He was listening, but she made a point of thanking Him every day for all that she'd been blessed with.

Through people at church, Ella became aware of some job possibilities. One was in a sewing factory, but Ella didn't have the faintest idea how to sew—either by hand *or* with a machine. Another job was a secretarial position for a legal office. Her father had been a barrister, but he had never talked much about his work, and she knew next to nothing about such things. And she certainly didn't have the skills to be a secretary, which required knowledge of shorthand and being able to use a typewriter. She'd never had any exposure to either. She was invited to interview for a position as the assistant to a cook in a large household, but it didn't go well. Ella felt confident that she could do the job and do it well when it mostly consisted of just handing the cook whatever she needed, and seeing that the completed dishes were given to the serving maids in the proper way. But for some reason, the cook didn't like the way Ella answered the questions, and she chose someone else to fill the position.

"Perhaps it was just a personality conflict, dear," Mrs. Pack said when word came that Ella didn't get the job. "When you work so closely with someone, you've got to be compatible in personality."

"Perhaps this cook is ornery and disagreeable and you're better off not working with her," Brother Pack said.

"I'm not fussy about working with people who are ornery and disagreeable," Ella said. "I just want to earn a sufficient living to care for myself."

"Your ambition is admirable, dear," Sister Pack said, "but you know you're welcome to stay here with us as long as you need."

"It's true," Brother Pack said. "We do enjoy having you here."

"You're very kind," Ella said as she had said dozens of times before, "and I'm more grateful than I could say, but I've got to earn my keep." Ella didn't add that while she knew these people were not put out by having her sleep in their house, and feeding one extra person was not a strain for them, they didn't have the extra cash to buy her things she needed, and she refused to be a burden to them or anyone else.

"Something will turn up," Sister Pack said.

The following week a friend of Sister Pack's said she needed some temporary help with some housekeeping while her maid was away for a few weeks due to a death in the family. Ella worked six days a week doing light cleaning and a little bit of simple cooking. She enjoyed the work and she liked the family she was working for. It was satisfying and not terribly difficult. She was able to earn enough money to buy herself some new shoes and stockings, and some new underclothing as well. She also bought a set of three lovely lace handkerchiefs. She kept one for herself, and wrapped the others up separately in some blue tissue paper she'd purchased. She wrote a note to Irene on some fine blue stationery she'd purchased, thanking her for all she'd done, and she wrote a separate note to Sister Pack for the same reason. On Sunday she gave the notes and handkerchiefs to these wonderful women, and she gave Brother Pack some horehound candy she'd purchased, knowing it was his favorite.

Brother and Sister Pack were delighted with their little gifts, but Irene got tears in her eyes when she folded back the tissue and saw the handkerchief. She read the note to herself while she held the handkerchief to her heart, then she hugged Ella tightly and told her how glad she was that they had become friends. Ella was glad too, but she couldn't see how her being Irene's friend had been any great benefit to Irene. She could only see how much this fine woman had done for her.

Later that evening, Irene and Ella sat together on Ella's bed, talking as if they were schoolgirls. Irene told Ella all about her home in Utah, which was located in the western United States. She talked of how the area had been settled by members of her church who had gone there to avoid religious persecution. Ella admired these people and their courage, certain she never could have sacrificed so much. But now Utah was well established, and according to Irene's descriptions, it was a lovely place to live, populated by many good people. Ella wondered what it would be like to go to such a place, where no one would ever know about her past, and she could be away from the city where she had so many difficult and painful memories. Irene lit up at Ella's mention of the idea, saying that if Ella could someday earn enough to get herself to Utah, she would make certain that she had a place to stay, and she would help her start a new life there. It seemed like a dream that was too far out of reach for Ella, especially when she had no job at all and wasn't likely to get one that would ever pay more than she needed to simply provide for herself. But it was still a lovely dream, and Ella lay in bed that night imagining what it might be like to go to America and start a new life.

When the temporary housekeeping job came to an end, Ella felt disappointed to let it go, feeling it was ideal, but she was glad for the boost it had given her. She still had a little bit of money put away should a need arise, and she devoted her time to searching for work. Even though the city was turning cold with winter, she went for long walks, going into shops and pubs and cafes, asking anyone who would listen if they had any work that she could do. But nothing turned up. Even though she was clean and nicely dressed, she still had trouble finding work.

She returned home discouraged again late one afternoon, glad that Sister Pack had insisted that she take an umbrella, since it had started to rain quite fiercely and Ella would have been drenched by the time she'd arrived. She came into the house after shaking the umbrella off as much as possible on the porch, deeply grateful to have a warm place where she could find refuge from the storm.

"Come in here, dear," she heard Sister Pack call. "Someone has come to see you."

Ella wiped her feet carefully on the mat inside the door before she stepped into the parlor to see a woman from church who looked familiar. Ella couldn't remember her name, but she was dressed very nicely, and Ella knew she was one of the members of the Church who had money. There were all different kinds of people that attended church together, and for the most part they seemed to interact very well. This woman reminded Ella of the kinds of women that her mother had once socialized with.

"You remember Sister Lynch?" Sister Pack said.

"Oh, of course," Ella said politely and took a seat. "How are you, Sister Lynch?"

"I'm very well, thank you. And how are you?"

"I'm well, thank you," Ella said.

"Sister Lynch came to call because she's been made aware of an opening that's become available with a family that her sister-in-law is familiar with."

"Oh?" Ella said, feeling some hope restored following her day of hopeless searching for work.

"Apparently they've had trouble keeping a decent nanny," Sister Lynch said, and Ella immediately wondered if that was due to bad luck with incompetent nannies, or because there was some difficulty with the job. But who was she to be fussy over such details? "I assured my sister-in-law that you were a lovely girl, and that you have fine manners and are quite respectable."

Ella smiled, wondering if the word *respectable* would be used in reference to her if people knew the whole truth about her past. As far as she knew, no one at church besides Brother and Sister Pack knew that Ella had been in the hospital because she'd given birth to an illegitimate baby. Ella preferred to keep it that way, but she hated the uneasiness she felt in wondering what people would think if they knew the truth. She just nodded and waited for Sister Lynch to go on.

"They would like to interview you tomorrow morning, if you're available."

"That would be wonderful!" Ella exclaimed, not holding back her enthusiasm. She would be so grateful to have *any* job, if only to be able to go forward with her life and stop feeling like she was taking advantage of Brother and Sister Pack.

"Lovely, then," Sister Lynch said and handed Ella a piece of paper with an address written on it. "Mrs. Blackhurst will be expecting you at nine o'clock. She told my sister-in-law that she would like to talk with you, and if she feels you're suitable, she'll have you meet the children right away. Do you have experience with children?"

Ella had to be honest. "Not very much, to be truthful, but—"

"Well," Sister Lynch laughed, "how hard can it be to simply watch out for a couple of children?"

"I'm certain I'll manage if they'll give me a chance," Ella said.

"I'm certain you will," Sister Pack said with enthusiasm.

That night Ella lay in her comfortable bed, staring at the ceiling, feeling a tight sense of dread that she couldn't understand. She'd been looking for a job and now she had the possibility of getting one. Perhaps she dreaded that it would just be another disappointment and she would still come away unemployed following the interview. Or perhaps she dreaded the possibility that she might actually *get* the job and that it would bring about changes in her life that she might not be prepared to face. She'd declared over and over—to herself and to others—that she was willing to take any kind of respectable work and she would not complain. With her limited skills and her complete lack of experience, she certainly couldn't afford to be choosy. But she felt wary of Sister Lynch's mention of this family not being able to keep a decent nanny. Ella told herself there was no good to be done in worrying about what that meant. If she got the job, she would take it on to the best of her ability and she would make it work. If she didn't get the job, she would just have to keep looking for work and hope that it wouldn't be too long before something turned up.

The following morning Ella was glad to have some money to pay the fare for a cab to deliver her to the Blackhurst home, since it was some distance from where the Packs lived. When Ella was standing before the front door, she was quite overcome with the huge and ostentatious structure before her. These people were not just well off, they were most definitely quite wealthy. As long as they were capable of paying her an honest wage for an honest day's work, she would be grateful. She took a deep breath, smoothed her skirt, and rang the bell.

An expressionless manservant answered the door and guided Ella to an elaborate study where she was asked to sit and wait for Mrs. Blackhurst. She waited for nearly twenty minutes before Mrs. Blackhurst entered the room in a dramatic flourish while she was barking orders at the maid, who followed her into the room then quickly left and closed the doors, leaving Mrs. Blackhurst alone with Ella, who stood to greet her potential employer. The woman had blonde hair that was styled too neatly for Ella to imagine even a strand ever being out of place. She wore a ridiculous amount of jewelry just for interviewing a potential nanny so early in the morning, and Ella wondered what she might wear to an evening event.

Ella immediately found the woman distasteful because of her obvious arrogance and the way that she questioned Ella, making it clear that she viewed the serving class as a people who were simply unequal to those for whom they worked. Ella thought about how she had once lived in a household that had hired help, but she couldn't recall her parents ever looking down on them or treating them unkindly. Mrs. Blackhurst asked Ella ridiculous questions like, "Are you afraid of snakes?" and "Do you have an aversion to eating green vegetables?" She seemed pleased when Ella answered no to both. The woman then began to ramble about her darling children—Donald, age seven, and Dorcas, age four—and how mistreated they had been by the last *several* nannies.

Ella was wishing with some fervency that she'd be told she was *not* suitable for the job, due to her obvious lack of experience with children—which Ella had made a point of emphasizing—when Mrs. Blackhurst announced with enthusiasm, "This is wonderful, then. I do hope you can start today. Of course, the job includes accommodations because naturally you'll need to sleep in a room near the children so that you can be on hand if you're needed in the night, and you must see them to bed and be available when they wake up. I'll give you cab fare to go home and get your things, and as soon as you return you can meet the children. I'll have Mrs. Cluff show you to your room and acquaint you with the household. She's the head housekeeper. I hope you'll find this all satisfactory, because I do so need you."

While Ella was envisioning herself enslaved to two difficult children every waking moment, she was ready to decline the position, feeling uncomfortable for reasons she couldn't completely define. Then Mrs. Blackhurst told her what the salary would be, and Ella nearly choked. She got by on a dainty little cough into her handkerchief, then heard herself saying that she was very glad for the job. During the cab ride back to the Packs' home, Ella imagined what she could do with the amount of money she could make if she could endure the Blackhurst children for even a year. Perhaps she could go to America and *really* start a new life. And perhaps these children weren't as bad as Ella might be imagining from their mother's description of all the traumatized nannies who had run off. But instinctively she felt a tremendous change in the air. When she'd gotten out of bed that morning, she'd not imagined herself actually moving out of the Packs' home before the end of the day. She hoped—and even prayed—that her transition into the world of working as a servant would not be too difficult or too painful. She tried not to think about what life had been like a couple of years ago. That had been another time and another world, and she had to face up to the fact that she could never go back to that life. She could only go forward, whatever that journey might entail.

CHAPTER FOUR
A Miraculous Coincidence

"I got the job," Ella told Sister Pack, who had been watching for Ella to return.

"Oh, that's lovely, dear!" she said with enthusiasm.

"But that means I need to hurry and get my things, because—"

"Your things?" she echoed, alarmed.

"Apparently having the job means living with the Blackhursts now," Ella said.

"Oh, I see," Sister Pack said as if she'd been informed of a death in the family and was trying to be stoic. This woman had been so kind and gracious, but Ella had perhaps expected her to feel some relief at having their boarder move out. Instead, she obviously felt regret at Ella's announcement that she would be leaving. In fact, she could tell that Sister Pack was trying very hard not to cry. She followed Ella to her room and tried to be helpful as Ella gathered her things together. When it became evident that Ella had nothing to actually put her things in, Sister Pack provided an old suitcase that was just the right size. Ella told her she'd bring it back, but Sister Pack insisted that she keep it. "Perhaps you will think of us when you see it," the woman said and wiped a tear. "And perhaps you'll come to visit when you can."

"Of course I will," Ella said and hugged Sister Pack tightly. "You've been so very good to me. I could never thank you enough." She smiled firmly at this woman who had become so much like a mother to her. "I'll come as often as time permits."

Sister Pack nodded stoutly and helped Ella gather the rest of her things. Brother Pack came to investigate the goings on, and he became very somber at the news of Ella's departure. They all shared a quiet lunch, none of them having much to say. After they'd eaten, hugs and farewells were exchanged, then Ella hired a cab to return to the Blackhurst home—*her* home now. She felt decidedly nervous and silently prayed throughout the drive that this would not turn out to be a terribly difficult endeavor. The amount of money she could make soothed her nerves, reminding her that whatever challenges she might face would surely be insignificant in comparison to what she had already survived. And at least she would have a roof over her head and food in her stomach, which was no small thing—no matter how she looked at it.

* * * * *

It only took a few days for Ella to realize that caring for the Blackhurst children was in its own way a nightmare. She continually measured each difficult situation in contrast to the nightmarish circumstances of her past, and she did her best to be grateful and keep perspective. But, *oh*! She'd never imagined that such spoiled, manipulative children could even exist! Ella's exposure to the parents of Donald and Dorcas made it easily evident why the children behaved the way they did. Mr. Blackhurst took no interest in the children, and had no involvement with them whatsoever. He expected his children to behave and make him proud, and since they rarely did either, he simply ignored them and tried to avoid them as much as possible. Mrs. Blackhurst was preoccupied with her social calendar, the beauty of her home, and the glory of her own reflection in the mirror. She *was* a beautiful woman; no doubt about that. But her obsession with it was downright annoying. She took the time to be involved with her children just enough to reinforce their bad behavior and teach them that they could get away with anything, no matter what the nanny said or did. Ella had no authority to discipline the children, but was expected to keep them under control. They continually got away with doing things to make Ella look bad in their parents' eyes. Mr. Blackhurst didn't care. Mrs. Blackhurst was just constantly reprimanding Ella for not *understanding her babies,* or being *insensitive to their refined natures.* But it seemed that given the difficulty she'd had in keeping a nanny, she was willing to overlook these problems so long as Ella kept the children safe and didn't allow them to interfere with any of the plans of their mother and father.

Ella was given very little free time. She had one afternoon a week when she was allowed to leave the children in the care of the housekeeper, but since the housekeeper loathed this part of her duties, she counted every minute of Ella's absence. In that time she had to do her own laundry and see to any of her own personal needs, which left little if any time for visiting friends or having relaxation. Even on Sundays she was expected to attend church with the Blackhurst family—a decidedly boring and unimpressive experience in contrast to going to church with Brother and Sister Pack. Ella was expected to keep the children quiet so that they could appear to be little angels when other churchgoers were observing them. She ate all of her meals with the children, since their parents shared *no* meals with the children. She taught them their lessons, bathed them, played with them, and did her best to keep them preoccupied and happy, the last part being the most difficult. They were the most miserable children she'd ever encountered.

In desperation, Ella went to visit Brother and Sister Pack, not only needing the reprieve of their home and their company, but seeking advice from good people who had raised a family. In order to use her time wisely, she did her laundry at their home so that she could accomplish this task while she visited, and Sister Pack was gracious, even eager, in helping her do it so that their time together could be put to the best possible use. Ella deeply appreciated their advice, and she found that by following it she could manage the situation a *little* better, but Mrs. Blackhurst still had far too much control without being involved enough to feel the consequences of her bad mothering.

The following week, Ella had managed to get her laundry done by staying up late two nights in a row after the children had gone to bed, so that on her afternoon off, she could meet Irene and visit. They had arranged through some messages back and forth to be at a certain tea shop at a certain time to share a leisurely lunch and visit. Ella was so glad to see her friend that she had trouble not crying when they embraced. As they sat together with a pretty tea service and lovely little sandwiches, Ella felt it was the best moment she'd had in her life in a long while—if not ever. Irene commented that she loved the British ritual of tea time and the dainty china teacups that were part of the tradition. Even though Irene didn't drink the strong tea that most British people were accustomed to, she enjoyed the ritual and wished that she could incorporate it into her own life when she returned to America. Irene talked about home with a tender nostalgia that was typical of such conversation. She got tears in her eyes as she talked of missing her children, and she told Ella all that her parents had written recently about what the children were doing. The conversation turned specifically to America, and Irene strongly encouraged Ella to seriously consider finding a way to get passage across the Atlantic, and then to take a train west to Utah. Irene made it sound so easy, and all Ella needed was to earn enough money to make the journey.

"Once you get to Utah," Irene said, "I'll take care of you and help you make a fresh start, and then we can be friends forever. It will be grand!"

Ella couldn't deny her intrigue with this idea. It was likely the only thing that made it possible for her to continue enduring her work with the Blackhurst children. Every hour of every day she imagined what she could do with the money she was earning. The possibility of using it to get to America, to the lovely valley in Utah where Irene made her home, made it all seem worth it.

Ella asked Irene *her* advice in dealing with Donald and Dorcas. Irene talked more about her three children at home, and how very much she missed them. She'd never had the horrible discipline problems that Ella was having, because she'd never allowed her children to behave that way to begin with. But her children were also very young. Irene just encouraged Ella to be loving to the children, since love was likely not something they received from *anyone,* and it was likely what they were craving, and the biggest reason they acted out so much.

"On top of that," Irene said, "they must have firm boundaries with consequences. That is how God deals with His children. It's surely the best example we can follow."

"The problem is that I have no control over the consequences," Ella said.

"You can only do the best that you can do," Irene said. "Prayerfully make your best efforts, do what you feel is best, and recognize that Mr. and Mrs. Blackhurst—and even the children—have their agency. Perhaps, whatever the outcome, you will have some kind of good influence on them. And if you don't, you'll know that you tried."

"It sounds so easy while I'm sitting here talking to you," Ella said, "but in all practicality, it's . . ." She didn't even know how to finish the sentence.

"I understand," Irene said, putting a hand over Ella's. "And remember that this is only temporary. You have better things to do with your life than put up with being treated badly by someone else's children."

"Do I?" Ella asked. "I'm intrigued with going to America, but truthfully I can't imagine doing much of anything with my life. I don't have any skills or—"

"Skills can be learned, my dear Ella," Irene said. "You have a strong will and a good heart. You can do great things with your life, if you just set your mind to it."

"I'd like to think so, but you might need to keep reminding me."

"Oh, I intend to," Irene said with a wink.

Ella found Irene to be incredibly wise and charitable, and she told her so. Irene laughed softly and said, "You're only around me just often enough to see the best of me, my dear friend. I can assure you that eventually what wisdom I have that might benefit you will all run out, and a day will come when you see that I can be terribly impatient and willful."

"Until I have the opportunity to be around you enough to see that side of you, I'll have to take your word for it."

"We all have weaknesses," Irene said, "and I have many . . . I can assure you." She laughed again, as if the very idea of being seen as *incredibly wise and charitable* was actually comical. Ella just wanted to add that Irene was also humble, but she kept it to herself.

With the combination of advice from Irene and Brother and Sister Pack—and her newfound efforts at prayer—Ella somehow found the will and ability to endure the exhausting and overwhelming challenges of her job. There were good moments here and there, and she tried to focus on those and give a great deal of positive reinforcement to the children when they behaved well and treated her with kindness. She continued to see her friends now and then, but not nearly as often as she would havev liked. Ella enjoyed her time with Brother and Sister Pack, but she most treasured every minute she might get with Irene—especially when they were so rare and all the more precious. Irene's work at the hospital—and all that she was learning—kept her very busy. She confessed to Ella that much of it was difficult and often very discouraging. At times she felt very homesick, and she'd even questioned whether or not she'd made the right decision in coming to

England. But she professed with fervency that in the deepest part of herself she *knew* it had been the right choice, and she didn't regret it. She knew that God wanted her to be here, and that the path of her life was in His hands.

Ella often pondered on Irene's faith and the idea that the path of an ordinary woman's life could be of any concern to God one way or another. Of course, Ella didn't consider Irene ordinary in any way. But she certainly wasn't famous or well-known. The work she did and the life she lived might go unnoticed by many, but to Ella—and to the many others who had benefitted from her kindness and faith—she had made a tremendous mark on the world. Ella would have never considered herself capable of making any noticeable contributions to this world, but Irene made her feel as if she could—even if it was impossible to imagine exactly *how* that might happen.

Ella found Irene's faith a great inspiration. Irene's belief in God and His hand being in the lives of His children was a sure and solid part of her character. She was a delicate woman in some ways—tender and soft-spoken. And yet she had a deep strength and determination that left Ella in awe. Just thinking of all Irene had accomplished in her thirty years of life helped Ella get through the difficult moments of her days—or rather the difficult hours. In fact, there were more hours that were difficult than not. But every hour was earning her a step closer to a new life and a new freedom, and she was willing to pay the price.

Christmas Day came and went with very little change in Ella's routine. The Blackhursts did give her a Christmas bonus, which was put carefully away with the rest of the money she was earning that wasn't absolutely needed. Brother and Sister Pack invited her for Christmas dinner, but she was not able to get away. But it turned out that on Boxing Day, she was able to spend most of the day with the Packs. Irene was there for a few hours, and they shared a lovely meal and had a marvelous time. Ella made up for it the next day, however, when Mrs. Blackhurst was in a highly agitated state over being left to care for the children the previous day while the servants had been given time off to have their Christmas celebrations. It took Ella more than a week to get the children back on track—if there was such a thing as having them on track at all.

On a bitter February day, Ella received a letter from Irene that she didn't have time to read until the children were finally asleep. The letter included what she called *a strange request.* She wrote, *Since we are unable to see each other very often, I thought it might be best to write and let you know of my wish for us to meet with a kindly gentleman with whom I have become acquainted. He is willing and able to come to dinner at the home of Brother and Sister Pack on the evening of your usual day off next week, and Brother and Sister Pack are eager and excited at the prospect. He is somewhat famous, you see, and a wonderful man. His name is William Stead, and he is a well-known journalist. He has been an advocate for many great causes on behalf of humankind, and among them he has shown an interest in the church to which I belong, and has been a good friend to the Mormons in this area. That is how I became acquainted with him. He has taken an interest in the work I've been doing on behalf of the poor and destitute here in London, and has asked me many questions. I shared a little bit of your story with him (without using your name, of course), and he was very compassionate and saddened that such things are happening to innocent young women. It is a situation he has been aware of for many years, and has, in fact, written about it and advocated for better opportunities that might help such things be avoided. He would very much like to meet you and speak with you, but only if you are comfortable with doing so. He believes that your story, which would remain entirely anonymous, might at some point in the future help the cause of other young women in your situation, and I personally feel that if you have the opportunity to speak with him, it might also help you to heal from the difficulties you have been forced to endure.*

I hope, my dear friend, that I am not being too presumptuous, and that you will not feel uncomfortable with my request. You are at liberty to decline, and I would completely understand. The decision is entirely up to you. If you are in agreement, I will arrange it, and I will be there with you, of course.

As for other matters, work at the hospital continues to keep me terribly busy, but I am learning much about the subject that I came here to learn. I am also learning much about life and its joys and miseries that I did not expect to be a part of my education, but I am deeply grateful that through God's hands I am learning these things. I will be forever changed, and forever a better person for these experiences. I miss my little ones so very much, but I know they are in good hands.

I hope that all is well with you, and that the challenges of your work will bring you closer to the goals and dreams you have before you. I want you to know that you are an amazing woman! When I think of all that you have conquered, I feel deeply privileged to call you my friend, and I look forward to seeing all the good that you will do with your life.

I will anxiously await your reply. With affection, Irene.

Ella cried as she read the letter, then she had to read it again and carefully consider what Irene was asking of her. For a minute or two she felt uncomfortable with the prospect of sharing her story with a stranger in such a way, then it occurred to her that she had no reason to not trust Irene, and if Irene felt that it was a good thing, then she was more likely to regret *not* doing it than she was to regret doing it. Irene had assured her all would be kept confidential and anonymous, and perhaps her story *could* make a difference to others. She liked the idea of that very much!

Ella once again read Irene's tender expressions of friendship at the end of the letter, shedding a few more tears as she wondered what she would have done, or where she would be, without Irene. Ella still had difficulty imagining that she might make something of her life in the way that Irene seemed to believe, but if Irene believed it, Ella felt that she should at least *try* to believe it.

Ella wrote Irene a lengthy letter in response, expressing her gratitude for their friendship and for all that Irene had done for her. She wrote a promise to do her best to live up to the potential that Irene seemed to believe was possible. Ella also told her that she would find it a privilege to speak with Mr. Stead, and she would keep the appointment. She had the letter sent out with the morning post and settled into her day, more able to cope while she held to the anticipation of getting away from the house to be among friends.

When the day came to have dinner at the Packs' home with Irene and Mr. Stead, Ella felt decidedly nervous, but she was grateful for the way Irene had taught her to pray. She still didn't know for certain whether God was hearing her prayers, but praying made her feel better anyway, and she prayed that this encounter would go well. She also knew she could rely on her trust in Irene, and if nothing else, the prospect of spending time with Irene and Brother and Sister Pack was always a delight.

Ella arrived at the home where she'd once lived to find that everyone else had already arrived. Sister Pack answered the door and hugged her tightly while she laughed with delight to see Ella.

"Come in, come in," she said. "Mr. Stead is such a pleasant man. What a great honor this is!"

At that very moment Ella heard the laughter of Brother Pack mingled with that of another man, and Irene's gentle laugh joining in. Ella entered the parlor and greeted her friends as they stood to give her their warm hugs, then she turned around to meet Mr. Stead. He was a nice-looking older gentleman, with a full, gray beard and a receding hairline.

"How lovely to meet you, Miss Brown," he said once introductions had been made and he'd offered her a warm and friendly handshake.

"A pleasure to meet you, Mr. Stead," she said in reply.

They went straightaway to the table to eat amidst pleasant conversation. Ella liked Mr. Stead and was very impressed with the great things he had accomplished in his lifetime. He was very humble about those accomplishments, which made Ella admire him all the more.

When they'd finished eating, Sister Pack insisted that she and her husband clean up while the others went into the other room, where they could share a private conversation. Once Ella and Irene were seated across the room from Mr. Stead, with the door closed, he said kindly, "I understand you've had some especially difficult challenges in your young life."

"I have, yes," Ella said, "although I'm sure there are many out there who have had it much worse."

"I'm certain that's true," he said, "but that does not discount what *you* have endured. I would very much like to hear your story, if you would be willing to share it with me. You only have to tell me what you're comfortable with sharing."

Ella had trouble getting started, but Irene helped by filling in some things that Ella had shared with her previously. Once Ella got started, she was able to tell this kind man all that had happened, discreetly omitting any embarrassing details. He was easy to talk to, and his compassion was genuine. Ella found some assurance in hearing him share experiences he had heard in the past of other young women who had been equally deceived and lured into horrible situations. It was nice to feel that she wasn't the only one who had been so foolish and gullible, and it was also nice to hear that Mr. Stead knew some of these women had gone on to lead good lives, and he felt confident that Ella could do the same. He believed that it was possible to take hardship and find value in it that could be applied to making a positive contribution to the world.

Mr. Stead made a gracious exit after expressing his gratitude to Ella and Irene for their time and their candor, then he expressed his gratitude to Brother and Sister Pack for their gracious hospitality.

"And I still intend to read that book you gave me," Mr. Stead said to Irene just before he left.

"What a nice man!" Sister Pack said.

"Yes, indeed," Irene said, then they all sat to visit for a while longer before Ella needed to return to her work, and Irene needed to return to the hospital.

Ella always hated saying good-bye to her friends—especially Irene. And she always hated going back to that dreadful house and having to associate with those difficult people. Even with the months that she'd worked there, she didn't even feel comfortable with the other servants. Having to spend every waking minute with the children didn't allow her the opportunity to interact with them as she might have liked. She felt mostly alone in her duties and in her dislike of them. Even with her efforts—at Irene's suggestion—to have a positive and loving attitude toward her work, she still felt unappreciated and mistreated. But she considered the fact that she could keep a smile on her face and never speak unkindly to others a huge accomplishment.

Ella returned to the Blackhurst home carrying with her a gratitude for her time spent with good people who genuinely cared, and that in itself gave her strength to move forward and more of an ability to strive for a positive attitude.

As the cold bite of winter began to show some hint of relenting to the healing power of spring, Ella was surprised to realize how long she'd actually endured what had to be one of the worst nanny positions in the great city of London. Through her occasional conversations with Irene—that didn't happen nearly often enough—Ella knew that Irene's time in London was winding down. Her training would be complete around the end of March, and she would be sailing back to America. Ella couldn't hold back tears when Irene told her, but she promised to always keep in touch through letters, and she was firm on Ella working toward joining her in Utah as soon as she could afford to do so.

The following day was one of the worst Ella had ever endured through the course of her employment in the Blackhurst household.

Donald and Dorcas were the most spoiled, unmanageable, and selfish children imaginable! And somehow they always managed to manipulate their mother into scolding Ella for something that one or both of the children had done that they shouldn't have done. Added to the children's especially bad behavior was Ella's preoccupation with Irene's impending departure. She wished that she could go with Irene now, but she simply didn't have nearly enough money saved yet to make the passage and then make the railway journey across America. Ella longed for a different job, but recalling her previous efforts in searching for employment, she knew it would be impossible to devote the hours to inquiries and interviews when she was occupied every waking moment with the children in her charge.

Mrs. Blackhurst went out for the afternoon, which was not at all unusual. But the moment she got home, she rushed into the nursery where Ella was playing a game with the children. Seeking out the children was *highly* unusual, and Ella wondered over the reason for this woman's excited fluster.

"Oh, my goodness!" she said, taking a seat as she dramatically tore off her fur stole and gloves and tossed them aside. "I have the most exciting news! Come and sit by Mother and let me tell you of the grand adventure we're going to have!"

The children moved to her sides on the little sofa where she sat. Ella took a seat across the room, wondering if this adventure would include Ella having to go along and keep the children in line. Already it held no appeal to Ella, if that were the case.

Mrs. Blackhurst appeared more animated than Ella had ever seen her. "Your father has arranged everything, and *we* are going on holiday to America!"

The children gasped, and so did Ella. Her heart beat hard and fast in her chest as she wondered if she was meant to go along. In the space of a couple of shallow breaths she was already considering how she could conveniently terminate her employment once her dreams of going there would be realized. But it only took another breath to realize that she was not likely to be included in such a grand adventure.

Mrs. Blackhurst took a deep, loud breath and said with even more animation, "But that's not the best part! We're to get to America on the *Titanic*."

"The what?" Ella asked, knowing the children were as ignorant as she was on why this would be the cause of such excitement.

"Oh, my goodness!" Mrs. Blackhurst said to Ella. "You really should remain more abreast of what's going on in the world."

Ella bit her tongue to keep from saying that if she were not consumed with the sole care of these children every waking minute she might be able to read a newspaper or converse with people about *what was going on in the world.*

"Oh, my goodness!" she said again. "The *Titanic* is the largest, the fastest, the most luxurious steamship in the world! And we are to travel on its maiden voyage!" She clapped her hands together and let out a laugh that sounded more diabolical than delighted, but the children were quickly caught up in her enthusiasm, suddenly asking question after question. "Just sit and listen," their mother said with her typical impatient tone, "and I'll tell you everything." She then went on and on about the impeccable reputation of the *Titanic* as being a great representation of man's ability to build anything. She spoke of it as absolutely being the *safest* way to travel to America, since it had been built to be practically unsinkable. She talked of how they would be staying in rooms on the ship that were equivalent to—if not finer than—the most luxurious hotels anywhere in the world. And she made a very strong point over the fact that sailing on the *Titanic's* maiden voyage had earned them great envy among all of their friends and relatives. It was something she would be able to brag about for the rest of her life.

Ella listened to Mrs. Blackhurst's oratory, considering that this was the most she'd conversed with her children since Christmas, except the children were not doing much of the talking. Ella still didn't know whether or not this adventure included her, and she had mixed feelings about whether or not she wanted it to. Going to America would be grand, but having some time to herself while the family was on an extensive holiday felt even more wonderful.

Mrs. Blackhurst then looked at Ella and said, "You must get the children's things in order and be packed and ready before the appointed day. We sail on April 10, and we'll be taking the boat train from here to Southampton."

"I'll have everything ready for the children," Ella said.

"And for yourself, of course," Mrs. Blackhurst said, as if Ella should have read her mind.

"I'm to go along, then?" Ella asked, her heart suddenly taking hold of the possibility of going to America as something she dared hope for.

Mrs. Blackhurst let out a ridiculous laugh that *did* sound diabolical. "Why, of course. It wouldn't be much of a holiday for me and Mr. Blackhurst if we had to fuss with the children all the time."

Ella felt angry on the children's behalf. It was no wonder they acted out so much when they heard their parents say such things. She felt sorry for them more than anything, but feeling sorry for them had not aided her in keeping them under control. She knew that well enough.

"We will be staying in America for more than a month before we return home, so be certain that you prepare adequately for yourself and the children."

"Of course," Ella said in a toneless voice that gave no hint to her secret enthusiasm. *America.*

That night Ella lay in bed, staring at the ceiling, trying to take it in. *America!* She felt guilty for already conspiring in her head how she would abandon her post once she got there. But, of course, she considered herself a responsible person, and she would simply give the Blackhursts an appropriate notice once they arrived. The worst possible outcome for them would be their having to care for their own children until they could find a replacement for Ella.

Ella longed to tell Irene the news, but she wanted to do it in person, and she couldn't get away until her usual afternoon off. She *did* send a note to Irene asking if they could meet in the usual tea shop, since she had something to share. Irene sent back a note saying she would be there, and that she *also* had news to share.

When the appointed day came, Ella waited in the tea shop for nearly twenty minutes before Irene arrived.

"So sorry I'm late," Irene said, hugging Ella tightly. "An emergency occurred and I had trouble getting away."

"Is everything all right?" Ella asked as they were seated.

"It is now," Irene said, "and the patient is in good hands." Irene pulled off her gloves. "Now tell me your news. I can't wait another minute."

"I think you should go first," Ella said, feeling the same way.

"Well, all right," Irene said, "although I'm afraid my news is more sad for us."

Ella felt deflated. "You're going to tell me that you're leaving England."

"That's right, I'm afraid," Irene said. "I'm very sad to be leaving for many reasons—most especially to be leaving you behind. But I'll be so very glad to get back home, and especially to see my babies again. I've missed them so dreadfully!"

"Of course," Ella said, trying to be compassionate—and positive. Her own news made it easier to be so. But she was waiting for the right moment.

"The big news is that I'll be sailing to America on what is said to be the largest and most luxurious ship ever built. And it's supposedly very fast, which means the journey might not be so tedious."

Ella held her breath, then let it out enough to ask, "What do you mean? What ship?"

"The *Titanic*," Irene said with a matter-of-fact nonchalance that was a lovely contrast to Mrs. Blackhurst's ridiculous enthusiasm. "Have you heard of it?"

Ella started to laugh so hard she couldn't speak. She kept a hand over her mouth while she glanced around to see if she should be embarrassed by such an outburst. Given that no one seemed to have noticed, she concentrated on what she'd just realized and kept laughing, unable to control it enough to get a word out.

"What is it?" Irene asked and laughed as well, even though she had no idea what was so funny. Or perhaps she just thought that Ella making a fool of herself was funny enough. "Ella, what is it?" she asked and laughed again.

"Oh, my dear friend," Ella finally managed, putting a hand over Irene's on the table. "It is the most miraculous coincidence! I came here to tell you that the Blackhursts are going on holiday and taking me along. We're sailing on the *Titanic*."

Irene gasped and jumped to her feet, which automatically urged Ella to her feet as well. Irene laughed as much as Ella just had as she threw her arms around Ella's neck.

"I can't believe it!" Irene said, forcing herself to sit back down.

"I can't either," Ella said, sitting across from her.

"It *is* a miraculous coincidence!" Irene said. "Although, I believe that what we often call a *coincidence* is just the hand of God orchestrating our lives."

"I like that idea very much," Ella said, "because I would like to think there's a reason He wants us to sail to America on the same ship."

"And once you get there," Irene said, "you must simply find a way to appropriately terminate your employment."

"That's exactly what I've been thinking," Ella said, "although I've felt terribly guilty to think of abandoning them to care for their own children while in a foreign country."

"You won't be *abandoning* them. You can give a fair notice once you've arrived. It's not in you to be unfair, my dear. Just pray about it and you'll know what to do. If God wants you in America—and I believe He does—He will help you in making it work out." Irene gasped as if an idea had occurred to her. "Perhaps you can get a railway ticket and come home with me."

Ella hardly dared admit how she'd been hoping for that exact thing. "Oh, that would be grand," she said. "I don't like the idea of being in a strange country by myself, but you must know how I would never want to be a burden to you or your family or—"

"You could never be that!" Irene insisted, then laughed again. "Oh, it's wonderful indeed!" She sighed as if she had just finished reading a satisfying book, then added, "And there are other miraculous *coincidences* at work here. I've just discovered that Mr. Stead is *also* sailing on the *Titanic*."

"You cannot be serious!" Ella said.

"It's true. He's going to some kind of peace conference in New York. I happened upon him recently when he came to the hospital in regard to one of his projects. And not only that, I've learned that a group of six Mormon missionaries will also be traveling on the *Titanic*. I confess that after my crossing to England, I'm not at all fond of being at sea, but I feel more reassured knowing the elders will be on board."

Ella recalled meeting some missionaries when she'd gone to church with Brother and Sister Pack, and she wondered if they might be among this group. She was also pleased to know they would be on board. She knew little about the Mormon Church, but she did know that the missionaries were considered to be very good and righteous men who sacrificed much to leave their homes to share the gospel. Surely they would be watched over and protected in their travels.

Ella enjoyed her time with Irene even more than usual. Where she had come to the tea shop believing it might be one of their last times together—unless Ella might ever miraculously make it to Utah—now she knew they would be sailing to America on the same ship. And even though Ella would be responsible for the children, she could still anticipate stealing away for some time with Irene, even if it was only late at night when the children were in bed. They made plans for that very thing, and even formed a plan of where and when to meet the first night of the journey. Even though they didn't have any idea what the layout of the ship might be, they did know the difference between the bow and the stern, and decided that they would meet at the very front of the ship at nine o'clock. They both hoped that the weather would be fair enough to allow for such a meeting, and they each agreed to be willing to wait for at least half an hour on the chance that there were unavoidable delays. They would try again the following evening should that attempt fail.

Ella and Irene parted with a tight hug and another bout of laughter as they once again expressed their awe and excitement over such a miraculous coincidence. The *Titanic*. Ella didn't care that it was large or fast or luxurious. She only cared that it would take her to America, and that Irene would also be on board. It could turn out to be the best thing that had ever happened to her.

CHAPTER FIVE
Man's Modern Marvel

ELLA WAS PLEASED TO FIND the children behaving a little better than usual. Asking them to behave so that she could get everything in order for their grand voyage to America apparently gave them great incentive. Ella was overwhelmed with the task of preparing the children for such a lengthy holiday, especially when their mother insisted that they needed to take practically everything they owned, *just in case.* Ella wanted to ask, *Just in case of what, exactly?* What could possibly necessitate a child needing so many changes of clothing, books they would never read, and toys that would never be played with? But Ella was meant to follow orders, and her opinion had no value, so she kept her mouth shut and worked at organizing multiple trunks that would go with them to America.

Ella could get *everything* she owned into the suitcase that Sister Pack had given her, but Mrs. Blackhurst gave her a new one, insisting that their nanny should not be seen with such an old and worn piece of luggage. Ella found the very idea ludicrous, when it was a perfectly good suitcase, but she returned it to Sister Pack, expressing her appreciation and hoping that someone else might be able to make good use of it.

Ella thoroughly enjoyed her final visit with Brother and Sister Pack, even though it was difficult not to be preoccupied with the fact that it was their *final* visit. Irene was there as well, and the farewells were difficult when it came time to leave. Ella just felt deeply grateful for all these people had done for her, and she told them so repeatedly. And she also felt grateful to know that this was not good-bye for her and Irene. She didn't know how she could possibly let go of her friend and wonder if she might ever see her again.

On the morning of April 10, Ella boarded the boat train to Southampton, holding the hands of Donald and Dorcas while their parents remained a few steps ahead. The children were remarkably quiet and well-behaved, perhaps in awe of the adventure upon which they were embarking. Ella hoped she might see Irene on the train, but it quickly became evident that the areas of the train were divided into first-, second-, or third-class ticket-holders—just as they would be on the ship. She knew that Irene was sailing second class, which was supposedly luxurious in and of itself, although the first-class passengers—such as the Blackhursts—would be traveling in some kind of sailing paradise. That was the rumor, at least. Ella would believe it when she saw it.

Throughout the train journey, Ella kept the children occupied with the view out the window. Once away from London, the lovely green countryside of England was a refreshing sight. When they disembarked from the train, Ella got her first glimpse of the *Titanic*. The enormity of it took her breath away and she found it difficult to get it back. *"Unbelievable,"* she muttered to herself, holding tightly to the children's hands. They too were so in awe that they stuck very close to her and had little to say. The noise and bustle on the pier was overwhelming as luggage and passengers were efficiently taken on board into their respective areas. Ella could quickly see a vast differentiation between the way that first-class passengers were handled, as opposed to those of third class; second class fell somewhere in between. Ella kept hoping she would catch a glimpse of Irene, or perhaps even Mr. Stead. Or the Mormon missionaries. But the crowds were vast, and she knew it wasn't very likely. Mr. Blackhurst had informed them earlier that with the crew and passengers combined, there would be well more than two thousand people on board. Ella could only think that it was a good thing she and Irene had determined a time and place to meet, or they would *never* have found each other.

Once on board, it didn't even feel as if they were on a ship. They were guided to large and beautiful staterooms that proved to Ella the rumors had not been false. The *Titanic* was indeed very spacious and luxurious. Ella would be sharing a room with the children, but the beds were lovely and comfortable, and there was plenty of room for all of the things that Mrs. Blackhurst had insisted they bring along.

They didn't bother unpacking anything before they went back to the deck of the ship, where it seemed to be some kind of tradition for the passengers on board to wave good-bye to the crowds gathered on the dock below. Given the fact that the *Titanic* was such a celebrated ship, and this was her maiden voyage, the roar of the crowds—both on the ship *and* on the dock—was quite a daunting experience. Donald and Dorcas were full of excitement, and Ella could only think what a challenge it would be to calm them down. She glanced around, wishing for a glimpse of Irene, but she had to keep her focus constantly on the children, and she also knew her friend would likely be on a different part of the ship.

There was a brief delay in getting underway, the rumor being that the massive force of the *Titanic* had pulled another ship away from the dock, snapping its ropes and causing a near collision. Ella couldn't see anything from where she was, but there was talk that all had been resolved, and the ship was soon underway, heading south across the channel to stop in Cherbourg, France. Once they had cleared the harbor, Mrs. Blackhurst sent Ella to keep the children occupied in their stateroom so that she and Mr. Blackhurst could socialize and become acquainted with the other wealthy passengers. Apparently there were some *very* wealthy people on board, and also some famous ones. Some were both. Ella only wanted to socialize with Irene, and she wouldn't mind a conversation with Mr. Stead or the Mormon missionaries. Beyond that, she didn't really care *who* was on board.

Just as Ella had predicted, all of the excitement of the journey had filled the children with excess energy. The subduing awe of the experience and getting underway had fled, and in its place was an uncanny need to tease each other into one fight after another. Ella endured the afternoon with the dreadful realization that being on the *Titanic* was no different than being in London, except that the available space in which the children could play was significantly less. She did take them for a walk on deck, leaving a note for their parents in case they should return. It helped get some of their wiggles out of them; but then they complained of the air being too cool, and they wanted to go back to their room. Ella felt disappointed, actually enjoying the fresh air coming off the sea. The view in the afternoon light was beautiful, and she longed to just stand on the deck and take it in as the *Titanic* cut its way smoothly over the water's surface.

The ship arrived in France near dusk, but Ella was barely aware of the occurrence, as busy as she was. She kept glancing at the clock, anxious to have the children down for the night so she could have some freedom.

She had spoken to Mrs. Blackhurst prior to sailing and asked permission to have her evenings free once the children were in bed. Her lady's maid, Patsy, had agreed to remain nearby to listen for the children once they'd gone to bed, since she had some hours of free time earlier in the day. This way Mr. and Mrs. Blackhurst could socialize as late as they wanted, and Ella could have some time to rejuvenate herself—time with Irene!

At five minutes before nine, Ella finally had the children settled down enough that she felt comfortable leaving them in the care of the maid, who was settling down in the next room with a good book. Ella thanked her and grabbed her coat, putting it on as she hurried down the long hallway, trying to get her bearings on which direction she should go in order to get to the deck at the bow of the ship. She marveled at what a very long walk it was, and twice she had to stop one of the crew and ask for directions. When she finally reached what they called the forecastle deck, she took in a deep breath of the sea air and felt a thrill to see Irene leaning against the rail of the ship, gazing out over the ocean. Ella had to use self-control to keep from shouting her name and squealing like an excited child. Instead she came up beside her and said, "Hello, my friend!"

Irene turned and laughed, and they exchanged a tight hug. "What a miraculous coincidence," Irene said and they laughed again.

They stood there together at the bow, just marveling at the size and magnitude of the *Titanic* and at the strange sensation of moving so quickly through the water. They strolled together at an unhurried pace while they talked about the day, the strange adventure they were on, and their impressions of this modern marvel on which they were sailing.

"To see something like this," Ella said, "you could almost think that man could build just about anything . . . do anything . . . go anywhere."

"We certainly live in an age of great advancements in technology—and in other things as well," Irene said. "I've personally seen such advancements in the field of medicine. There is an understanding of it in ways that have never been explored before. But I've learned that no matter what power we as human beings might think we have, God is always in charge. Everything the best doctors are capable of doing is powerless if it's a person's time to go. And the best possible health care would be useless without the body's ability to heal. Only God is responsible for those things."

"How very true," Ella said.

"We have so many wonders in our day and age," Irene went on as if she'd thought about this a great deal. "Wonders like the *Titanic*. Just think of the things we have that didn't exist when we were children. Well," she laughed, "when *I* was a child."

"There's less than a decade's difference in our ages," Ella reminded her.

"Yes, but a decade can bring about many changes. Think of all we have in our modern world. Electricity. The telephone. Automobiles."

"And sailing palaces that can take more than two thousand people across an ocean in a week's time."

"Exactly," Irene said. "I would only hope that man can recognize that everything he has that gives him the capacity to build and apply such things can come only from God. If man has a great idea, it's because God gave it to him. I sincerely hope that mankind has the humility to recognize that, and not get too full of themselves."

"You amaze me," Ella said.

"Why is that?"

"You just . . . think so deeply about things that would never even occur to me. It's fascinating. That's one of many reasons I enjoy talking with you."

"It's good to be able to talk to someone who isn't bored with my ideas," Irene said.

"Oh, never!" Ella said.

Irene took Ella to her second-class cabin, where Ella declared, "Oh, it's lovely!"

"It *is* lovely, isn't it."

Together they examined the cabin's features, marveling that the bed had never been slept in, and everything was completely new. Its fineness was evident in every detail of the decor, and the room provided everything that could possibly be needed.

"I've spoken with some of the third-class passengers," Irene said, "and they tell me that their accommodations are finer than the homes they left behind."

"Left behind?"

"Many of them have sold everything to make this journey; they're immigrating to America."

"Oh, how exciting!"

"Yes, it is," Irene said as they sat together on the bed like a couple of little girls. "Are *you* immigrating to America?"

"I hope so," Ella said.

"You hope so?" Irene countered. "You're the one who has to decide if you'll stay there."

"I *want* to, but . . ."

"But?"

"I just don't know if it's right."

"Right to stay in America? Or right to quit your job?"

"Both, perhaps."

"Well, you can pray about it and get an answer for yourself, Ella. The Spirit can guide you in this decision. The way is there for you if you have the courage to take it, but you need to know for yourself if it's the right path for your future."

"And how do I go about that, exactly?" Ella asked.

Irene had taught Ella much about prayer and recognizing God's hand in her life, but this time she went into more detail about how it was possible to discern the answers to prayers through the still, small voice of the Holy Spirit. She shared some examples from her own life that helped Ella understand a little better the practical application of such knowledge. Ella especially enjoyed hearing how desperately Irene had struggled with the decision to go to England to become a midwife. Ella hadn't realized until then that Irene's husband and mother-in-law had been very much against her decision, but Irene's parents had supported her to the point that they had mortgaged their home to provide the money she needed to make the trip and pay for her education. Irene talked again about how her children were also staying with her parents, and how grateful she was to know that they were in good hands.

"It's been difficult in many ways," Irene said, "but I know beyond any doubt . . ." her voice quivered and tears sparkled in her eyes, ". . . that this was the right choice for me. I don't know the path of my life from this day forward, but I know that it has purpose, and that this journey was important to that path."

"Your faith inspires me," Ella said.

"You have a lot more faith than you think you do," Irene said.

"Do I?"

"Oh, absolutely! Which reminds me, have you ever read much in that book I gave you?"

"The Book of Mormon?" Ella asked. "Only a little here and there. I don't get much time for reading."

"I understand," Irene said. "But I do hope you'll take the time to read it when you can. Did you bring it with you?"

"I did," Ella said and laughed. "Actually, I brought with me everything I own . . . on the chance that I decide to stay in America."

"Well, I hope you decide soon. And I'm hoping you'll decide to come home with me."

"It's very tempting," Ella said, wondering how she would go about telling her employers that she intended to leave them without a nanny.

Ella asked Irene about the Mormon missionaries, and she was disappointed to learn that they'd not sailed on the *Titanic* after all.

"As I understand it," Irene said, "one of them was unable to leave, and he told the others to go ahead, but they agreed that they would wait and all sail together."

"I hope that's not a bad omen," Ella said.

"I'm certain there's a good reason for it," Irene said, "but whatever that reason might be, our lives are in God's hands, and we mustn't worry."

"Of course," Ella said, trying to push away any concern she might have felt, since she could find no reason to feel anything but glad to be with Irene on her way to America.

When both women started to get tired due to the late hour, Irene helped Ella find her way back to a place on the ship that she recognized so that she could return to her room. They shared a parting hug, and Ella quietly entered her room to find the children sound asleep. Patsy had gone back to her room, and Mr. and Mrs. Blackhurst had just returned from their late-evening socializing.

Ella slept well but was dismayed when the children woke early and were full of energy and mischief. Mrs. Blackhurst had scolded her twice before noon, and Ella felt great incentive to quit her job and go west with Irene. Still, she wondered if it was the right thing to do. For some reason it *didn't* feel right, but she couldn't figure out why. She felt good about staying in America, but when she considered going home with Irene, it nagged at her in a way that Irene had described as the kind of negative feelings that might mean it wasn't the right answer to her prayer. But logically, whether she went west with Irene or not, she still intended to stay in America, and that meant quitting her job sometime in the near future. She just wondered if she should at least wait until they'd arrived. Ella would like to have somewhere to sleep, and if Mrs. Blackhurst was angry over her decision, that might not be an option anymore. As it was now, her bed was in the same room with the children, and being on a ship, there was nowhere else to go. For now, she decided to just wait and pray about the matter some more. At least she knew she had a fair amount of money tucked safely away in her luggage, so that whatever she decided to do, she would not be destitute.

The ship made its final stop in Queenstown, Ireland, where some passengers disembarked and others came on. The ship was too large to come too close to port, so passengers were ferried to the ship. The children wanted to stand on the deck and watch the excitement. Ella was only glad that it kept them occupied. When the view became tedious, she was glad to feel the *Titanic* moving again toward the open ocean. They were now on their way to America, venturing out across the massive Atlantic with power and speed.

Shortly after a late lunch, a miracle happened when Mr. Blackhurst told Ella that he wanted to spend more time with the children while they were sailing. Therefore, he was giving her a few hours off in the afternoons as well as time off following the children's bedtime. Ella thanked him and left right away, glad that she knew how to find Irene's cabin. She hoped that she would be there. Given such a precious opportunity, she didn't want to waste it by being alone. Once they arrived in America, she had no idea what to expect. But this brief oasis of time on the *Titanic* was a treasured chance to spend some leisurely time with Irene.

Just as Ella was about to knock, the door came open and Irene was standing there, ready to go out. Both women gasped at the same moment, then laughed together from the way they'd startled each other.

"Did you quit your job?" Irene asked facetiously.

"Not yet," Ella said. "But I am going to be given time off in the afternoons while we're sailing."

"Oh, how delightful!" Irene said and pulled the door closed to her cabin. "That means you can come with me."

"Where are we going?" Ella asked, following her through the labyrinth of hallways and stairwells, wondering how Irene could keep her sense of direction.

"I've become acquainted with the most delightful people," she said. "I was just going to the third-class dining saloon. It's much more fun there than being around those stuffy people who spent enough money on this voyage to feed many families for a year."

"Indeed it would be!" Ella said.

During the next couple of hours, Ella got to know a number of families with children. It seemed to be the families with children that Irene felt drawn to. Some did not speak very good English—or no English at all—but Irene communicated with smiles and gestures and simply by playing with the children. Those who *did* speak English were quickly engaged in conversation about where they'd come from, what had made them want to go to America, and what they would do when they arrived. Ella loved to see how Irene was so genuinely interested in these people and their lives. It seemed she learned something new from Irene each time they were together.

When they left the dining saloon, Ella glanced at her watch to realize she still had some time. Irene was pleased and said, "Come with me." She took Ella by the hand. "I doubt that anyone will be there this time of day."

"Be where?"

Irene just laughed and led the way through more hallways and stairwells, then through a set of elegant doors and down another hall.

"Are we supposed to be here?"

"Just trust me," Irene said, and Ella lost track of where they were going. The ship was a literal maze of endless decks and hallways and stairs. But Irene apparently knew the way, as if she were a hunting dog with a strong scent to follow. She paused outside of an open doorway, then peered carefully around the corner before she declared, "See, we're all alone."

The two women entered the room, and Ella gasped to see the elegant decor of the parlor in which they stood. Once again she could hardly comprehend that they were on board a ship. When standing in such a room, it felt as if they were in a very luxurious hotel. Ella then realized that the main focus of Irene's attention was the beautiful grand piano. She let go of Ella's hand to carefully fold back the cover from the keys. She then reverently touched the keys in greeting before she sat at the bench.

"You play?" Ella asked, feeling a sudden thrill at the prospect of such an opportunity. Irene was always full of surprises.

"I do," Irene said and let out a delighted laugh, as if being at a piano brought her great joy. "I confess that I actually registered myself on the *Titanic* as a musician."

"Even though you are professionally a nurse? Well, a midwife now."

"Yes, and I hold a great respect for my profession, but . . ."

"In your heart you are a musician?"

"Something like that," Irene said and put her fingers on the keys. Immediately something magical happened, and Ella sank into one of the lovely chairs nearby to just take in the ethereal sound that floated into the air as Irene's fingers lovingly caressed the ivory and ebony. At first Ella was fascinated with watching Irene's hands, and how effortlessly they made the music come to life, then she closed her eyes and felt drawn into a different world—a world where suffering and evil didn't prevail; a world where there was no fear and no pain. Irene had made her believe that such a place *did* exist, and that the trials endured in this life would bring them to a better place. Ella wanted to believe that, and hearing Irene's music filling the air around her made it easier to believe. She thought of all this dear friend had taught her, and all the hope she had found through her association with this great woman. Her thoughts, combined with the music, brought the sting of tears to her eyes, but she welcomed the sensation, feeling in touch with her emotions in a positive way for the first time in years.

Irene eased from one song into another, and Ella was grateful to not have the experience end right away; she enjoyed indulging in it for every minute that Irene was willing to play. But eventually Ella had to get back to work, knowing that if she wasn't there when Mr. Blackhurst tired of the children, she would be facing the wrath of Mrs. Blackhurst.

The following day during her time off, Ella and Irene were able to explore the *Titanic* like a couple of children in a palace. There were some areas of the ship where they were not allowed to enter, but they managed a peek at one of the two grand staircases, which left them both breathless. They discovered that the amenities available for the first-class passengers included a swimming pool, Turkish baths—whatever that might mean— as well as private promenades for the highest-paying passengers. There was even a hospital, of which they were given a gracious tour while one of the nurses there was engaged in friendly conversation with Irene over their common knowledge and interests.

The enormity and luxury of the *Titanic* was difficult to take in, but its beauty and majesty certainly had a delightful effect on two women who were enjoying their time together in a way that made them feel like little girls on a grand adventure.

At the conclusion of their explorations, they went again to the parlor, but this time they found a few middle-aged women there visiting. Ella felt deeply disappointed and could see that Irene felt the same. Irene whispered to her, "I hear there are four other pianos on the ship."

"Five pianos?" Ella whispered back. "On a ship?"

"Apparently."

"But how would we find them?" Ella asked. Then without waiting for Irene's permission, she approached the women in the parlor and said, "My friend here is very talented at playing the piano. Would you mind very much if she were to play? We don't want to interrupt your visiting, but—"

"Oh, that would be lovely," one of the finely dressed women said. Ella motioned Irene toward the piano, winking at her as she crossed the room.

Ella once again made herself comfortable, admiring the beautiful decor of the room while she took in the beautiful music. The other listeners were immediately entranced as well, and they applauded between songs, encouraging Irene to continue playing. Ella hated pulling herself away to return to work, but she kept hearing Irene's music in her head while she cared for the unruly little Blackhurst children, and it kept her spirits up through the remainder of the day, until she had the reprieve of putting them to bed.

Ella met Irene at their usual place on the deck that evening. They ambled slowly about the ship, chatting comfortably about a myriad of topics.

"I dare say it's getting colder," Irene said. "Aren't you freezing? That coat is lovely but just too thin to keep out this kind of cold."

"I'm fine," Ella said. "The company is keeping me warm, and we'll go inside soon enough."

The next day was Saturday, and the highlight of the day was once again being with Irene. They visited with their new friends in third class, then they went to the parlor where Irene played the piano, and they visited with some people there as well. When they left the parlor, Ella was glad they still had some time, because she wanted to talk to Irene about her ongoing contemplations in regard to the decisions she was trying to make. They were barely out the door, however, before they came face-to-face with Mr. William Stead.

"Ladies!" he said with a pleasant smile. "What a remarkable coincidence!"

"Indeed," Irene said at the same time that Ella said, "Oh, it is." Then they both giggled like a couple of girls, which made Mr. Stead laugh.

"Since we've come upon each other this way, I wonder if you would both do me the honor of a stroll around the deck. With such a lovely lady on each arm, I'd be the envy of every man on board."

The women both laughed softly at his sweetness, and they heartily agreed to the stroll. While they were ambling comfortably in the chilly afternoon air, Mr. Stead told them that he'd had somewhat of an eerie sensation while sailing on the *Titanic*.

"Why is that?" Ella asked.

"Well, you see," he said, "many years ago I wrote a little piece of fiction about a disaster at sea. No, come to think of it, there were two different stories. Both stories were quite disastrous, and I'm hoping that there isn't some strange meaning to them for me now."

"Tell us about them," Irene said.

"Well, it's been many years ago," Mr. Stead said, "and I've done a great deal of writing since that time, but one was written from the point of view of a survivor. It was about two ships that collided at sea, and many people died because there was a shortage of lifeboats."

"Are there enough lifeboats on *this* ship?" Ella asked, immediately alarmed.

"I can't say that I know the answer to that question, but I doubt that my silly little story has any bearing on our current situation. It's just that I thought of it earlier and found the memory somewhat eerie."

"And what of the other story?" Irene asked.

"Something about a ship colliding with an iceberg, as I recall," Mr. Stead said.

Ella shuddered and noted that Irene did as well.

"And I think that now would be an excellent time to change the subject," he said with a little laugh. "Tell me about your plans when you get to America."

Irene talked about her family, and how she was looking forward to being reunited with many friends and loved ones. While Irene was talking, Ella realized that she needed to get back to work. She told Mr. Stead how very good it had been to see him again, and she lightly told him that she hoped his stories didn't come true. Ella said she would see

Irene later in the usual place, then she hurried back to the stateroom to care for the children.

That evening, while standing at the bow of the ship, Ella told Irene that she felt good about staying in America, but less certain about going west to Utah. "It doesn't quite make sense to me," Ella said, "because I *want* to go with you, but I just . . . I don't know."

"If you're worried about being a burden, you mustn't be."

"I *have* worried about being a burden," Ella said, "but I've come to know you well enough to know that you wouldn't have invited me to come if you didn't want me to."

"That's right."

"And I would hope I've proven that I'm willing to work to support myself."

"Absolutely," Irene said.

"So, it's not that. It just . . . doesn't feel right. I can't leave the Blackhursts without giving them fair notice, and we'll be in New York the middle of the week. So, for now, my plan is to give them notice a few weeks before they plan to return to England, and perhaps I'll come to Utah then—depending on how I feel."

"That sounds very reasonable," Irene said, "even though I'll miss you dreadfully."

"We'll keep in touch through letters always," Ella said.

"Of course we will," Irene insisted and the subject was changed. Ella enjoyed listening to some stories about Irene's children, and she hoped that she would one day have the opportunity to meet them.

The following day was Sunday, and Ella had the opportunity to attend a church service with the family. Of course, she'd been brought along to keep the children from misbehaving, which was not an easy task. Due to their tendency to engage in mild forms of mischief, rather than any kind of reverence, Ella wasn't able to concentrate on the service as much as she would have liked, but she enjoyed singing the hymns and was still glad she'd been able to go.

That afternoon she especially enjoyed her time with Irene. They walked and talked and Irene again played the piano while Ella and a few other people in the parlor enjoyed listening. They went down to visit with their friends in third class, then Ella returned to her post with the children.

Ella once again spent suppertime trying to convince Donald to eat his vegetables, at the same time struggling to keep Dorcas from crawling under the table. What happened next was surely the most infuriating moment of Ella's life. Dorcas slipped from her chair while attempting to once again slither beneath the table. Ella grabbed her arm to try to spare her from the fall, but Dorcas immediately started screaming. She'd obviously bumped her head, but instead of allowing Ella to offer her some comfort over the injury, the child started screaming at the full capacity of her high-pitched voice, "Ella hurt me! She hurt me!"

At the very same moment, Donald apparently realized he had a great opportunity to stir the pot a little more on Ella's behalf. He turned his plate upside down, sending his food in every direction across the table, at the same time yelling, "Ella got mad at me and spilled my food!"

Of course, Mrs. Blackhurst's investigation of the tumult resulted in *her* yelling in a voice that strongly resembled those of her children, "I've had enough of your ill treatment of my children. You are finished. You're fired! I don't want to see your face again!"

"We're in the middle of the Atlantic Ocean," Ella said. "Where do you think I would go?"

"I don't care where you go, but get your things and get out." She made a disgusted noise while comforting her wailing children, who were even in that moment eyeing Ella with mischief, away from their mother's view. "Good luck to you when you get to New York and you're completely on your own," Mrs. Blackhurst snarled. "I hope you *starve!*"

Ella bit her tongue so hard it nearly bled. If she responded emotionally to such a remark, she would say something she would regret, or cry like a baby. While she was struggling to prevent herself from doing either, Mr. Blackhurst entered the scene, nonchalantly asking, "What *is* all the fuss about?"

"I've had it with this woman!" Mrs. Blackhurst said to him. "She'll be leaving immediately!"

Mr. Blackhurst looked at his wife and the two wailing children. He looked at Ella, then at his wife again. "If that's what you wish, my dear. I'll make your excuses this evening."

"What?" Mrs. Blackhurst countered.

"If you're watching the children, you clearly won't be able to attend the—"

Mrs. Blackhurst made an astonished noise that stopped her husband midsentence. He just walked away. Mrs. Blackhurst looked at Ella as if she were consciously swallowing her pride enough to take back what she'd just done. But Ella felt her own pride take over. She'd been abused and insulted enough.

"Good-bye, then," Ella said and left the room. Within a few minutes she had her minimal belongings packed and was on her way to Irene's room, hoping her friend wouldn't mind if she spent the night there on the floor. She didn't know what she *would* do when she got to New York, but she was done dealing with the Blackhursts and their selfish arrogance. She deserved better than that!

"You deserve better than that!" Irene insisted after Ella had told her about the encounter.

"That's exactly what *I* thought," Ella said and couldn't help chuckling, now that it was over and Irene was being so supportive. "You know, my friend, before I met you, I would have never believed that. I would have believed that I *didn't* deserve any better. You've changed me, and I'm grateful."

"Well, if you can see that you don't need people like the Blackhursts, then it's a change for the better, indeed."

"But maybe I *do* need them," Ella said. "I have some money saved, but not very much, and—"

"I thought we'd already discussed this," Irene said. "This just makes our plan all the easier. You can sleep here for the few days we have left of the journey, and you can come with me to Utah. Now you don't have to worry about *what* to do, and whether or not you should quit your job once you get to America. It's been decided for you."

Ella gasped at the thought. "I admit that it all sounded like a lovely idea, but I just couldn't imagine it really working out." She looked intently at Irene. "Are you really certain you want me to come home with you? Wouldn't that cause a problem for—"

"I'm absolutely certain," Irene said. "You can start a new life there. My parents will *love* you!"

Ella considered the possibility more than she'd allowed herself to do before. "What if I don't have enough for the railroad ticket, or—"

"I'll loan you enough for the difference," Irene said. "Let's worry about that when we get to New York. For now, you are no longer burdened by those poor little spoiled children. We should enjoy the remainder of the evening. Come along. Let's go for a walk. Perhaps we could go and visit our new friends. Those children have been brought up right. They're a joy to be with."

"Indeed they are," Ella said. "Perhaps they can help me get the bad taste out of my mouth."

"Perhaps," Irene laughed and led the way to the third-class dining saloon where supper was over but many people were still gathered there in laughter and conversation. Ella was quickly able to forget about her nasty encounter with Mrs. Blackhurst, and deep inside she felt a warm relief. Her decision had been made for her. She was going to America, and she was going to begin a new life!

CHAPTER SIX
The End of a Dream

LATE IN THE EVENING, ELLA and Irene went back to Irene's cabin after she had found a member of the crew and asked if she might be able to get some extra blankets and a pillow. In the cabin Irene made up a tolerable bed on the floor, then said, "I'll sleep on the floor tonight, and you can sleep on the floor tomorrow night."

"I will sleep on the floor *every* night until we get to New York," Ella insisted. "I'll not have you giving up your bed for me."

"I'm so happy to think of you coming home with me, that I'm glad to give up my bed for you."

"Well, I won't have it!" Ella said, and they teasingly argued over the matter in between taking turns brushing their teeth.

They were both digging out their nightgowns in order to change for bed when Irene said, "Did you feel that?"

"What?" Ella asked, her heart quickening with a sudden memory of Mr. Stead's tragic stories.

"I think the engines have stopped," Irene said, looking around as if the reason might present itself right there in the little cabin. "I've gotten used to the constant hum of the engines, but . . ."

"You're right," Ella said. "Something's different. I hope nothing is wrong."

Irene looked contemplative while she seemed to be listening, and Ella remained quiet. "Let's go find out what's happening," Irene said.

"I'm sure it's nothing," Ella said. "Wouldn't we be better off waiting here?"

Irene was silent a long moment and said, "I feel like we should find out."

"Then let's find out," Ella said, not about to quibble with Irene's instincts, or her hearing the Spirit, or whatever it might be. They both put on their coats and hurried to the deck where they found nothing apparently out of the ordinary.

Together they stood there for a minute or two, saying nothing, looking around as if they expected something to happen. A few late-night strollers ambled past, but no one seemed concerned. Ella sensed that Irene felt concerned, and she had to wonder if her own feelings of concern were because of that, or whether they came from within herself. Both, she concluded.

"What are you thinking?" Ella finally asked.

"I don't know," Irene said. "Let's walk for a few minutes. I don't think I can sleep yet."

"Good idea," Ella said, and they walked toward the bow of the ship then around to the starboard side, where they found some commotion taking place, but it was laughter that came to their ears.

"What in the world is that?" Irene asked, taking hold of Ella's arm. They both stopped to consider what they were seeing.

"It's ice," Ella said and they watched with fascination as some people on deck were kicking around large chunks of ice that slid over the deck like toys.

While Ella was wondering how ice might have ended up on the deck, a man in uniform came running toward them.

"Excuse me," Irene said, stepping into his path, "I can see you're in a hurry, but . . . is something wrong? The engines have stopped."

"We've come very near an iceberg," he said, walking as he spoke, "but I'm certain everything's all right. No need to worry, ma'am."

"Thank you," Irene said, and the man hurried on.

"Do you think there's no need to worry?" Ella asked.

Irene thought about it. "I don't know, but . . . whether or not there is, I doubt our *worrying* about it will change anything."

"That's true," Ella had to admit.

"Let's just . . . walk. I feel restless."

"Good idea," Ella said again. "Although it's awfully cold. Does it feel colder to you?"

"Yes, it's definitely colder. Let's just keep moving."

They walked slowly toward the stern, but since it was a very large ship they probably got only about halfway before Irene turned to go back the other way for no apparent reason. As they were nearing the bow again, Irene stopped walking and said, "Does it feel to you as if we're walking downhill?"

Ella looked over her shoulder, then ahead. She took a few steps and said decidedly, "Yes." She then gasped. "Something *is* wrong." Her concern jolted into a form of panic in an instant. She took hold of Irene's arms and looked hard into her eyes as if she might never have the chance to do so again. "What if something is *really* wrong, Irene? What if—"

"We must keep our wits about us," Irene said, but Ella could tell she was having similar thoughts. "Keep walking. Let's talk about this." But neither of them had anything to say, as if not putting their worst thoughts to words might keep them from being a reality. Ella was thinking about Mr. Stead's stories, wondering if they'd been some sort of strange premonition. She felt sure Irene had similar thoughts, but neither of them spoke. It seemed the more they walked, the more there was a sense of walking uphill—now that they were going in the other direction.

They both stopped again at exactly the same moment, and Ella took a sharp breath just before she heard Irene do the same. A short distance ahead, crewmen in uniform were removing the canvas cover from a lifeboat.

"Heaven help us," Irene said and took Ella's hand as if there was not a moment to lose. "We must tell the others."

"Who?" Ella asked.

"Everyone!" Irene said, as if she personally intended to save each and every person on board.

"I must warn the Blackhursts," Ella said, surprised at how her difficult feelings over the situation did not lessen her desire to see that they were all safe.

"That's where we're going first," Irene said, and they hurried toward the first-class staterooms where Ella had been staying with the Blackhurst family. As they entered the hall, they were both taken aback to see chaos forming as crew members were knocking on doors and telling people to dress warmly, put on their life belts, and get to the deck.

As Irene and Ella pressed on toward the Blackhursts' rooms, a man said to them, "Ladies, please return to your rooms and get your life belts."

"We will, thank you," Irene said and they moved on through a growing crowd moving in the opposite direction.

Ella entered the stateroom without knocking to find Mr. and Mrs. Blackhurst arguing about whether or not they should heed the warning. Mrs. Blackhurst was prone to stay in her comfortable room, certain it was nothing. Mr. Blackhurst insisted that it was better to be safe than sorry.

"I agree," Ella said, and the two of them came out of their argument enough to realize they were not alone.

"What on *earth* are you doing here?" Mrs. Blackhurst snarled.

"I've come to tell you, you need to do as you've been told," Ella said.

"I don't believe there are enough lifeboats for everyone," Irene added, and Ella looked at her sharply, wanting to scream but not knowing what to say. Their eyes met, and Ella felt a foreboding chill that made her start to shake from the inside.

"I'm certain it's nothing," Mrs. Blackhurst insisted.

Ella thought of the children and felt desperate. She looked around and noticed some of Donald's marbles on the floor. "It's not *nothing!*" Ella said and put a marble on the table. Mr. and Mrs. Blackhurst gasped in unison as the marble promptly rolled off the table. "The bow is sinking. Please get the children dressed and get to the lifeboats."

Mrs. Blackhurst rushed into the other room to wake the children. Ella followed her and took a long glance at each of them, praying they would be all right. She got out the life belts and tossed them onto the children's beds, then she grabbed her own and followed Irene back to her cabin.

"Please tell me what you're thinking," Ella said to Irene.

"I'm thinking that our lives are in God's hands, Ella, and whatever happens this night is beyond our control."

"And if we die?" Ella asked.

She expected Irene to perhaps assure her that they weren't going to die, that everything was going to be all right. But she simply said, "Then it is God's will."

Ella grabbed her arm to stop her. "How can you say that?"

"Ella," Irene said in a calm voice that had a soothing effect on Ella, "faith is not having the ability to change God's will, it is having the ability to *accept* God's will. Right now I feel like I need to be with the children . . . I need to help the children."

"Of course," Ella said, grateful for the distraction, "the children." She thought of all the sweet little faces of the children they'd become well acquainted with, all the families in third class. She wondered what might happen to them, but she couldn't think of that now.

Irene was surprised at the tremendous rush of thoughts swirling in her head as they hurried into the cabin where she first found her life belt, but had a strange sensation as she picked it up that it would do her no good. She felt more concerned about what she could do to help others through whatever might be happening, and knew that she had to see that Ella was safe. It wasn't the first time that she'd had impressed upon her mind the great potential of this dear friend of hers, but in that moment it came back to her with even more clarity. Irene needed to make certain that Ella's life would begin this night, not end. And there were others who needed her as well. She felt it as if she could literally hear their voices calling her name.

Feeling compelled to act quickly, she said, "Get your money, Ella. Put it inside of your clothing where it will be safe, then put on your life belt. Leave the rest."

Ella's temptation to panic was lessened by Irene's calm ability to give orders. Ella found her money and tucked it inside her chemise, near the waistband of her skirt, where it was secure.

"Put on your coat," Irene ordered and Ella did. Irene glanced at her and said, "That's not going to be warm enough." She said it as if she knew exactly what was going to happen. Ella didn't comment. She then put on the life belt, wondering what good it might do if the water was colder than the air outside. She couldn't think about that!

"Come along," Irene said, and Ella followed blindly behind her, glad that she seemed to know where she was going and what she was doing, because Ella felt as if she were lost in some kind of mental fog. She felt an urge to ask Irene a thousand questions about life and love and God and faith, and wished that she had thought to ask more of these questions in the time they'd spent together. But she couldn't get a single syllable out of her mouth.

Ella was surprised to realize they'd returned to the hallway where the Blackhursts' staterooms were located, which was now mostly deserted.

"What are we doing?" Ella asked.

Irene just went into the stateroom, opened the closet, and took out one of the three coats hanging there that belonged to Mr. Blackhurst. "Put it on," Irene ordered and Ella did.

It was large enough to fit over the top of the life belt, but she had to say, "How can I steal his coat?"

"You're just going to borrow it," Irene said. "I don't think he's going to miss it. Besides, you need it more than he does. He can only wear one at a time, and he's got one on already, I'm sure."

They were quickly back in the hallway and heading toward the third-class area where they had made so many friends. Irene kept hold of Ella's hand, feeling responsible for her but also feeling an urgency to get to the children—and their mothers—and to help them in any way that she could. As they hurried blindly down some stairs, she gasped at the realization that they had just stepped in water—ice cold and ankle deep.

Their eyes met as the shock seemed to take hold of them both in the same instant. Irene's thoughts raced even faster, but they were clear and defined and she felt surprisingly calm. She was more concerned about *what* to do than what the outcome might be.

"Don't just stand there," Irene ordered, and turned Ella around on the stairs. "We've got to get out of here. Getting on one of those lifeboats is our only hope of surviving this."

"What about the children?" Ella demanded, resisting Irene's firm tugging. "What about—"

"You mustn't think about that now," Irene said, exerting more effort in moving Ella quickly along.

Ella stopped in her tracks and stubbornly resisted Irene's efforts to budge her. "What on earth do you mean?" she asked, as if Irene might actually have a sensible response to such a question.

Irene came back down two steps to face Ella directly. She knew that this moment was profoundly important, and she needed to make herself impeccably clear. "Listen to me well, my friend," Irene said. "I don't know how all of this will end, but I know what I have to do, and I know what *you* have to do."

"How could you possibly know *that*?" Ella insisted.

"I've explained to you more than once how such a thing is possible, but now is not the time to quibble over details." Irene felt the sting of tears in her eyes, but they were more from resolve than any kind of fear. Knowing there wasn't time to explain further, she headed up the stairs again, dragging Ella along. "We must hurry," was all she said.

Irene felt a harsh rush of fear course through her as they came onto the deck to be assaulted by panic and chaos, but she took a deep breath, prayed for strength and guidance, and honed in on the target. She knew what she had to do. She had to get Ella on one of the lifeboats, and then she had to do all she could to help the children. But she knew Ella would never knowingly go without her, and she specifically asked that God's hand would guide her in what she was about to do. And she prayed that Ella would forgive her.

Amazingly, a path cleared for Ella to be put into a lifeboat just before it was lowered. She knew that Ella would be expecting Irene to take the one remaining seat, but Irene ushered a young woman into that spot then stepped back, fighting the urge to break down and cry like a baby. There was no time for tears. All she could do now was shout her farewells from the deck, and ignore the sound of Ella's protests as their separation became imminent.

"Dear Father, give me strength!" Irene whispered, taking one last look at Ella before she hurried back into the bowels of the ship, determined to give aid wherever she could. She felt surprisingly calm and in too big of a hurry to be concerned about how this night might end for her. Ella was safe. She felt peace over that. She had never doubted that her life was in God's hands. It always had been. And she had made peace a long time ago with knowing that her decision to make this journey had been right. She was where she needed to be; there had to be purpose in her being there. Striving to feel the guidance of the Spirit in how she might find the people who most needed whatever her skills and her presence might have to offer, she felt surprisingly calm and ready to face whatever might be waiting for her.

* * * * *

Ella became conscious of every breath she took, fearing that she might die simply from the shock of all that her eyes and ears were taking in. For all that she couldn't deny the reality of what was happening, her mind refused to accept it. The sights and sounds were astronomical, incomprehensible, and unspeakably hideous. She wanted to look away, as if she might be able to block out what was happening. But her eyes were locked on the *Titanic*, and no amount of willpower could pull them away. She wondered where Irene was. Had she made it safely onto one of the lifeboats? Or was she one of the many people that could still be seen on the decks of the ship, even from this distance? Ella could hear screams and wails of terror and dread, and she prayed that Irene's voice was not among them. But even if Irene were still aboard, Ella imagined her maintaining a firm and solid courage. Her grace and dignity would surely sustain her in any situation. But Ella couldn't even entertain the possibility that Irene hadn't gotten off the ship. It made the terror even more terrible—the implausibility of all of this even more implausible!

"I'm certain your friend is all right," Ella heard Mrs. Olsen say at the same time she felt the hand on her arm tighten, bringing her to a strange awareness that she wasn't alone. She'd met Mrs. Olsen only a short while ago when she'd found herself sitting next to the woman, who was also apparently on her own in the lifeboat. She was a middle-aged woman who had already been very kind to Ella, and had asked polite questions after observing Ella's tearful reluctance to be parted from Irene. But now conversation had ceased. The passengers of the little lifeboat had become eerily silent in contrast to the noises coming from the ship in the distance.

"Of course," Ella said, as if it might offer Mrs. Olsen the same comfort that she'd been attempting to give Ella. But comfort was difficult to give—or accept—with the veritable view before them.

Ella watched in stunned silence with the others as the stern of the *Titanic* began to lift clear of the water in direct correspondence to the bow sinking lower and lower into the dark mouth of the ocean. It was easy for Ella to imagine the great ship being balanced on a set of scales, with the weight of inevitability swallowing the prideful vessel in a determination to prove that nothing in this world is nearly as invincible as it might seem. The outcome grew ever more undeniable. Many lives would be lost this night, and those who might survive—should there be any—would never be the same. Ella wondered for a moment about her own chances for survival. Her feet were so cold that it wasn't difficult to imagine frostbite setting in. But her misery and its possible long-term effects were utterly insignificant in contrast to the suffering before her eyes—suffering that was only about to begin.

Ella continued to watch the stern of the ship moving slowly higher as the counterbalance of the bow made any other motion scientifically impossible. She could feel the dreaded anticipation of those who were still on board, knowing that—in consideration of science—the rising of the stern was soon to become catastrophic, in and of itself. The ship suddenly went dark, which made Ella realize that the electricity that had kept the lights on had remained functional in a miraculous way right up to this point. Now the ship was only a dark silhouette, its stern eerily suspended against the night sky. Ella cried out in a voice that joined in haphazard unison with those around her as they all realized the *Titanic* was breaking in half, the weight of the stern being too much for the sinking bow to hold in suspension any longer. Ella had no idea how many minutes unfolded as the ship cracked and broke, then the stern settled back onto the ocean, looking for a long moment as if it might be able to float on its own. The sight of the ship was vague, but it hovered amidst a marked increase in the distant screams and cries of the doomed. The sinking half of the ship then sank very quickly, and the stern rose rather abruptly, pointing its great propellers toward the night sky before the ship dropped as if it were being swallowed by a great beast. All who were left alive were now in the freezing water, and the collective wailing of their misery rose like a din from the bowels of hell. The ocean gurgled violently where the ship had disappeared, and then it was hard to imagine that an enormous ship had been just there minutes earlier. The crewman who had been assigned to man the oars commented on the time as he glanced at his watch with the use of the battery-powered light in his hand. Ella was stunned to realize that only two and a half hours earlier she had been sitting in Irene's cabin with her when they'd realized the engines had stopped. Unbelievable! Incomprehensible!

The cries of the abandoned and freezing passengers became so unbearable that Ella had to cover her ears and squeeze her eyes closed. It had become too much, especially when she had to wonder if Irene's voice might be heard among them. When her hands helped only a little in muffling the sound, she began to hum. It was a hymn she'd heard sung in church earlier that day. She wasn't terribly familiar with it, and she couldn't remember the words, but the tune was now firm in her mind. She had a vague sense that she wasn't humming alone, but she felt too frightened to open her eyes or move her hands from her ears, so it was impossible to know for sure. Again she felt no sense of time, except that it seemed a brief eternity passed while she hummed that song over and over and over. A hand on her arm forced her to acknowledge how tired she'd grown of humming. She opened her eyes only when she knew they were looking at Mrs. Olsen.

"It's over now, dear," the woman said, and wiped tears away with her sleeve before they could freeze on her face. Ella reluctantly eased her hands away from her ears, hearing nothing but a silence that was hallowed by the keen sense of death in the air. As Ella allowed herself to fully take in what that meant, she wanted to sob and scream. But the silence was contagious. The survivors didn't seem any more capable of uttering a sound than those who had been silenced by death.

The stupor shared by the passengers in the little boat in regard to what had happened became replaced by a growing concern over what would happen now. First one person spoke up, then another, speculating over their whereabouts and wondering if they would be rescued by some other vessel upon the sea, or left there in the freezing Atlantic air to experience death by freezing in a slower form than their fellow passengers of the *Titanic*, who had already been freed from their misery and had supposedly moved on to a better place. Again Ella wondered if Irene might be among them. She desperately wanted to think of her as being alive, and of their reunion at some moment in the near future. But at the same time she found it terribly easy to imagine Irene now in some angelic form, hovering near Ella, offering a strange, enigmatic kind of comfort and hope that she might actually survive this and be glad that she had. At the moment neither seemed possible.

Ella couldn't feel her feet, and her hands were dividing their time between covering her ears and taking refuge beneath her arms to warm up again. If not for Mr. Blackhurst's coat, she would be utterly frozen instead of just miserably cold. She wondered if Mr. Blackhurst had survived. For all that she'd disliked him—and stolen his coat—she would have never wished him any ill will, and the thought of his not surviving made her stomach churn. She hoped that Mrs. Blackhurst and the children had gotten safely into a lifeboat, but she wondered how miserable they might be at the moment. Mrs. Blackhurst was likely more comfortable than most in her lush fur coat, and the children certainly would have been adequately clothed. She would likely never see any of them again, but she was glad to think they would be all right—provided the survivors might yet be discovered by some other seaworthy vessel.

The people in the boat were organized into taking turns rowing with the idea that it would help keep them warm. It *did* help in that regard, but they all quickly became too weary to do so, especially when they had no compass and had no idea in which direction to row, or if moving at all would make any difference to their chances of survival. The harshness of the cold air and the shock of what they'd witnessed seemed to lure them all again into a numb kind of silence. The stillness of a glassy ocean gradually gave way to a definite swaying of the little boat. While Ella found herself thinking that death would be preferable to enduring this another hour, she wondered if the others felt the same way. But surely no one would dare voice such a thought. Not yet, at least. For now she had to hold on to the dwindling yet still flickering hope that she might still have a life before her—even if she had no idea what that life might entail.

* * * * *

Jonathan Moreau settled into the usual night shift, glad that he'd gotten some good sleep during the day. His body was finally starting to adjust to this nocturnal lifestyle. Being the newest member of the *Carpathia*'s crew, he had no choice but to work at night, and his job consisted of being on hand to do all of the tedious things that no one else wanted to do. Having been taken on almost at the last minute—as a favor from the friend of a friend—he was simply grateful to have the job, and glad to finally be at sea. It was something he'd been craving for some time now, and the salty air felt refreshing to him after the noise and chaos of growing up in the heart of New York City.

After making certain that all of the officers with higher rank than his—which meant almost everyone—had fresh coffee and all necessities at hand, Jonathan was ordered to take the usual stroll around the decks to simply make certain all was well. There was a peaceful and pleasant rhythm to the ship this time of night. Some passengers, mostly men, were laughing and talking; some were drinking, some were playing cards. Most of the passengers had gone to bed by now. Jonathan found nothing amiss. The night was crisp and cold, and the waters were still.

He made his way around the entire perimeter of the ship, taking a unique route that included going up and down some stairwells and stopping here and there to ponder the ocean or the sky. Both felt very dark and ominous out here. He'd grown up in a port city, but until he'd been on board this ship with the horizon of America no longer visible, he'd never comprehended the immensity of the ocean. But he liked the way it was giving him a lot to think about, and the stillness in which to do it. For quite some time he'd felt at odds with his life, as if something were missing, but he'd not been able to figure out what it might be. Going to sea had seemed a good way to try to solve that problem, even though his parents had protested strongly. Their voyage to America nearly thirty years earlier had been difficult and traumatic, and neither of them had any desire to ever contend with the great Atlantic again. But they were convinced that their son's need to go to sea was temporary, and he would soon come to his senses and come home and settle down to help run the family business. He knew it was a typical story: a son resisting the expectation of stepping into his father's shoes. But he didn't know how his version of the story would end. He had a great deal of respect for his father, and he even loved the family business and believed he could do it well. It was this vague unsettled feeling inside of him that left him wondering if it was right—as if some unknown voice were screaming from within his mind, calling him to sea like some kind of siren. He only hoped that he could find the answers and not end up senselessly wandering the globe as his mother had tearfully predicted he might do. He had no desire to senselessly wander the globe. What he wanted was to understand why he'd felt the need to leave home, and why he'd felt it with such urgency. Well, now he was here, and he looked to the ocean and sky as if they might present the answers.

Jonathan became aware of some kind of commotion on the ship, and he felt an assault of nerves as he wondered if something was wrong. Perhaps the siren's call had led him into a dangerous situation; perhaps he would lose his life to the Atlantic and never return home again. The very idea—while it seemed ludicrous and dramatic—made him suddenly a bit homesick. He wished to be safely at home now, asleep in his bed with the comfort of knowing that his family members were all safe beneath the same roof. A strange chill rushed over him, and he hoped it wasn't some kind of foreboding premonition.

Jonathan was moving toward the sound of many voices in harried tones when he saw an officer running toward him.

"What's happening?" Jonathan asked, and the officer barely slowed down enough to answer the question.

"Cottam got a distress call from the *Titanic*. Apparently she's going down."

"The *Titanic*?" Jonathan echoed in disbelief. The newspapers had been full of talk about this great ship and her maiden voyage to America. In fact, one of the many ploys his parents had used to try to keep him from going to sea was that he'd miss the *Titanic's* arrival. He'd really had no interest in such an event, and this tactic had not swayed him. But he knew the ship's reputation for safety, and he felt sure this news had to be some kind of mistake.

"Captain Rostron's changing course to answer the call. He's ordered all engines full throttle." The officer was running backward now, away from Jonathan. "He wants all hands on deck. Get blankets, coffee made . . . and all that." He turned and disappeared, off to give important orders, no doubt.

Jonathan stood there for a long moment. The chill he'd had only a minute ago did a repeat performance, this time more boldly. He didn't have time to consider what the personal implications of this might be. There was work to be done, and he quickly joined himself with the crew in making every possible preparation to bring hundreds of passengers on board, along with their luggage. To say the *Carpathia* would be crowded was to make a gross understatement. As Jonathan had heard through the grapevine of officers and crew, Captain Rostron had cut off the heat from the passengers' rooms in order to give more power to the engines. He had given orders to make ready every possible means of rescue they had available, and he wanted every man ready to aid and assist. And then they waited.

It was said that the *Carpathia* had been fifty-eight miles from the coordinates received over the wireless in regard to the *Titanic's* location. The captain had estimated it would take approximately four hours to get there, and he expected to find a sinking vessel when he arrived. Jonathan was at the rail as they drew near to their destination. The sky was barely taking on some hint of light with the promise of day when they arrived to find nothing but more ocean and sky. His own sense of foreboding grew in proportion to the confusion he felt that was shared by those around him. Talk among the others was that perhaps the message had been a mistake, or perhaps the coordinates had been wrong. Surely this couldn't be right. The largest steamship in the world could not have simply disappeared. Then a light was spotted in the distance, then another. Jonathan heard a number of expletives being spoken around him that expressed his own growing shock and disbelief. Then someone uttered the truth of what they were seeing. "Those are lifeboats."

"How can that be?" another voice demanded, as if a great voice from heaven might provide the answer.

Orders began flying to "Get the ship closer," and "Get those people on board as quickly as possible and get them warmed up." The sense of busyness ensued again, allowing the opportunity to avoid thinking about the unthinkable. But it was true, and it could not be denied. The *Titanic* had gone under. She was no more. And it was doubtful that her every passenger and crew member had gotten into the small number of lifeboats that were appearing, scattered about on the horizon. Lives had surely been lost here, and a hovering sense of death seemed to linger in the air.

When the first lifeboat was finally guided to the side of the *Carpathia*, the reality descended more fully upon the rescuers. The eyes and expressions of the survivors said what no words ever could. Something unspeakable had happened here, and for some reason that Jonathan couldn't begin to comprehend, he'd managed to put himself right in the middle of it.

CHAPTER SEVEN
Rescued

ELLA WASN'T SURE IF SHE'D drifted off to sleep, or if her mind had just been wandering into a place so deep that she'd temporarily lost all awareness of her surroundings. Perhaps she *was* freezing to death. But as she looked around to be assured that she was still a survivor of the *Titanic,* she felt a tiny ray of hope—and warmth—in the evidence of dawn's light settling over the Atlantic. She could now see other lifeboats around them, and in the distance was a ship. *A ship!* She was apparently the first in her boat to notice it, because as she sat up straighter and pointed in that direction, those sitting around her seemed to force themselves to move and take note of their surroundings.

"A ship!" Mrs. Olsen verbalized what Ella hadn't had the voice to speak, but the woman's weariness of body and spirit came through clearly in her inert and weakened tone.

Ella put her effort into focusing on the ship as a beacon of tangible hope. As the lifeboat was rowed slowly closer to the floating mass, it gradually became more clear. They were close enough to hear voices coming from the deck of the ship before Ella was able to read the name on the side: *Carpathia.* She uttered the name over and over in her mind, etching it into her memory as the representation of despair being replaced by hope. But her hope felt abstract, difficult to grasp, and perhaps without purpose. The largest part of her spirit was drowning in the belief that death would have been preferable to facing whatever minute possibility she might have of creating any kind of value in her life from this moment on. Irene had convinced her that there was hope of a new life in America, of putting the ugly past behind her. But Ella felt all but certain that Irene had perished with the sinking ship. What would she do now? Where would she go? And how could she go on if the only person who had ever truly believed in her was no longer alive?

Ella held back as others around her scrambled to be lifted from the lifeboat. She was glad to be on the far side of the little boat, and huddled there in her stolen coat, suddenly feeling cold again when she'd felt practically nothing for hours. She became focused more on her own shivering than what was going on around her, until she was nudged and looked up to see a man in uniform, standing in the lifeboat beside her. A quick glance told her that they were the only two people there, except for a sailor from the *Titanic* who wore an expression of determination that seemed to say he would be the last one off.

"I'm sorry," Ella said in a raspy voice that indicated the cold air she'd been breathing. "Did you say something?"

"I asked if you're all right, miss," the man said. His accent was American, reminding her that this entire endeavor had been with the hope of getting to the promised land. That's what Irene had called it. *The promised land.* Could it possibly hold the promise of anything good for her? Or was she destined to end up in a position of barely surviving— again? It was becoming the theme of her life. Given the present moment, the thought gave her a sharp chill that increased her shivering.

"Miss?" the man asked.

"Forgive me," she said. "I'm just . . . tired." She stood abruptly, not wanting these men to have to wait for her any longer. She'd forgotten that she hadn't been able to feel her feet for hours. She'd forgotten that they'd been wet when she'd climbed into the boat. But now her feet failed her, and she would have fallen flat on her face if she'd not fallen into the arms of the man in uniform. She considered it providential that he was young and strong, and she suddenly and inexplicably felt safer than she'd felt since her father had taken his own life. Her temptation to feel embarrassed was immediately dispelled by the kindness in his voice as he reassured her that everything would be all right now.

Ella realized she must have been drifting in and out of consciousness when she found herself lying on the deck of the *Carpathia* and couldn't recall getting there from the lifeboat. The blanket she was wrapped in felt heavenly. She heard voices speaking around her with sporadic phrases. *Her shoes are frozen. Her feet must have been wet. Get the doctor . . . quickly.*

"We've got to cut them off," she heard in the familiar voice of the sailor who had saved her.

"No!" she protested, struggling to raise her head and grasping on to the arm closest to her side, then realizing it was his as she looked up and once again saw the same eyes. "Not my feet."

She heard him chuckle and wondered what on earth could be so funny at a time like this. "Not your feet," he said gently but with a smile. "Your shoes. We're going to cut off your shoes and get your feet warmed up. I'm certain they'll be fine."

Ella nodded and let her head drop back down to the blanket beneath her head. Her relief gave the moment a hint of humor, but not enough for her to exert any effort to even smile. She became aware of some pain in her feet as her shoes and stockings were peeled away, but perhaps pain was a good sign. She'd no sooner had the thought than she heard someone say the very same to her. A doctor presumably. She missed Irene and wondered if she might be on the *Carpathia* somewhere; she wondered if she might still be alive. In her heart she knew the contrary was true, and she wanted to curl up then and there and cry like a baby. Given her depth of shock and fatigue and the temperature of her body—not to mention being surrounded by strangers—she held back the temptation and tried to be grateful to be alive.

Jonathan felt a strange inclination to stay at this woman's side, even though there were hundreds of survivors that needed attention.

"Come along," he said, scooping her into his arms again, blankets and all.

"Where are you taking me?" she asked, but not with any alarm.

"Someplace a bit warmer than out here on the deck." While many survivors were scattered on the decks, most of them hadn't actually been wet when they'd gotten into the lifeboats. He figured that justified his extra care of *this* survivor, even though he knew that was only part of the reason.

He laid her down on the carpeted floor of a parlor and made certain one of the two blankets around her was tucked tightly around her freezing feet. "Can I get you something warm to drink? Something to eat?" he asked.

"No . . . thank you," she said and met his eyes with such a haunted gaze that he felt as chilled as if he'd dived into the Atlantic water on which they were floating. "I'm wondering if . . . my friend . . ."

Jonathan saw moisture brim in her eyes just before she looked away. "They're taking names of all the survivors," he explained. "Once everyone is accounted for, we can see if she's on board."

She looked at him again, silently expressing a measure of hope that he doubted he would ever be able to satisfy. "Are there other ships? Is it possible that she could be on another . . ."

"It appears that we are the only one," he said gently and watched the news sink in. He didn't want to tell her what he'd heard, that some crewmen from the *Titanic* had transferred people from one lifeboat to another, going back with an empty boat to look for survivors. They'd found only a few passengers clinging to an overturned collapsible lifeboat. Everyone else they found was floating in his or her life belt, frozen to death. He simply added, "All of the survivors in lifeboats have come aboard the *Carpathia*." He then heard himself promise, "When you've had some rest, I'll help you find out whether or not your friend is on board."

"Oh, thank you," she said, as if he might actually be able to find Irene alive.

"You rest now," he said. "I'll bring you something to eat when they serve breakfast."

"Thank you," she said again and closed her eyes to rest before he stood up and walked away, glancing back more than once, not only to look at her, but to consider why he felt so drawn to her. He could see very little of her face through the tiny opening in the blanket wrapped around her, but his memory of it was clear. It was a fine and beautiful face, in spite of that distant, haunted look in her eyes.

Once left alone, Ella felt so agitated by the memories of the previous night that she felt sure she wouldn't be able to sleep. There were sounds of people around her crying, some frantically asking about loved ones and speculating over their possible rescue. But Ella felt sure that what she'd been told was true. All who were lucky enough to survive were already aboard the *Carpathia*. Once the chaos was sorted out, most of these people would realize that their loved ones were not here. Ella held on to a tiny possibility that Irene had made it, but in her heart she knew it likely wasn't true. She recalled so well that look in Irene's eyes the last time she'd seen her. Resignation? Determination? A final good-bye? Ella couldn't be sure, but instinctively she knew Irene had gone down with the ship.

Ella kept her eyes closed, pretending to be asleep even though she wasn't. She figured it was the best way to remain undisturbed and to keep to herself. That tactic proved beneficial when she came awake to the realization that she'd actually been sleeping. Disoriented by her surroundings, it took her several seconds to connect a chain of events in her mind that brought her to this place and this moment. She saw the feet and legs of a man in uniform and looked up, hoping to see the handsome, young sailor who had been so kind to her. She saw someone else, but he too had a kind smile.

"I wonder if I could get your name, miss," the man said with a British accent.

"Ella Brown," she said, sitting up while she made a futile attempt to straighten her hair, as if doing so might actually matter in such a situation.

"And what class were you sailing, miss?"

"Um . . ." It took her a moment to realize what he meant. "First class," she said, and almost added that she'd been a servant there, but she didn't want to be connected again to the Blackhurst family in any way, so she left it at that.

"Thank you, Miss," the man said. "There's hot coffee and tea and some brandy available over there," he motioned with his arm to the other side of the room, where a line was forming, "if you'd like some to warm you up. They'll have some breakfast served soon."

"Thank you," she said but decided to stay where she was for the time being. A distinct ache in her feet added to her lack of incentive. She was glad to be lying near a wall and out of the way. The amount of people in the room made it evident that the *Carpathia* was very crowded. She wished that it could be *more* crowded, that more people could have been saved. Or better yet, she wished that the *Titanic* had been as unsinkable as she'd claimed to be. Tears stung her eyes, but she fought them back. There were many people crying, and her tears would have been understandable to anyone who might care to notice, but her emotion seemed the only thing she had any control of, and she had to hold on to it.

"Did you get any rest?" Ella heard and looked up to see her rescuer.

"A bit, thank you," she said.

He squatted down in front of her but kept one hand behind his back. "I've got a surprise for you."

"Really?" she said, and he produced a fine pair of ladies' shoes from where he'd been hiding them.

Ella gasped and he said, "A kind woman noticed the doctor cutting away your shoes. She took them to compare the size. Since she's traveling with her sisters and daughters, she figured that one of the women would have an extra pair that would work, and here you are."

"How very kind," Ella said, taking the shoes. She'd not worn anything so fine since her family's fortune had disappeared. "I should thank her."

"She insisted on remaining anonymous," the man said, "and I promised her I would not reveal her identity." He reached into his coat pockets and pulled something out of each one. "She also sent thin stockings," he held out one hand, "and thick ones," he held out the other, "in order to suit your preference, or to help the shoes fit better with one or the other."

Ella took the stockings as well. "Thank her for me . . . should you get the chance."

"Already done," he said and smiled, although she couldn't miss the shock and sadness in his eyes.

Ella tried to ignore that and said, "You've been so kind. You must tell me your name."

"Jonathan Moreau," he said. "And you are?"

"Ella," she said.

"Only Ella?"

"Ella Brown. A very plain name."

"A lovely name," he said, "for a lovely woman."

A part of Ella felt reluctant to trust a stranger with such personal conversation. But she felt instinctively comfortable with him and forced away her tendency to be distrusting.

"Where are you from, Ella?" he asked.

"London," she said.

"And you were going to America to . . ."

"Is this an official inquiry, or personal?"

"I'm asking because I would like to know. That's the only reason." Ella looked down, and he added, "I don't want to upset you. I just can't help wondering."

"I was hoping to make a new start with my life," she said, deciding any other details could wait.

"With your friend," he stated rather than asked. Ella nodded but couldn't look at him without luring tears too close to the surface. "Did you see her get on a lifeboat, Ella?"

Ella shook her head, finding it harder to hold back the tears. Jonathan Moreau took her hand, which took her enough by surprise that it aided her courage in being able to say, "I thought she was getting in right behind me. The boat was crowded, but we could have made room. She seemed determined to stay . . . for some reason . . . I don't understand. I hoped that she would get into another boat, but . . ."

"But you don't think she did?"

Ella shook her head again. She squeezed her eyes closed in an effort to block out the images, but it only brought them closer, and she opened her eyes again. "There were so many people left on board when it went down. So many."

Jonathan didn't tell her the numbers that had already been estimated according to the information they'd received from the members of the *Titanic's* crew that had survived. Instead he told her, "The *Carpathia* is returning to New York to take the survivors. The captain wants to hold a brief service on deck before we set out. Are you up to it?"

"I think so," she said, not wanting to miss such a thing—especially in light of her belief that Irene had perished. She thought of the faces of other people who had become familiar to her during their days at sea. She wondered how many of them were meant to be honored in this brief service.

Jonathan was kind enough to wait for her while she put on the gift of new stockings. But her feet were far too tender to want to attempt putting on the shoes. She chose instead to wear *both* pairs of stockings and just carry the shoes. She tied the laces together and looped them over her arm, holding a blanket tightly around herself as she walked tentatively on aching feet toward the tremendously crowded deck where the service was to be held. Ella hardly recognized the ocean and sky surrounding them as the same black abyss that had surrounded her through the night. The pain in her feet, combined with a heady effect from thoughts of all that had happened, made her grateful for the way Mr. Moreau offered his arm for support. She took it and thanked him, and tried not to be embarrassed by the way she held so tightly to him through the service. He said little as he helped her back to her safe little spot, then he promised to check on her as often as he could in between doing his work and getting some snatches of rest here and there. He kept his promise and made certain that she was as comfortable and cared for as she possibly could be.

By the end of the day, Ella knew for certain that Irene's name was not on the list of survivors now aboard the *Carpathia*. Neither was Mr. Stead, nor any of the people that Ella had come to know by name. Not one! Not one person that she had become acquainted with during the passage had survived—except for the entire Blackhurst family. She was glad to know they were well, but what about the others? The children! The mothers! *Irene!* She felt utterly lost in her grieving, but so was everyone around her. The survivors of the *Titanic* were all lost and in shock. Some were barely able to speak, if at all; others couldn't stop crying. Ella was somewhere in between. The passengers and crew of the *Carpathia* were rallying around the survivors and exhibiting many kindnesses. People were sharing their cabins and their clothes and their bedding. Ella was grateful for her gift of shoes and stockings, even though she was still just carrying the shoes around, and she was grateful for the extra pair of warm stockings she could wear in the parlor where she was content to remain most of the time.

After twenty-four hours on board the *Carpathia*, Ella began to realize that Irene was truly gone. The hours that preceded ending up in a lifeboat in a black, silent ocean began to haunt her more vividly. She felt afraid to close her eyes at all, and she began to shake without warning for no apparent reason, as violently at times as if she were freezing. Mr. Moreau—who had insisted upon her calling him by his given name—had been so gracious and kind that she couldn't imagine what she would have done without him. But Jonathan had a job to do and needed rest in between his shifts, and she was most often left alone. Mrs. Olsen, the kindly woman whom Ella had met on the lifeboat, had sought her out and had been very friendly—the problem being that Mrs. Olsen was a little *too* friendly. She talked incessantly about the drama, uttering the same things over and over. Ella appreciated the fact that some people needed to do so in order to come to terms with such an event, but she found it difficult to listen to Mrs. Olsen's retelling the tale over and over. The woman was also quite preoccupied with getting home to her twin terriers, Baxter and Dexter. She was certain the little dogs had been very lonesome without her while she'd been on her tour of Europe, and they were probably worried about her, considering the fact that the news of the *Titanic* going down had surely reached the newspapers via the wireless. When Ella pointed out the obvious—that Baxter and Dexter were unable to read the papers—Mrs. Olsen matter-of-factly insisted that the servants were surely talking about it, and the dogs would overhear them. Ella just nodded and listened while Mrs. Olsen once again rehearsed how terrible the drama had been for her. Ella couldn't dispute that; they'd been sitting side by side in the lifeboat. But upon hearing the detailed oratory—again—Ella found it difficult to keep her head from spinning, and she couldn't manage to keep her hands from shaking.

Ella was deeply grateful when a woman Mrs. Olsen had made friends with interrupted them and drew her away. Mrs. Chadwick was a passenger on *Carpathia* and she was generously sharing her cabin with Mrs. Olsen. The two had a good deal in common and plenty to talk about—much to Ella's relief.

The third day on board the *Carpathia*, Ella was doing her best to avoid Mrs. Olsen, but hadn't been very successful. The weather had been foul with frequent rain or fog; therefore, people were huddled indoors with no room to spare, and were taking advantage of the opportunity to go on deck in between bouts of rain as much as possible. The fresh air was cold, but at least it was fresh. Ella was annoyed by having her opportunity to get out on deck intruded upon by the melodramatic Mrs. Olsen before she even got to the door. She was grateful beyond words when Jonathan rescued her from yet another histrionic interchange by asking her if she could assist him with something.

"How did you know?" Ella asked as they stepped out onto the deck.

"Know what?" he asked.

"That if I'd been left in her company another minute I would have probably resorted to some inappropriate outburst."

Jonathan chuckled. "Just a hunch."

"She means well," Ella justified, "and she's a kind woman at heart. She was a great comfort to me on the lifeboat, but . . ."

"I understand," Jonathan said. "You don't need to explain, but if you—"

Ella gasped when she caught sight of a familiar face, a woman standing at the rail with two children. *Mrs. Blackhurst.* Ella abruptly turned to walk in the other direction, glad that Jonathan quickly followed, but not wanting to explain.

"Is there someone you don't want to see?" he asked. "Besides Mrs. Olsen?"

Ella glanced up at him, then straight ahead. If she expected him to go along with her trying to remain hidden, she owed him an explanation. "I was sailing on first class because I was working for . . . these people. I was hired to care for their children. I can assure you that, of my own accord, I would have never been sailing first class. I likely wouldn't have been sailing at all."

"I take it your employment didn't go well."

"To say the least," Ella said. "They were dreadfully unkind; the children as well as the parents. I endured it because I needed the money. When they told me they were sailing to America and wanted me to come along, I considered it worth all that I would have to put up with. My friend was—"

"Irene."

"Yes, Irene." Ella had to swallow hard after saying her name. "Irene was returning to her home in America and invited me to come along, but I would have to earn the money for passage. When it turned out that we were both sailing on the *Titanic*—and we hadn't even planned it—we felt sure that it was destiny. Now . . ."

"You don't have to talk about that," Jonathan said, ambling slowly beside her. "Tell me more about these awful employers of yours."

"You must think me very petty and self-centered."

"Not at all," he said, surprised. "Why would you believe that I would?"

"Sometimes I *feel* petty and self-centered. I'm afraid I have a long history of things not working out very well in my life, and sometimes I can feel very sorry for myself."

"I don't know what happened to you before Sunday night," he said, "but that in itself warrants some feeling sorry for yourself. I feel sorry for you, and don't take that to mean that I'm being patronizing or giving you some unwarranted pity. I can't imagine how you're even holding yourself together. Given what I've witnessed with many of the other passengers, I believe you are a very courageous woman."

Ella took that in and could only say, "You're very kind, Jonathan. I hardly know what to say when you're so kind."

"You don't need to say anything," he said and smiled before he looked ahead as they continued to walk slowly. "How are your feet? I notice you've graduated to wearing shoes."

"They're much better, thank you. Although, I think it will take some time for them to stop aching."

"Naturally," he said. "Tell me when you've had enough walking."

"I'm fine, thank you," she said.

"Tell me more about this family who hired you."

Ella sighed. "The evening of the . . . accident . . ." Even as she said the word, Ella wondered how the sinking of the *Titanic* could ever be referred to as an *accident*. It was like calling a hurricane an unpleasant rainstorm. Nevertheless, it was an easier word to say than other words that might have been more adequately descriptive. "We had a disagreement. The children accused me of behaving in a way that I have *never* behaved, and Mrs. Blackhurst was furious with me, believing that her precious darlings would never lie. It was far from the first time such a thing had happened, but this time she terminated my employment. I was secretly relieved because I'd been planning to quit once I got to America anyway. This made it less awkward for me. Then it . . . happened. The rest is . . . well. . . the rest I would rather not talk about."

"Perhaps you *should* talk about it."

"Perhaps," Ella said, "but . . . not yet; not . . . now."

"I understand," he said. "And you just saw Mrs. Blackhurst?"

"Yes, with the children. I'm glad they're all right, but I don't want to see them."

"And Mr. Blackhurst?"

"I wasn't sure if he would be on a lifeboat. It was only women and children—at least on that side of the ship. I've heard that on the other side of the ship, they were letting men into the boats. There was so much chaos, but . . . his name is on the list of survivors. I would never wish him ill, but if we see him, please don't point out that I'm wearing one of his coats."

Jonathan looked down at the oversized long wool coat she was wearing. "Are you?"

"I stole it when Irene insisted I needed something warmer than what I had available."

"He can only wear one at a time, right?"

"That's exactly what Irene said." Ella almost laughed, but it turned to an unexpected rush of tears instead, and she stopped walking to turn her back to Jonathan and put a hand over her mouth to keep from sobbing. She felt his hands come gently to her shoulders.

"I'm so sorry, Ella. I wish I could have prevented it. I'm only glad that I'm here now."

"I'm glad for that too," Ella said once she'd gathered her composure somewhat.

They walked on a little farther, mostly in silence, until Ella declared that her feet *were* hurting, and he escorted her back to her little spot in the parlor where she'd been sleeping on the floor. "I'll check on you," he said, as he always did at parting.

"You're very kind," she said, which was her usual response. He'd made certain she always had something to eat, and he'd been so kind and gracious. Looking at him now, she could almost imagine Irene in what might be heaven, giving some kind of angelic orders that had urged Jonathan Moreau to be the one to lift her up out of the lifeboat and to be so good to her. Without him she would have felt completely alone. She reminded herself that once they arrived in New York City, she *would* be completely alone. But for now, she was grateful for this man's friendship, and said for at least the hundredth time, "Thank you."

"A pleasure, Ella," he said and walked away. She couldn't deny that he was a handsome man, and he looked very fine in the dark-blue uniform that was typical of the officers and crew of these ships at sea. His hair was somewhere between blond and brown; perhaps *sandy* would be the right word to describe its color. She hadn't discerned the color of his eyes, but she knew well the penetrating effect they had.

The following day, Ella was taken off guard to hear that the *Carpathia* would be arriving in New York City that evening. For all of the crowdedness and lack of privacy aboard the ship, Ella had come to feel safe there. Being among the survivors, she had been taken care of and treated well. The *Carpathia* had become a little world of security. It had come to represent deliverance and escape from death itself. She had known that being aboard this floating township was temporary, but she felt entirely unprepared to step off of it and face the great unknown of America. Wondering what she would do made it harder to keep her thoughts from Irene. She was grateful beyond measure for Irene's directive to put her money beneath her clothing, and to know that it was still safely there. She'd had the opportunity to clean up since boarding the *Carpathia*, but she had no change of clothes. She'd imagined buying a railway ticket with that money, and traveling west with Irene to a place where her friend had assured her she could find peace and acceptance and a new life. Now she didn't know what to do. She wasn't destitute, but she had nowhere to go. She could only hope to find work in New York and find some way to survive before her money ran out. Irene had once told her that angels were all around, willing and able to assist, working as God's hands to bless people's lives. Ella wanted to believe that. But she wondered where the angels had been when the *Titanic* had gone under with hundreds of people still on board. She wondered why angels hadn't made it possible for Irene to be spared. Ella would have gladly traded places with her. Irene had a home and family to go home to, people who needed her and missed her. Ella wouldn't have been missed, and she would have been spared the dilemma of now having to face the need to provide for herself and carve some kind of life out of nothing. Nothing. That was what she had, that was who she was. Nothing. The echoes of the *Titanic's* dying passengers taunted her with the belief that it would have been far better if she'd not gotten into a lifeboat, and someone else would have taken her place. As it was, she had no choice but to find a way to survive. And with any luck, her future would not be *too* laden with misery.

Shortly after Ella had finished eating her lunch, Mrs. Olsen found her, making a big fuss that drew the attention of many people around them.

"Oh, you poor, dear thing," she said. "I wonder every minute I'm not with you if you're doing all right. You must let me take care of you." Ella wasn't at all surprised by the next words that came out of her mouth. "Now, I *insist* that you come and stay with me once we've arrived in the city. I know for a fact that you have nowhere else to go, and I simply *insist!*"

Ella looked around herself to see the pitiful glances of others who now—thanks to how well Mrs. Olsen's voice carried—knew that she was a woman without means or family. Would she never be able to get away from that fact? Overwrought by this dilemma, Ella turned back to look at Mrs. Olsen.

"You can stay as long as you need to, precious. We'll get along famously. You and me and Baxter and Dexter. Oh, they'll be ever so pleased to make your acquaintance."

Ella listened to Mrs. Olsen ramble on about her dogs, wondering what on earth to say to the woman—or what to do. She was grateful for the offer; she truly was. But she felt certain it would take very little time for Mrs. Olsen's dramatic antics to wear her nerves very thin. On the other hand, she couldn't forget that she had nowhere to go. For all that she had the security of some money tucked away, she couldn't imagine navigating her way around a strange city in a foreign land.

Mrs. Chadwick approached and apologized for interrupting, but Ella could have hugged her. She needed time to think about the best course to take before she gave Mrs. Olsen an answer. Logically, Ella couldn't see that she had any choice. She knew well enough that having a safe place to sleep and food to eat were no small thing, and not to be taken lightly. Enduring the company of Mrs. Olsen was not such a high price to pay for being offered this blessing. She really was a very kind lady; there was no doubt about that. Ella felt certain as she wandered the deck, huddled in Mr. Blackhurst's coat, that she should graciously accept Mrs. Olsen's offer, which would at least give her comfort and security until she could get her bearings and explore other options.

Ella stood at the rail, enjoying a reprieve from the rain, wishing she could look out over the ocean and think about *anything* besides the *Titanic* going down. Of course, looking at the sea in the light of day was entirely different than the cold, black monster that had taken so many lives. But it was still the same ocean, the same monster. It occurred to Ella that it *would* be good to get her feet on dry land, and she hoped to never set foot aboard a ship again. But that meant making a life for herself in America. She had to find a way to make it work. She just had to!

"Hello," she heard and turned to see Jonathan Moreau standing a short distance away, leaning his arm on the rail as if he'd been standing there for an hour, just watching her. He had a subtly dreamy look in his eyes that made her stomach flutter, but the sensation was immediately smothered by a tight knot that reminded her she would be wise to avoid any romantic hope with him or any other respectable man. He'd been kind and he was undeniably a handsome man, but he was probably caught up in the experience of rescuing a damsel in distress, as much as she might have come to feel some closeness to him being her rescuer. Whatever he—or she—might be feeling, was temporary and she knew it.

Temporary or not, she was glad to see him now. "Hello," she responded, wishing it was in her to give him more than a faint smile.

Before another word could be exchanged between them, she heard her name being called in a near-shrieking voice that she recognized immediately. She cringed before she forced herself to turn and acknowledge Mrs. Blackhurst, who was running toward her as if she'd come upon a beloved friend.

"Oh, Ella!" she cried and took hold of her shoulders. "My dear, sweet Ella! We thought you had perished. I'm so very, very glad to know that you made it. Oh, you dear, sweet girl!"

Ella couldn't think of a single word that might come out of her mouth that wouldn't sound rude or inappropriate. So she just let Mrs. Blackhurst talk, knowing there had to be a reason for her enthusiasm—a *selfish* reason.

"I was entirely wrong," Mrs. Blackhurst continued. "I should have never let you go like that. If we'd only known what was going to happen . . ." She pressed a handkerchief over her mouth to suppress some emotion, but Ella had trouble believing it was entirely genuine. She'd seen such behavior from the woman many times *before* they'd survived a sinking ship. "The thing is, Ella, I must insist that you return to your position. It's the only right thing to do. I simply can't allow you to be on your own this way in a strange land, not when we are the reason you were on the *Titanic*, and—"

"Did your husband survive?" Ella asked in a gentle voice, trying to ignore all else that was going through her head. She had seen his name on the list, but she felt it was polite to inquire.

"Why, yes, he did. We were very fortunate."

"You were indeed," Ella said, wondering if Mr. Blackhurst would insist on getting his coat back. Or perhaps it would be recognized through the course of this conversation and Ella would need to hand it over.

"Given that we've all come through just fine," Mrs. Blackhurst went on, "we must let bygones be bygones and get back to things as usual."

Ella knew what that meant. Within twenty minutes of this humble request, Mrs. Blackhurst would be back to barking orders and constantly harping with impatience at Ella and the children, who would be unconditionally allowed to mistreat Ella in every possible way. Ella knew that Mrs. Blackhurst didn't want the responsibility of caring for the children, and Patsy was likely complaining about having to wait on Mrs. Blackhurst hand and foot *and* keep the children from annoying her. Ella didn't even have to wonder if this woman's request had any sincere regret or humility in it. She knew it didn't. Simple as that. But it wouldn't do for her to stand here and say everything she *wanted* to say. It was best to just decline her offer and move on.

"I thank you very much for your kindness," Ella said, pleased with the even tone of her own voice, "but I've made other arrangements." Mrs. Blackhurst's astonished expression didn't deter Ella's cool explanation. "Since you were indisputably clear on having fired me, naturally I would not have assumed any possibility of returning to your employment."

Mrs. Blackhurst's eyes filled with a familiar venom. In a low voice that could not be overheard by any passersby, she muttered, "You're an ungrateful little—"

"Oh, and take this," Ella said, removing the coat. She suddenly didn't want it anymore. It had served her well, but she didn't want having it in her possession to weigh on her conscience—or to remind her of these people who represented everything she'd come to loathe about the life she was trying to leave behind.

"What in the world?" Mrs. Blackhurst demanded, taking the coat as it was forced upon her.

"It's one of your husband's many coats. I borrowed it."

"Why, you little *thief!*" she growled, not as softly as her last insult.

"The ship was sinking, Mrs. Blackhurst. If I'd not taken the coat, it would now be at the bottom of the Atlantic. Have a lovely day."

CHAPTER EIGHT
Survival

ELLA TURNED TO WALK THE other way, only to practically run into Jonathan. She'd completely forgotten that he'd been nearby when the conversation began. She heard Mrs. Blackhurst exude disgust before she'd hurried away, and Ella hoped to never encounter her or any member of her family again for the remaining hours of the journey.

Jonathan fell into step beside her. "*Who* was *that?*" he asked, sounding almost amused.

Ella tossed him a quick glare and kept walking. "I already told you about that. I was working for her and her husband, in charge of their odious children. That's why I was on board the *Titanic*. They were going to America for a grand holiday. They were hideously rude and unkind, and I'd rather starve than go back to working for them."

Jonathan chuckled as if her explanation were truly humorous. She glared at him again but kept walking. "I'm not making fun of you," he said. "I think you stood up to her brilliantly back there. I've never met her before and I could still see right through her."

Ella relaxed a little and slowed her pace once she'd glanced over her shoulder to be sure Mrs. Blackhurst wasn't in hot pursuit. "Well, that's somewhat comforting," she said.

"So you have other arrangements?" he asked, and she felt confused until he added, "When we get to New York? You have other arrangements?"

Ella sighed. "Mrs. Olsen has offered to let me come and stay with her."

"Mrs. Olsen? Are you sure you're up to that?"

"I don't know that I have a choice . . . at least for now. She does wear on my nerves, but she's a very kind woman, and she's been very good to me. Perhaps the problem is more that my nerves are so raw."

"That's a common ailment around here, I'd say."

"I should be grateful that I have such an offer. You know what they say: beggars can't be choosers."

"Is that what they say?" he asked. "Well . . . I don't really see you as a beggar."

That's because you don't really know me, Ella thought but couldn't bring herself to say aloud. She would hope for some possibility of seeing him again at some time in the future. But if he knew the truth about her, she knew that such a hope would never come to pass.

"And truthfully," he said, "I came to find you because I wanted to let you know that you *do* have other options . . . at least one, anyway." He stopped walking, and she did the same and turned to face him. "It may not be much better than Mrs. Olsen's, but . . . I'm hoping you'll at least consider it."

"I don't need you to feel sorry for me, Mr. Moreau," she said and walked on, knowing immediately that her comment hadn't been fair, but her first impulse tapped into places inside herself that were sensitive and uncomfortable.

"I'm Mr. Moreau now?" he asked, walking beside her. "I thought we were friends."

"We *are* friends," she said, "but . . ."

"But what?" he asked. "I don't know how you were raised, Ella, but I was raised to be a Christian. Given my beliefs, I could not walk away from this ship without knowing that you will have your needs met. Would you want me to ignore such beliefs?" He took hold of her arm and stopped her so that he could face her again. "Ella," he said in a gentle voice, "I *do* feel sorry for you. What you have been through is unimaginable. But my motivation is not based in pity—not that there would be anything wrong with that."

Ella tried to glare at him again, but the look in his eyes was so genuine she had to look away.

"What are you going to do now?" he asked with such sincere concern that Ella struggled to keep tears from surfacing. "Be honest with me."

"I'm not certain," she said and forced a smile. "I'm sure I'll manage." She sighed and looked around at the people surrounding her, most of them with that hollow expression in their eyes. She knew that every survivor would be attempting to get the help he or she needed to move beyond this day with the hope of recovering.

"I suspect you're well accustomed to *managing*," Jonathan said, startling her to the fact that he was watching her, "but you'll soon be in a strange city with nothing and no one."

"Which makes Mrs. Olsen's offer very appreciated."

"And as kind as she is, she would drive you crazy in a day; admit it."

"Yes, but . . . perhaps I can stay there just until I can find work and—"

"Or you could come home with me," Jonathan blurted before he lost his nerve—again. He didn't want to lose track of her. He didn't want to think of her being on her own with no one to look after her. And most of all, he wanted to be *the one* to look after her. In that moment he felt certain that if he could only devote his life to being her protector and provider, he would be a happy man. If that were true—and he couldn't bring himself to believe otherwise—then he couldn't possibly walk away from her now, simply with the hope of possibly seeing her again.

"I beg your pardon!" she said, her voice astonished and her eyes wide.

Jonathan felt horrified to realize he'd been misunderstood. "No, I don't mean . . . I mean . . . what I *do* mean is that . . . that you could stay with my family . . . until you decide what you want to do, and—"

"You're married?" she asked, sounding even more suspicious.

"No, I'm not married, Ella. I mean my parents; my brothers and sisters."

"Oh, I see." She chuckled and glanced away, but not before he saw a relief in her eyes that gave him an inkling of hope that she might have some of the same feelings for him as he had for her.

"The house is crowded, but my parents are always thrilled to take in guests. They believe that offering hospitality to someone in need will bring a blessing upon their home. That means if I bring you home with me, I will be in good favor with my parents."

"Are you not in good favor otherwise?" Ella asked, wanting desperately to accept his invitation, but not wanting to appear as desperate as she felt.

Jonathan looked away as he said tonelessly, "They weren't happy about my choice to seek out work at sea." He looked at her again. "They'll be glad to know that I've changed my mind about that."

"Have you?" she asked, so deeply relieved by his offer that her knees nearly buckled.

"I don't think I'll ever be able to go to sea again," he said with an unmasked trauma in his eyes that stirred the same feelings inside Ella.

Ella wanted to say that she understood how he felt. She wanted to say how grateful she was to know that she could leave the *Carpathia* and be in his care, as secure and safe as she'd come to feel with him. She wanted to cry in his arms and tell him that she was so glad to not feel alone in that moment—physically and emotionally. All she could manage to say was, "Yes, I know what you mean."

He reached out a hand toward her. "And my parents will be very happy to have you under their roof. My sisters will love you. My mother will coddle you. My father will feed you better than you've ever been fed in your life."

"Your father?"

"He does most of the cooking for the little restaurant that has been the family business since my parents came to New York right after they were married. We live above the restaurant, so the house usually smells like whatever is being served downstairs." He reached his hand a little closer toward her. "Come home with me," he repeated. "I'll take very good care of you. I promise."

"What about your brothers?" she asked.

"What *about* my brothers?" he countered, confused.

"You told me how your parents and sisters might feel about my coming; you didn't mention your brothers."

Jonathan chuckled. "My older brother is married. He and his new wife live nearby. My younger brother will probably fall in love with you, but he's only fourteen so you'll have to let him down easy." This made Ella smile. He couldn't resist adding, "But if he naively believes he can set his sights on you, he's going to have a fight on his hands." This made Ella blush slightly, which made Jonathan smile. "Say yes," he said, still holding his hand out toward her. "Say that you'll come home with me."

Ella looked at his hand, then his face, then his hand again. Her distrust of supposedly kind strangers battled with her desire to accept his offer, and even more so to believe that his intentions were not only honorable, but perhaps romantic in nature. She'd never felt this way about a man, and had perhaps come to believe that she never would. Recalling that Irene had told her more than once that she needed to learn to trust again, Ella slipped her hand into Jonathan's and felt both warmed and comforted by his smile and the corresponding squeeze of his fingers.

"I would be very grateful," she said, "but only if you'll promise that I can earn my keep. Perhaps you can help me find work and—"

"We'll worry about that once we get settled, but . . . I'll do everything I can to help. If you're so determined to be self-sufficient, I'm certain we'll figure something out."

"Thank you," she said, trying to be gracious. "Your kindness continues to astound me."

"Why should it?" he asked, and Ella thought of a way to answer that question that would lead into a tirade of her distrusting attitude toward men—and perhaps humankind in general.

Instead she just eased her hand from his and walked on, saying lightly, "Mrs. Olsen will be gravely disappointed."

"I'm certain that she and Mrs. Chadwick will be keeping each other company."

"I'm certain they will," Ella said.

Jonathan left to get some sleep before his night shift began. Ella returned to the rail of the ship, deeply grateful to know that she would not be left on her own in a strange place. Her fear of leaving the *Carpathia* had lessened significantly. At supper, Mrs. Olsen found her and insisted on sitting with her to eat. She was disappointed when Ella declined her offer, but she smiled and winked when Ella told her she would be staying with the family of Jonathan Moreau.

"Who could turn *that* down?" Mrs. Olsen said with an annoying chuckle. "Perhaps love is in the air."

"He's a very kind man, Mrs. Olsen. I wouldn't presume to think that his offer has any romantic implications."

"Think what you like, precious," the woman said with a conspiratorial smile, as if she knew some great secret to which Ella might be oblivious.

Thankfully the subject turned to talk of Baxter and Dexter. Before supper ended, Mrs. Olsen gave Ella a little piece of paper with her home address written on it, and she made her promise to come and visit. Ella put the paper in the pocket of her lightweight black coat, the one she'd worn when boarding the *Titanic*. She'd worn it underneath Mr. Blackhurst's heavier and more durable one. She hoped that she wouldn't be facing much cold between now and the time when she would be getting settled in at Jonathan Moreau's home in the city.

The *Carpathia* eased into the New York harbor late in the evening, while it was once again raining. Ella was glad to have Jonathan standing beside her when a new reality began to settle in. Even from where she was holding back in a place where she could stay dry, she could see a boat full of newspaper reporters that had been there to meet the arriving ship. It sailed at the *Carpathia's* side into the port, with men calling out to the passengers, begging for information, offering money for eyewitness accounts, and even tempting people to jump in the water and come over to their boat in exchange for a substantial payment for their story.

"It's horrible," Ella said.

"I fear it will only get worse," Jonathan said.

The thousands of people gathered on the piers to meet the *Carpathia* seemed evidence that what he'd said was true. Thanks to wireless communication, news of the *Titanic* tragedy had reached America long before the ship carrying the survivors and rescuers. Ella knew she would be utterly terrified to step off the ship without a man at her side. And she told Jonathan so. He just humbly replied, "I'm glad to be able to help. We won't be leaving the ship until after breakfast, however. I need to finish my last shift through the night, and you need to get some sleep. Perhaps by the time we disembark, the frenzy will have died down a little."

"We can hope," she said, relieved by the plan.

They walked away from the view of the chaotic pier while Ella wondered what it would feel like to have dry ground beneath her feet again. The very thought almost spurred her to tears, but she fought them back. There would be other times to cry, but not now.

Ella didn't sleep well that night. She was plagued with bad dreams that kept waking her up, and she had trouble falling back to sleep with the distant sounds of the city that were unfamiliar after days at sea. She wondered what life in New York City might be like as opposed to life in London. She wondered what the Moreau family might be like, and she hoped she wasn't getting herself into a situation that might simply be a different kind of awkward than that of staying with Mrs. Olsen. Either way, it was only temporary. She would quickly need to find work to support herself and find a way to move forward with her life. Ever since she'd made plans to come to America, she'd considered New York just a stopping place before moving on. Of course, she'd planned to move on to Utah where Irene would have been there to help guide her into making a new life. But she couldn't think about that. Thoughts of Irene provoked her to tears more than anything else. She simply couldn't bear to think about her being gone, and the impact her absence would have on so many people—including herself.

The following morning Ella felt decidedly nervous to leave the *Carpathia*. She longed to have her feet on dry land, and she longed to put the entire nightmare of this drama at sea behind her, but the uncertainty before her made it tempting to want to never disembark this ship that had become a temporary home to her. She wondered if a woman could get a job on such a vessel but, of course, realized her entire way of thinking was absurd.

The ship had become very quiet since most of the passengers had disembarked the previous evening or earlier this morning. Ella waited in the parlor where she'd been sleeping, knowing that Jonathan would find her there when he was ready to leave. A couple of hours after she'd eaten her breakfast, she looked up to see him there, dressed in very average clothes. It was the first time she'd seen him wearing anything besides his uniform. In response to her silent assessment, he said, "I thought the uniform might draw unwanted attention."

Ella nodded but didn't want to talk about the reasons for such a comment. He held out his hand and she took it, glad for the safe feeling that radiated from his touch.

"Are you ready?" he asked.

"I'm trying to be," she admitted.

"One day at a time," he said, and they walked off the *Carpathia* onto the pier. Within minutes they had immersed themselves discreetly into the busyness of New York City, where no one would suspect they were witnesses to the most talked-about event in decades. Ella was glad to know that this was Jonathan's home and he was comfortably skilled at finding his way around. She couldn't even imagine how she would have managed to be here on her own with very little money to her name. More than once they passed boys selling newspapers, shouting headlines about the tragedy of the *Titanic*. Ella realized she was trembling and knew that Jonathan couldn't help but notice as he continued to hold her hand, but he just squeezed it more tightly, and they kept walking, as if the story held no interest for them.

"Let's get a cup of tea or something, shall we?" he said. "Then we can hire a taxicab to take us to the house. We *could* walk from here, but it would be a *long* walk."

"That would be lovely," she said in regard to the cup of tea *and* not having to take a long walk. Her feet were much improved but still tender. She had no desire to tempt them into aching any more than necessary.

Ella said nothing else as she walked through the crowds with her hand holding tightly to his. She was grateful for his insight in having a small reprieve before going to meet his family. She wanted a little time to become accustomed to the idea before she was plunged into the situation. She was far more grateful than she could have ever told him, to feel her hand in his and to know that she wasn't alone in this strange place. Her mind once again considered her alternatives. She could have stayed with the Blackhursts and at least have had a roof over her head and food in her stomach. But the degradation of being in their presence seemed more than she could bear, even as desperate as she felt. She could have gone home with Mrs. Olsen. She truly was a kind woman, and Ella was glad to know that God had offered her more than one choice in this situation. But for all of her kindness, the woman was just much too talkative, and Ella knew once again that living under the same roof with her would have created a different sort of bondage from which she might have found it difficult to break free. She put a hand in her coat pocket where she felt the note Mrs. Olsen had given her, and knew that going to stay with her was an option should any problems arise in regard to staying with Jonathan and his family. But for now, she felt comfortable with the choice and grateful it was an option.

Ella quickly found walking through the crowded streets to be challenging and tiresome. She was glad when they entered a little tea shop of sorts, and relieved to find it almost devoid of customers. The whispers of a quiet conversation in a far corner were a sweet reprieve to the noise and bustle outside. She was reminded of all the times she'd met Irene in a tea shop, but she pushed the memory away and slammed a door on allowing herself to feel any associated grief. Jonathan ordered tea for two and some biscuits, but Ella admitted, "I don't know that I'm very hungry."

"Perhaps you should just eat a little . . . to keep up your strength. I'm certain we'll be fed well once it's supper time, but I'm afraid we'll be arriving after lunch is over."

Ella nodded, thinking more that she should eat to calm her nerves as she thought of meeting his family. In the absence of noise surrounding them, the silence between her and Jonathan became starkly noticeable. Again she found him watching her, but she was surprised to acknowledge that his doing so didn't make her uneasy. Trying to be practical about the situation, she asked, "Why are you being so kind to me?"

"Am I?" he asked, and just then the tea and biscuits were brought to their table.

Jonathan smiled at the woman once she'd set everything on the table. "Thank you," he said, and she smiled in return and then left them alone.

"Yes, you are," Ella said while he poured the tea from a lovely china teapot into matching cups that were dainty and elegant and reminded her of the days before her father's death; and they reminded her of Irene. She pushed all memories away.

"Whatever I might be doing, Ella, I can assure you that it comes very naturally."

Ella picked up her teacup only to realize that her hand was shaking, and she set it back down very quickly. She was unable to avoid the way it rattled against the saucer as she set it there. Jonathan couldn't help but notice, and his eyes showed concern.

"It's been days," she said, looking down as she set her hand flat on the table in an effort to steady it. "You would think I could stop shaking."

"I think it's a wonder you're not shaking a lot more than you are. I think that your courage and dignity are quite remarkable."

Ella felt deeply touched but wasn't certain she agreed, and she didn't know how to respond. He put his hand over hers on the table and asked, "Does it happen often?"

"Less and less," she said, "but still too often."

"Give it time," he said, and she noted that his hand over hers had a soothing effect. She eased her hand away and made another attempt to lift the cup, this time more successfully.

She took a sip of tea, closing her eyes to feel the gentle steam rising to her face. She'd come to love every little evidence of warmth. She cradled the warm cup in her hands. "So, you're naturally a kind person, then," she said, returning to their previous conversation.

"Not necessarily, if you must know. What I meant is that it's very easy to be kind to you. From the moment I lifted you out of that lifeboat, I've wanted nothing more than to be certain you were cared for . . . and safe."

Ella's heart quickened at the tender—and seemingly personal—implication. Then she told herself that she could be reading some meaning into his words that had not been intended. Perhaps he was more naturally caring and kind than he gave himself credit for. Perhaps her being in need awakened a hidden hero within himself. Whatever his reasons, she couldn't think too much about that right now. She only smiled and made no comment before she tried one of the biscuits that had been brought with the tea. It was entirely different from what would be called a biscuit in England; more breadlike, but warm and fluffy and delicious, with butter and honey. Jonathan seemed to find some pleasure in her enjoyment of the biscuits, but his only comment was, "Wait until you taste my father's pastries. He's truly a genius when it comes to what he can do with flour and sugar and an oven."

"How delightful," Ella said and took another sip of tea, trying not to feel nervous at the prospect of moving in unannounced with his family. But given the options of the Blackhursts and Mrs. Olsen, she had to feel grateful. Jonathan Moreau was a very nice man. And he spoke so highly of his family; surely it couldn't be too bad. And it was only temporary anyway. She would find work, and she would find a way to make it on her own.

When they had finished their tea, Jonathan settled the bill and Ella thanked him. She pointed out that she did have *some* money; she certainly wasn't as penniless as she had been at other times in her life. But he insisted on paying anyway, and she didn't want to make too big of a fuss. She hoped he knew that it was her intention to find work as quickly as possible, and not be a burden to him or his family. The thought hovered with her as he took her hand again before they stepped back outside onto the noisy street. They had nothing to say to each other while he hailed a taxicab, then he opened the door for her to slide onto the automobile seat first. He slid in beside her and told the driver the address of his home. "Moreau's Bistro," he added.

"Oh, I know the place," the driver said with enthusiasm. "Best crepes in the city."

"Crepes?" Ella asked Jonathan quietly. She'd never heard the word.

"You'll see," he said with a smile and once again took her hand. She found it both comfortable and comforting to have her hand in his, but it brought to mind once again what she needed to say. It had to be clarified before she moved into his home and took advantage of his family.

"Jonathan . . . I need to say something."

"All right," he said, looking directly at her in a way that could have been unnerving, but it wasn't.

"I'm very grateful for what you're doing for me, but . . . I want you to know that . . . I'll find work as soon as I can, and I'll find a way to make it on my own."

He looked astonished, then leaned a little more toward her. "That is the last thing you need to be worrying about right now. When you can get through a day without shaking, we'll talk about the next step."

Jonathan hoped that by then she might be convinced to become his wife and that he would be able to take care of her for the rest of his life. But he knew it was far too soon to be expressing such thoughts, especially with what she'd been through.

"What if I *never* stop shaking?" she asked in barely more than a whisper, not wanting the driver to overhear.

"You will," Jonathan said, squeezing her hand more tightly as if he could prove to her that he could be at her side and offer comfort and reassurance for as long as she needed him.

Ella turned to look out the window, wondering where all of this would lead.

As if the driver had been looking for silence from the backseat in order to make conversation, he said with some excitement, "Can you believe what happened to the *Titanic*?"

Ella shot a startled glance at Jonathan, silently asking him to save her from this conversation. With no thought beyond an instinctive need to cling to him, she put her free hand on top of his, the one that was holding her other hand. He covered it with *his* free hand. "What about it?" Jonathan asked, falsely cool while he held Ella's shaking hands in his.

"Sank like a rock," the driver said, and Ella shuddered from the memory such words provoked. Jonathan put an arm around her shoulders and she gratefully leaned against him while he managed to hold both of her hands in one of his. "It's in all the papers," the driver added as if it were the most exciting thing he'd ever had the opportunity to gossip about. "More than fifteen hundred souls went down with her, they say."

Ella shuddered again and turned her face toward Jonathan's shoulder, fearing she would let out an audible cry otherwise. "It's all right," Jonathan said quietly to Ella, then more loudly, "It's unconscionable."

"It sure is!" the driver said and shook his head, making a disgusted noise. "Sure makes me glad to have my feet on dry land."

"Yes, it sure does," Jonathan said and tightened his arm around Ella's shoulders at the same time he tightened his grasp on her hands.

Ella forced herself to breathe deeply and push the nightmarish images from her mind. She tried to think instead about meeting Jonathan's family, then her attention was drawn to how close he was holding her, and the tangible strength and comfort she drew from his nearness. She looked up at him, startled to find his face very close to hers, and to see that he was watching her too. She wondered for a moment if he might kiss her, and she was stunned to realize that she wanted him to—until a memory almost as horrible as the sinking of the *Titanic* jumped into her mind, provoking a wave of nausea. She turned her face abruptly away and sat up straight, muttering quietly, "Forgive me."

"For what?" he asked, equally quiet.

She wanted to say, *For being so stupid and gullible and ruining my life long before I ever met you.* She amended her words to a quiet, "Thank you," implying her gratitude for his efforts to keep her together. Then she felt starkly relieved when the taxicab came to a halt.

"Here we are," the driver declared with the same enthusiasm he'd used in declaring the news that a great ship had sunk *like a rock*. "Be sure to order some crepes," he added.

"Thank you," Jonathan said and handed the man money to pay for the fare. "Keep the change."

Jonathan opened the door, and the driver said, "Thank you, Mr. uh . . ."

"Moreau," Jonathan said and got out.

He took Ella's hand to help her out of the taxicab and to her feet. "You're shaking again," he said to her as the automobile drove away.

"I'm a little nervous," she said, wishing she could credit her shaking to simply that.

She knew he was well aware of the truth, but he was kind enough to humor her. "No need for that," he said as she looked up at the lovely café with a sign above the windows that read in elegant red letters, MOREAU'S BISTRO AND BAKERY.

"It looks very nice," she said with zest.

"It *is* very nice," he said, "but you're still shaking."

Ella looked down at her hand in his, then up at his face. "How are you going to explain your bringing me home like this? We're standing here holding hands as if we're sweethearts or something, but . . ." Ella regretted putting a voice to the implication that something romantic might be evolving between them, and she didn't know how to finish that sentence.

Jonathan saved her when he said, "But it's too soon to be talking about such feelings . . . especially with all that you've been through. I'll tell my parents the truth. I always have."

With that he led her toward a door right next to the bistro that blended discreetly into the woodwork surrounding the front of the café. He opened it and motioned for her to go ahead of him. She entered to see a narrow enclosed staircase going up, and nothing else. Jonathan closed the door behind him and said, "Go on up." She started up the stairs and he followed, since it was too narrow for them to walk up side by side.

When they got to the landing, he opened the door and motioned for her to go ahead of him, but she said, "You go first."

"Very well," he said, and she followed him into a little parlor. It was clutter free and decorated in tasteful simplicity. He whispered, "Papa will be downstairs working, along with most everyone else. But my mother would never forgive me if I didn't come to find her first." He winked to verify his exaggeration just before he closed the door.

Only a moment after the latch closed, a woman appeared in the doorway from what was obviously the kitchen, wearing a long apron on which she was wiping her hands. She was dark haired and slender, and her face bore a strong resemblance to Jonathan's.

"Hello, Mama," he said, and she flew into his arms as if he'd returned from war.

"My Jonathan," she said, embracing him tightly, her eyes squeezed closed. Even with those two words Ella could hear the thick French accent. She took his face into her hands, and Ella was glad that Mrs. Moreau had eyes only for her son, which allowed Ella to remain unnoticed until they had the opportunity to exchange proper greetings.

"What are you doing here?" she asked, as if he were in trouble. "Was your ship not on its way to Austria?"

"It turned back," he said and kissed both of his mother's cheeks while she kissed his in return. "Have you not seen the papers?"

Mrs. Moreau gasped and put a hand over her heart. "Papa said a ship went down, but we knew it was not yours and we did not worry anymore."

"Our ship came back to New York . . . to bring survivors."

Ella began to shake at that last word, but since he glanced her way at the same time, she fought to subdue the evidence of it. Mrs. Moreau's eyes followed in the direction of Jonathan's glance, and she gasped again. "A young lady?" she asked, glancing at Jonathan then back to Ella. "You have brought a young lady?"

"Yes, Mama. This is Ella. I told her that she could stay here for a while. She has nowhere else to go."

Ella could see Mrs. Moreau putting the pieces together in her head, then she gasped *again*, more loudly. "Oh, mon cheri!" she said, taking hold of Ella's shoulders before she pressed a kiss to both of Ella's cheeks. "You poor, dear child. Of course you must stay with us. Jonathan did right to bring you here." She looked at her son without letting go of Ella's shoulders. "And she is so pretty, no?"

"Yes, Mama," Jonathan said with a smile and wink toward Ella, "she is very pretty."

"Oh, *ma chéri*," Mrs. Moreau said again, putting her arm around Ella and guiding her toward the sofa. Ella didn't know what the words meant, but they sounded very endearing. "You must tell me everything." She urged Ella to sit down then sat beside her. "What you must have been through!" She took Ella's hand and patted it gently.

"Perhaps she doesn't want to talk about it right now, Mama," Jonathan said, and Ella saw a glance pass between mother and son that seemed to have hidden meaning. "It was very traumatic."

"Another time, then," Mrs. Moreau said. "Perhaps you are tired. Or hungry."

"Do you want something to eat before supper?" Jonathan asked Ella.

"No, thank you," she said. "I'm fine, but . . . I . . ."

"You would like to lie down?" Mrs. Moreau guessed when Ella hesitated. She didn't want to admit how very little sleep she'd gotten since the nightmare had begun, but she was more motivated by the desire to be left alone for a while in order to get her bearings and put her composure firmly in place.

"That would be very nice, thank you," Ella said.

Jonathan's mother said to him, "Let her use your room. You can sleep in your old bed. She can have privacy there, no?"

"Thank you, Mama," Jonathan said and took Ella's hand to help her to her feet.

"Yes, thank you so much, Mrs. Moreau. Your kindness is so—"

"It is nothing but pleasure to have you here, *ma chéri*. We will wake you before supper. And please, you must call me Lisette."

"What a lovely name . . . Lisette," Ella said, and Jonathan led her into a narrow hall, then up another flight of stairs, then another.

"The house is small but has three floors above the bistro," he explained. "The parlor and kitchen and dining room are on the first level. The next level has my parents' bedroom, and my younger sisters', and the bathroom." He pointed it out as they passed by. "At the top," he said as they arrived there, "are three other bedrooms." He stood in the little hall and pointed at the doors. "My sister Sally and her husband Frank are using that room. This is where I will be sleeping along with my brother Lucas." He pushed the door open slightly and she could see two single beds.

"Is that a problem?" she asked, thinking of all the times that people had given up beds for her.

"Not at all. I shared this room with Lucas for most of my life, until our older brother, Sebastian, got married and moved out, just a year or so ago. I took over his room, but I'm more than happy to let you use it now." He opened the door to the specified room where she saw a larger bed, a little dresser, and a chair. There was barely enough room to navigate around the furniture, but the room was tidy and comfortable.

"It's lovely. Thank you," she said, squeezing his hand, since it was still conveniently holding to hers.

He smiled. "As my mother said, it is nothing but pleasure to have you here."

"She is very dear."

"Yes, she is," he said, "as long as you can steer clear of her curiosity. While you're resting I'll go try to ease it a bit so she won't plague you with questions."

"Thank you," Ella said again, grateful beyond words. "Oh, what does it mean . . . what she called me?"

"*Ma chéri?*" he said with a perfect French accent, and she nodded. He smiled again. "*Chéri* means precious or darling. It would be something like calling you 'my dear.' She doesn't generally use such endearment with someone she's just met. You should be flattered."

"I am," Ella said.

"Do you need anything?"

Ella glanced around. "No, thank you."

"I'll see you later, then," he said and left her alone.

CHAPTER NINE
The Best of France

ELLA TOOK OFF HER SHOES and closed the curtains to darken the room a bit. She tried to get comfortable, then crept quietly down one flight of stairs to the little bathroom. She found the house to be tidy and decorated in a variety of colored paints and wallpapers, but tastefully done. While the house was obviously quite old, it was in good repair and there was evidence of modern electricity and plumbing having been added.

Ella went just as quietly back up the stairs and once again tried to get comfortable, but just closing her eyes brought to mind the horrible sounds and images that refused to be blocked out. Her hands began to shake and, being alone, she made no effort to hold it back. The trembling reverberated through her entire body and she wrapped her arms around the spare pillow, wishing she could cry. But her tears seemed frozen somewhere deep inside, and she feared what might happen when they finally melted.

* * * * *

Jonathan took a few minutes to mentally prepare himself for the inevitable conversation with his mother. He was glad for this time of day when they were alone in the house, and he hoped it would last more than a few minutes. The comings and goings of his siblings could be unpredictable. He felt so grateful to be home again and to have a place to come home to that thinking about it created a swelling in his chest that he knew was the precursor to possible tears. He'd never been one to cry easily—not since he'd passed into his teen years, at least. But he'd fought the temptation many times since he'd stood on the deck of the *Carpathia* to come upon the dark, empty ocean where the *Titanic* had gone down. Now he needed to tell his mother the story or she would ask too many questions of Ella, and he knew Ella wasn't strong enough to handle it.

Jonathan stepped quietly into the doorway of the kitchen where his mother was stirring something in a pot on the stove and humming quietly. It was a familiar scene and it warmed his heart.

"Hello," she said, turning to look at him. "Your father is a genius with his crepes and pastries, no? But he can never compete with what your mother can do with soup." She laughed softly, perhaps nervously; he knew she had other things on her mind, and her attempt at casual conversation was an effort to make him feel more comfortable.

"Papa would never dispute that," he said and sat down on one of the two chairs at opposite sides of a tiny table. The family dined in the other room. This table was used only for food preparation that could be done sitting down or for face-to-face conversations over a cup of tea or coffee. As if his mother had predicted this conversation, she set a cup of steaming tea in front of him, then got one for herself and sat down.

"It is good to have you home safe, my Johnny. I missed you."

"I haven't been gone very many days, Mama."

"No, but I worried for you. I did not understand this need you felt to go to sea, but I think I understand it now."

"Do you?" he asked, wishing *he* did.

"You needed to find the lovely Ella and bring her home with you, no?"

Jonathan hadn't wanted to admit that he'd had the same thought. The tragedy of the whole experience was still so prominent on his mind that it was difficult to believe his purpose for sailing on the *Carpathia* might have been some kind of fate or destiny in regard to Ella. He'd like to think so, but right now they were both far too traumatized to think about destiny—she far more than he. "Perhaps," was all he said.

"Talk to your mama," she said, putting her hand over his. "Tell me what happened that has left such clouds in your eyes."

Acknowledging that he might have *clouds in his eyes*, Jonathan once again felt that temptation to cry, but he fought it back and cleared his throat, knowing he had much to tell her and no guarantee of how much time they might have alone.

"I was on the night shift," he began. "Being one of the newest members of the crew, my duties mostly entailed just being on hand to do whatever I was ordered to do. My previous shifts had been relatively boring, and I'd felt more like a waiter than a sailor, getting this thing or that for the men who were sailing the ship while the captain slept."

"Then your experience in the bistro came to good use," she said somewhat facetiously, but again Jonathan recognized her effort to put some normalcy into a conversation that had her very agitated. He could well imagine that she was having some of the same thoughts he'd been having. What if it had been the *Carpathia* that had hit an iceberg and gone down with most of her crew still aboard? Of course, she didn't know the whole story yet, but she still had likely sensed that he'd brushed way too closely against death to not be shaken.

"As far as I understand it, the captain was awakened when a distress signal was wired from the *Titanic*. The captain immediately changed course and got all the engines running at maximum speed to get there as quickly as possible. He even ordered power to be cut off from heating the passenger rooms so that more power could be converted to the engines. He gave orders for all kinds of preparations to be made to bring aboard the passengers and luggage from the *Titanic*, and we all expected to arrive at the coordinates and find a sinking vessel, but . . ."

Jonathan felt suddenly closer to getting choked up than he had since the drama had unfolded. Or perhaps it was accurate to say that the words forming in his mind threatened to choke him if he dared utter them. Perhaps uttering them might make them more real, less deniable. He felt a dose of empathy for Ella's reluctance to talk about what had happened. But he cleared his throat and forged ahead, knowing his mother would not let up without hearing the whole story, and if he didn't tell her, she would press Ella. And he didn't want that to happen. His mother meant well, but her overt curiosity would not mix well with Ella's present state of mind.

"What we found," he sighed, leaning back and folding his arms over his chest, "was nothing."

"Nothing?"

"There was . . . nothing but . . . cold, black ocean. Deathly silence." He regretted the metaphor as soon as it had passed his lips, but he couldn't take it back. "I think the captain must have been wondering if he'd gotten the wrong coordinates, or if the message had been wrong altogether. Then we spotted a light, and we realized it was a lifeboat. That's when we all began to realize what had happened. We worked as quickly as we could to get all of those people on board and to help them. They were freezing and exhausted. Some were in shock, some were sobbing uncontrollably, some were trying to behave normally. But they all had the same look in their eyes. A hollow . . . distant . . . kind of look. They'd seen something horrible; something that no human being ever expects to see in a lifetime. They'd watched the ship sink. They'd watched people go into the water and listened to them screaming and crying until they froze to death."

"Heaven have mercy!" Lisette muttered before she put a hand over her mouth. Jonathan didn't look directly at her, or he never would have been able to finish.

"We took seven hundred and five passengers on board out of the lifeboats. Many of them believed that their friends and loved ones were on *other* lifeboats, but quickly discovered they weren't." He hung his head and barely managed a steady voice. "More than fifteen hundred people died." He heard his mother gasp behind the hand over her mouth. He ignored her and hurried to finish. "Ella was in one of the lifeboats. Her friend Irene didn't make it. Irene had been in London training to be a midwife. She was returning to her family in Utah—her parents, a husband, three children."

Jonathan sighed again. "I felt immediately drawn to Ella. Most of the survivors had someone. They'd been in the lifeboat with a family member or friend. But Ella was completely alone. I tried to watch out for her, make certain she was all right, and . . . I confess that I was deeply hoping she would agree to come home with me when we docked in New York. I suspected that she had nowhere to go. So . . . here we are."

Once he stopped talking, Jonathan realized his mother was crying. He wasn't surprised, but he didn't know if he could keep it from becoming contagious. He stood up and went to the window, looking down into the familiar street below. "I'm never going to sea again. I've looked at the ocean my whole life. Growing up in a port city, that's what you do. But until you're out there it's impossible to fully comprehend its power. I know you crossed the ocean to get to America; you're the one who told me that. But I had no idea. And it didn't fully sink in until I realized that the ocean had completely swallowed a massive vessel . . . a small floating city . . . in less than a few hours. If I do nothing more in my life that has any value, I will help Ella get past this and make peace with it . . . if such a thing is possible."

Jonathan ran out of things to say, which made him more keenly aware of his mother's sniffling. From the corner of his eye he could see her dabbing at her eyes with her apron. "I thank God above that you are safe," she muttered.

"I've done that a thousand times since the moment I realized what had happened. It could have been me. Except for those who were manning the oars of the lifeboats, the entire crew—including the captain—went down with the *Titanic*. I can't close my eyes without wondering what it must have been like for them."

Lisette kept dabbing at her tears, and Jonathan stopped himself from the temptation to ramble on with details that were better left unspoken. "Mama," he said, turning toward her, "I want to ask a favor of you."

"Anything," she said, looking up at him.

"Don't ask Ella about it. I'm telling you what happened so you'll know. If you have questions, talk to me privately. I know you're just curious and concerned, but . . . she's not ready to talk about it. Do you understand?"

"I do, yes," she said and nodded. "That poor, sweet girl."

"Indeed," he said and turned back to the window.

Jonathan felt grateful the conversation had wound down when he heard footsteps bounding up the stairs and knew it was his little brother. Lucas was fourteen but looked more like eighteen. He had similar coloring to Jonathan but his features were more in favor of their father. He burst through the door of the parlor and shouted, "Mama, Mama! The *Carpathia* is back in New York! Everyone's talking about it and . . ." Lucas saw his brother and laughed, throwing his arms around Jonathan's neck. "You *are* here!" Lucas said and laughed again. "We were hoping!"

"Yes, I'm here," Jonathan said.

"And you were on the ship that rescued the *Titanic* survivors?"

"Yes," Jonathan said, "but don't go making that into something exciting. What happened was horrible."

"Sure," Lucas said as if it had just occurred to his youthful mind that it *was* horrible. "Sure it was. Sorry."

"It's okay," Jonathan said. "I understand it's in all the papers."

"It sure is," Lucas said. "That's all people have been talking about down-stairs, but no one figured out until this morning that *your* ship was in the news too."

"I'd prefer the entire city not know that it was *my* ship," Jonathan said.

"Avoiding that might not be so easy," Lisette said. "You know how your papa likes to talk."

"Yes, I know," Jonathan said, concerned with how this might affect Ella.

"Johnny has brought a young lady home with him," Lisette said to Lucas. The boy's eyes widened, then he smirked at his brother.

"A lady? You? I thought you were done with the ladies since—"

"There's no need to bring up the past," Jonathan interrupted. "Ella is quite lovely, and you need to mind your manners." He chuckled and lightly slapped his brother on the shoulder. "She's been through a great deal, and she doesn't need to have *you* flirting with her."

Lucas's eyes widened again. "She was one of the—"

"Yes," Jonathan said tersely, "but we'd prefer to keep that quiet."

"Oh," Lucas said. "Sure. You'd better tell Papa that. He's already waiting for you to come through the door, so you'd better go let him know you're back."

"The lunch crowd will be gone by now," Lisette said. "You should go talk to your papa." She nodded at Lucas. "Your brother can cover for Papa while he has a visit with Johnny. Run along now. Both of you."

Jonathan smiled at his mother and followed Lucas down the stairs, out the door onto the street, then into the door of the bistro, only a few steps away.

"Look, Papa!" Lucas called like a child much younger than fourteen. "Johnny's come home!"

Bastien Moreau looked up from behind the glass case that displayed a wide array of breads and pastries. "My Johnny!" he said and came around the counter, drawing the attention of a few customers, but they were strangers and quickly went back to their quiet conversations.

"Hello, Papa," Jonathan said as his father took hold of his shoulders and they exchanged a quick kiss on each cheek.

"Is it true, then?" Bastien asked. "About the—"

"Perhaps we could talk quietly while Lucas looks after the customers and—"

"Is that our Johnny?" they heard a feminine voice call, and Jonathan's sister came through the door from the kitchen, covered with flour. Marie was seventeen and had many young men competing for her affection. She was dark haired and beautiful like their mother. Ten-year-old Violet followed Marie out of the kitchen, also covered in flour. She was showing signs of turning into a beauty like her sister, but her coloring was blonde like their father's—although Bastien had become so bald that there was no recognizing the color his hair had once been. The girls made a striking contrast with their hair color, even though their features showed that they were undoubtedly sisters. They each took their turn at throwing their arms around Jonathan's neck and declaring how glad they were to see him, as if he'd been gone for months. After sufficient greetings had been exchanged, Bastien assigned the three children to their posts and guided Jonathan to his favorite table in a front corner by the window. Thankfully, the only remaining customers were seated far enough across the room that Jonathan and Bastien could converse privately.

"Now, what is this about your ship being in the papers?" Bastien asked.

"It's not *my* ship," Jonathan clarified.

"Yes, yes, yes. I am glad to see you back, but I know you should be nearly to Austria by now, and here you are back in the city. Tell your papa what has happened."

Jonathan repeated the story he had told his mother, although with fewer details. He knew that his mother loved details, while his father often grew impatient with them. He just wanted the important facts, so that's what Jonathan told him. He was pleased to hear that his son had brought a young lady home with him, and he promised to keep quiet about the fact that she was a survivor of the *Titanic*.

"I cannot promise, however, what people might already know about *your* involvement in all of this. Many friends and customers knew that you sailed on the *Carpathia*, and now it is in the headlines of every paper."

Jonathan sighed. "I'm not worried for myself, but Ella is very fragile right now."

"We will take good care of her," Bastien said, and Jonathan smiled. How grateful he was to have kind and generous parents! He just hoped that Ella took well to the family and didn't feel too uncomfortable—or overwhelmed.

* * * * *

Ella came awake with an audible gasp, her heart pounding. It took her a long moment to realize that the screams she'd been hearing had only been in her dream, and it took her a minute longer to fully orient herself to her surroundings. The bed where she found herself was a sweet comfort compared to the carpeted floor of the ship parlor where she'd been sleeping, but still she found it difficult to relax. It took minutes of breathing deeply to calm the agitation in her stomach and to slow her accelerated heart rate. She told herself the same things she always told herself. The people who had died on that horrible night were no longer suffering, no longer miserable. In most ways she envied them. In spite of that, she was safe and warm and she never had to go to sea again. But there was an underlying reality she had difficulty acknowledging. The fragility of human life, and the way a loved one could be snatched away without warning, left Ella continually uneasy for reasons she couldn't quite define but couldn't escape. She found herself wondering what she would do if something happened to Jonathan. She couldn't deny that she was growing to care for him. He had quickly become her only stability in this world. What if she lost him for any number of reasons? What if the house burned down? What if she or any member of this family became the victim of a violent crime? The world was full of hideousness, and the pride of humanity in believing that they could somehow be spared from tragedy or avoid being victimized was simply ludicrous. Ella tried to talk back to herself, as if there were two people in her head, one trying to convince the other that such thinking was nonsense, and she had to believe that everything would be all right. She wondered if the tragedies she'd already faced decreased the odds of ever having to face tragedy again, or if she was an ill-fated soul, destined to lead a troubled life, with disaster following her wherever she went. The other part of her tried to dismiss the latter as ridiculousness, but her life to this point left little assurance from which to draw.

Realizing she needed to use the bathroom again, she crept quietly into the hall and down the stairs, hoping not to encounter anyone, but when she headed back up the stairs a few minutes later, she found Jonathan sitting on a step about halfway up.

"I'm lying in wait for you," he said facetiously. With more seriousness he added, "I hope I didn't startle you. I heard you come out of your room."

"I'm fine," she said.

"Did you get any rest?"

"Some," she said and forced a smile. "You?"

"I've been catching up with the family. I'm pleased to say that they're all glad to have me back."

"It must be nice to be so loved by so many people," she said.

"It is, yes," he said, but his expression seemed to indicate that he was reading something deeper into her meaning.

Realizing he *could* read something deeper, she hurried to add, "Is there something I can do to help . . . in the kitchen, or . . ."

"Not today," he said. "We'll talk about that when you've settled in a bit. I'm afraid you'll have to expect to be treated like a guest for at least a day or two."

"I must earn my keep, Jonathan."

"I'm certain my father will put you to work in the bistro, if that's what you want. It always manages to keep the whole family busy in one way or another."

"Do the children go to school?"

"They do lessons at home," he said. "We've all done some bouts of public school, but my mother was actually a school teacher in France. She enjoys teaching her children the basics. They've all been given the choice, and they all seem to enjoy working on lessons in between their shifts of working in the bistro. I'll be back to work there tomorrow, I think."

"Is that a good thing?"

"Yes, it is, I believe. Supper will be a little while yet. Would you like a bit of something to tide you over?"

"No, thank you," she said.

"We generally eat late after the bistro is closed up so that we can all have supper together. Lunch is altogether different—every day but Sunday, when the bistro is closed, of course. Everyone is on their own for lunch, usually getting whatever suits them from the fare downstairs; taking turns for a lunch break."

"It sounds delightful," she said.

Jonathan stood up. "Would you like to go see it? The rest of the family has now heard all about you and they can't wait to meet you."

"Oh," she said, self-consciously smoothing her hair. "Might I have a minute to . . ."

"Of course. Take your time. My mother wanted you to know that you're welcome to use any of the hairbrushes—or anything else you need—that are in the bathroom. And if you need something you can't find, please let one of us know."

"She's as kind as you are."

"It's taken me a while to learn from her good example, but I think I'm finally catching on."

"What do you mean?" she asked, intrigued to think that he might not have always been the way he was now.

"Some other time," he said and motioned with his hand for her to pass him on the stairs. "Freshen up and we'll go downstairs."

Instead Ella went back to the bathroom where she unpinned her hair, smoothed it out with a brush, then pinned it again, thinking about her own hairbrush that was now at the bottom of the Atlantic. And her clothes. And the book that Irene had given her. She forced the thoughts away and focused on her task. She came out and couldn't see Jonathan, but she went down the stairs and found him waiting in the parlor.

"You ready?" he asked, holding out a hand.

"I hope so," she said, "although I feel a mess. It's been days since—"

"You look lovely," he said. "Mother told me she'll arrange some private time for you to have the bathroom later so that you can take a long, hot bath." He smiled. "My mother believes that any problem is more easily solved after a long, hot bath."

"Do you think she's right?" Ella asked as they went out the door and down the stairs.

"I think that it does give a person a chance to step back from life a little and think more clearly. I can't deny that it has some merits."

They went out onto the street, took a few steps, then Jonathan opened the door to the bistro. As he did so, Ella noticed that painted on the door were the words *The Best of France*. She found the slogan quaint, and given what she had already seen of Mrs. Moreau, she had to think it was true in many respects. She was *so* French, and *so* delightful.

A little bell tinkled above the door, and Ella saw a man standing behind a glass case that displayed many baked goods. He turned at the sound and showed a broad smile. His bald head was shiny and his countenance bright. He was of average height and slightly heavy in build, but perhaps that was from living his life among French pastries.

Before Mr. Moreau could get around the counter, two young women came gingerly through a swinging door that obviously led into the kitchen. Their curious eyes were all on Ella, but she felt Jonathan squeeze her hand, and her nerves were calmed. Meeting his mother had gone well; surely this would too.

"This is Ella," Jonathan said.

The girls both said hello at the same time and stepped forward eagerly, as if meeting her were truly exciting. Mr. Moreau held back, but Ella was aware of a wide smile on his face.

"These are my sisters," Jonathan said to Ella. "Marie is seventeen. And Violet is ten."

"You're very pretty," Violet said and was elbowed by her sister.

"Don't embarrass her," Marie whispered, but it was loud enough for everyone to hear.

"She *is* very pretty," Mr. Moreau said, stepping forward with an outstretched hand. His accent was as thickly French as his wife's, whereas the children all sounded like Americans. "It is so dear a pleasure to have you come to our home," he added before he kissed her hand, then he held it while he kissed both of her cheeks.

"You're so very kind," Ella said.

"My father," Jonathan said, motioning toward him while he still held to one of Ella's hands, and Jonathan kept hold of the other. "Bastien Moreau. He'll insist that you call him Bastien. Everyone does."

"Hello, Bastien," Ella said.

Bastien smiled more broadly—if that were possible—and finally let go of her hand. "Sit, sit. We must have tea, and you must choose a pastry, no?" He motioned toward the glass case that beautifully displayed the most glorious array of baked delicacies Ella had ever seen. "Choose one," he said. "Anything." To his daughters he said, "Back to work, *mademoiselles*. And bring tea, please."

"Yes, Papa," they both said in near-perfect unison.

Bastien motioned again toward the pastries. Ella felt overwhelmed and tossed a quick glance toward Jonathan, who said, "Let's start with a napoleon. We'll share one."

"Ah, she will love it, no?"

"I believe she will," Jonathan said and guided Ella to a quaint iron chair with a round seat. The chairs had all been painted red, and the round tables had cloths over them that were white with red flowers on them. The curtains at the windows were of the same fabric, tied back with red ribbons.

While Jonathan was helping her with her chair, Bastien was getting the pastry out of the case. Jonathan sat down, and his father brought two pretty little plates to the table, each bearing half of a napoleon, with its puffy and creamy layers looking like a piece of art. He set down little napkins and delicate forks, then said with pride, "You will be wanting another half, I think." He winked at his son and said, "We will have to fatten her up with fine French foods, no?"

"I think we should keep her delightfully content," Jonathan said, smiling at Ella as his father took a third chair to sit with them. "Whether or not she gets fat is up to her, I suppose. I think she would be beautiful no matter what."

"*Oui, oui,*" Bastien said and laughed. Then Ella realized he was waiting for her to taste the pastry.

With everything she'd heard so far—even from the driver of the taxicab—Ella was expecting it to taste good, but she was pleasantly surprised as the combination of textures and flavors immediately danced in her mouth. "Oh, it's wonderful!" she muttered with her mouth full, her fingers over her lips in order to not display bad manners.

"Ha!" Bastien said and slapped his thigh with another laugh. Ella loved this man and she'd only known him a few minutes. "It is the best of France, no?"

"I have nothing to compare it to," Ella said to him, "since I've never been to France, but it's certainly one of the best things I've ever tasted."

"Ha!" Bastien said again, as if her approval were the greatest triumph of his life. "I am very glad you found this lovely girl and brought her home to us," he said to Jonathan as if he might keep her forever. Ella wanted to think that he might. Was she so starved for a sense of belonging? For a family? Or just afraid of the future beyond this moment and the security of Moreau's Bistro and sharing a napoleon with Jonathan?

The girls brought the tea, one carrying the china teapot—white with red flowers—and the other carrying a tray with matching cups and saucers and a little pitcher of milk. Ella's sense of security and belonging deepened as they set the tea service on the table, each of them behaving as if being in Ella's presence were a great honor. A voice in the back of Ella's head told her not to get too comfortable, and especially not to believe that this was all as good as it seemed. But the weary and traumatized part of her dominated, and she could only take in the pleasure of the moment and find much-needed reprieve from the thoughts and memories that haunted her every moment—sleeping or awake—when she wasn't distracted by something else. Right now was a lovely distraction and she relished it.

The girls went back to the kitchen to work, and Ella realized that Lucas was back there as well when a customer came through the door and Lucas came out of the kitchen to sell them the pastries they had come to buy. Once the customers had left, he approached their table and Jonathan introduced him to Ella. He had a mildly entranced look on his face while he told Ella how good it was to meet her, then his father sent him back to work.

Bastien asked Ella some questions about her life in England. She simply told him that she was an only child, her parents had passed away, and she had been working as a nanny when she'd sailed for America. He asked nothing about the tragedy of the *Titanic*; in fact, he didn't even make a comment about it. Ella could tell that Jonathan had given instructions to avoid the subject, but she was fine with that. She couldn't bear to even think about it; she certainly didn't want to *talk* about it. Realizing that the version of her background that she was telling to Bastien was no more or less than she'd told Jonathan, she wondered how long she might be able to conceal the truth about her past. Would it be possible to develop lasting relationships with these people and not share such things? She would either have to open up to them eventually, or she would have to lie. It wasn't in her to make up something false about herself. The other option was not to develop lasting relationships. She glanced at Jonathan, then at his father, then she looked around at her quaint surroundings and wished to never leave. But perhaps believing she could stay was a fantasy she would do well to avoid. She resigned herself once again to enjoy the moment and not think too far ahead. Jonathan himself said that she needed some time.

The flow of customers began to increase as the hour moved toward evening and people came in to eat a French dinner. Bastien went back to work, but Jonathan remained seated, looking around as if he were taking in the experience in a way that belied the fact that he'd grown up here.

"What are you thinking?" Ella asked.

He smiled at her and said, "That I'm glad to be back, and . . ." He hesitated, sighed, and looked away, which made her think he'd been going to say something that he'd reconsidered, likely because he didn't want to bring up anything difficult for her.

"And glad that you didn't die at sea like most of the crew of the *Titanic*?"

He looked surprised, then said, "Yes, actually. That's exactly what I was thinking. How well you know me."

"I hardly know you at all," Ella said. "It's a logical assumption. How could *any* man not think such thoughts after what's happened?" She realized she was talking about the subject she preferred to avoid, but it felt easier to talk about how it affected *him* as opposed to how it had affected her. But then, this man was just incredibly easy to talk to.

Lucas approached the table wearing a smile that reminded Ella of his father. He had a little plate that he set down, saying to Jonathan, "Papa said she should try the crepes."

"Oh, she should!" Jonathan said while Lucas stared at Ella, still smiling, and the moment became mildly awkward. Ella looked away, and Jonathan said to his brother, "Thank you, Lucas. I'm certain you're needed elsewhere."

"Sure," Lucas said. "Uh . . . yeah, sure. Bye."

Jonathan chuckled as Lucas walked away, glancing at Ella over his shoulder. "I told you he would fall in love with you," he said to Ella.

"Oh, he's much too young for me," Ella said in an attempt to lighten the awkwardness.

"Yes, he is!" Jonathan said.

"And how could you have known he would fall in love with me?" she asked facetiously but with mock severity, as if his little brother's crush were actually a serious matter.

Jonathan looked at her with no sign of humor and said, "Because he and I are very much alike, and I did."

Ella's heart began to pound. She knew he meant it, but she also knew that he had no idea what kind of person she really was. She wanted to tell him that she had fallen in love with him too, but she didn't even know if it was true. She felt attracted to him, but how could she consider such feelings when nothing in her life was the same as it had been—or had been expected to be. The *Titanic* had changed everything, and she could hardly get her bearings. She felt Jonathan's hand over hers on the table, then she looked down to watch the way he took hold of her fingers.

"You don't have to comment on that, Ella. You don't even have to think about it right now. I just wanted you to know." She managed a subtle nod. He cleared his throat and added, "You need to taste the crepes."

"I hear they're the best in the city," she said and picked up her fork.

"This one has strawberries and cream rolled inside, but they come in many varieties. The sweet crepes are used for desserts, but there are savory crepes that we fill with all kinds of wonderful things."

"How delightful," Ella said, then realized her hand was shaking as she tried to lift the fork to her mouth. She hadn't even been thinking about the trauma—until she saw herself shaking and it all rushed back into her conscious mind.

She set the fork back down and Jonathan said softly, "It's all right, Ella."

She let go of the fork and put both hands in her lap, as if that might force them to be still. She nodded and bit her lip, suddenly finding it difficult to hold back the temptation to cry. She didn't know if it was her continual subconscious battle against the memories of surviving a shipwreck, or Jonathan's implications of love. Or maybe it was her knowing that eventually she would just break his heart when he realized that she was not likely the woman he might believe her to be. She concluded that it was a combination of all three as she looked down and blinked hard in an effort to force back the threat of tears.

"Do you want to leave?" he asked.

"No, I'm fine," she said and forced a smile as she lifted her head, having conquered the present threat.

CHAPTER TEN
Shipwrecked Heart

JONATHAN WATCHED HER A LONG moment as if he needed convincing, then he held the forkful of crepe in front of her lips. She opened her mouth and let it slide onto her tongue, immediately impressed. "That is divine," she said. He smiled and fed her another bite, as if he would be glad to help her avoid the need to use her trembling hands. He put a bite into his own mouth, using the same fork, then he gave her another bite.

Ella chewed and swallowed and attempted to steer the subject away from the feelings blossoming between them—or the trauma that had brought them together. "What a lovely place," she said, looking around her at the people talking and laughing and enjoying good food.

"Yes, it is," he said, his countenance bright with nostalgia.

"May I ask what made you want to leave here? You don't have to tell me if you don't want to."

"I don't mind telling you," he said, looking at her. "You're welcome to ask me anything you like." He sighed and leaned back in his chair. "I still haven't figured it out; well . . . not for certain, anyway. I just . . . felt like I had to get away from here. My father has always wanted his sons to work with him . . . to take over the business in time. That's the way it is with fathers and sons, I suppose. Sebastian, my older brother, never liked cooking; never took to it. He's working on the docks and seems to enjoy the physical labor. Not that cooking and baking aren't physical in a way, but . . ."

"I understand," she said.

"I've taken a number of odd jobs around the city, trying my hand at anything but making food for other people to eat. Then a friend of mine heard about an available position on the *Carpathia*. I made the decision impulsively. My parents were upset, but I just . . . went." His eyes grew distant again.

"I'm very grateful you did," she said, and his eyes moved to hers abruptly, showing an intensity that caused her breath to catch in her throat. They were back to that subject again, but she wondered if it was even possible to avoid it. She was moving in with his family, and if she didn't feel so completely comfortable with him, she might have chosen to stay with Mrs. Olsen instead. If she forced away the fogginess of trauma that was dominating her brain, she could never deny her own attraction to this man or her desire to have him near.

"I'm very grateful as well," he said and she felt a deep comfort and relief. "That's the point, Ella. At least I think that's the point. I think I was supposed to be on that ship. I think I was supposed to be the one to carry you off that lifeboat. I never believed in fate before; destiny—whatever you want to call it. But I do now. At least I think I do."

"You think?" she asked, feeling herself tremble for an entirely different reason.

"I suppose that depends on the outcome," he said, his eyes still intense.

Ella felt warmed—even fluttery inside—at the implication. But a part of her just couldn't believe that such a man would really want to settle down with a woman like her. And she felt absolutely certain that if he knew the truth about her, he would *never* even *consider* such a possibility. She was torn between telling him the truth and getting it over with, or keeping the secret forever buried in her heart. Both possibilities felt unbearable. For now, she just smiled, then looked away, unable to bear the warmth of his gaze for another second.

"So, what will you do now?" she asked, wondering if that would lead the conversation closer to or farther from his intentions in regard to their relationship. Not feeling ready to discuss it herself, she steered the conversation in the other direction by adding, "Will you look for work elsewhere or—"

"No, I don't think so," he said, looking around the bistro with that nostalgia coming back into his expression. "I don't believe I could find anyplace better than this to spend my life." He leaned his elbows on the table and chuckled. "And surprisingly enough, I'm rather good at doing all the things my father has taught me."

"You can make crepes as well as your father?" she asked with a gentle laugh.

"Not quite." He laughed as well. "But with some practice . . ." He laughed again, as if the idea made him deeply happy.

"Your parents will be pleased to hear your feelings about that, I'm certain."

"Yes, I'm certain they will. I just want to be absolutely sure before I tell them. I don't want to let them down again." He reached his hand across the table, and she drew one of hers from her lap in order to hold it. "I just need a little time."

"I understand," she said.

He met her eyes with his. "Yes, you do. Remarkable, don't you think?"

"What is?"

"The way you understand. You understand me unlike anyone I've ever known. How is that, Ella?"

"I don't know," she said and realized that she *did* understand him—without even trying. And he understood her. The thought of ever leaving him—of ever leaving *here*—was too painful to even consider. And she'd not even been here for a day. How could such feelings be possible? But he didn't know the whole truth about her, and she felt sure that once he did, he would be horrified. His parents would likely toss her into the streets.

They were both surprised when Lisette approached the table and said, "You have had your share of time with her." She took Ella by the hand and urged her to her feet. "We now have womanly matters to attend to. We will see you at supper."

Ella shrugged and said to Jonathan, "It seems I will see you at supper."

"Good luck," Jonathan said with a smile, glad to see Ella smile back at him. Now that he'd warned his mother not to assert her curiosity over the trauma that Ella had survived, he felt completely comfortable leaving Ella to her care. Lisette Moreau was a gentle and caring woman, and she could surely do more for Ella than he would ever have the sense to do. He decided to take a walk and reacquaint himself with the neighborhood. It was difficult to believe he'd only been absent a number of days. He felt as if he'd lived a lifetime since he'd left here to sail on the *Carpathia*. He was a different person, and he had the possibility of a different life before him— different than he'd ever considered before.

Ella followed Lisette up the stairs to the house, through the parlor, and up the next flight of stairs to the bathroom, where a wonderful aroma met Ella's senses.

"Now," Lisette said, "I have told everyone that the bathroom will not be available for at least an hour. There are facilities in the bistro should anyone need them." She gave a little wink. "The tub is full. The water is hot. The bath salts in the water are the fragrance of roses. My favorite. You will find some lovely soap and shampoo there that will refresh you after such a difficult week. You will have plenty of time to relax before supper, and if you are late for supper no one will mind at all." She then motioned to some clothing laid out over the top of a wicker laundry hamper. "I have left some clothes for you; everything you should need. I think they will fit well enough."

"Thank you," Ella said and meant to expound but Lisette hurried on.

"You came with nothing. I assume your things were lost."

"They were, yes," Ella said.

"There is no worry, *ma chéri*. We will shop tomorrow and get some things for you. A woman needs to have her own things, and to feel they are special so that *she* will feel special." She winked again. "A long, hot bath with the smell of roses is the remedy for many ailments, and something soft to wear against your skin will make you feel better. Put your dirty clothing in the hamper, and we will take care of that another day."

"Thank you," Ella said again, and again meant to say something more, but Lisette closed the door.

"Lock the door, *ma chéri*," she called, then Ella heard her descending the stairs.

Ella was quickly submerged to her chin in the hot, rose-scented water. The heat felt healing, and she wondered if she would ever be able to feel cold again without being reminded of sitting in that lifeboat, watching the world as she knew it sinking into nothingness. She ran her fingers idly through the water, pondering the contrast of how pleasant and soothing water could be, when she knew firsthand the destructive power it held when it carried the weight of an ocean. Closing her eyes, she found herself thinking about all of the fine decor and furnishings of the *Titanic,* and tried to imagine what they might look like now, lying in a heap of rubble on the ocean floor. Then her mind drifted to the people who had drowned, and she imagined their bodies scattered among that rubble. She gasped at the horror of the thought, and her eyes flew open, forcing her back to the reality of the quaint little bathroom in the Moreau home in New York City—on dry land. Even with keeping her eyes open, Ella couldn't help but think of

Irene. She wondered how exactly she might have died. Of course, it didn't matter—except that Ella preferred to think that she might have gone quickly and not suffered. She knew for a fact that the people who went into the water wearing life belts had suffered a great deal in the twenty or thirty minutes it had taken them to freeze to death.

With wet hands, Ella wiped tears from her cheeks, forcing her thoughts away from the death and destruction that had forever altered her life. She tried to think happy thoughts, and her mind went immediately to Jonathan Moreau and his lovely family. She thought of napoleons and crepes and rose-scented bath water. She thought of going shopping with Lisette and felt certain it would be a delightful experience. She was grateful once again to know that she had some money, and she wished she could thank Irene for having the foresight to tell her to take it with her. She felt certain these good people would do everything they could to help meet her needs, but she didn't want to feel like a burden, and she didn't want to be too terribly indebted to them or anyone else.

"Thank you, Irene," she whispered, not certain whether or not she might hear the words, but feeling better for uttering them.

When the water began to cool, Ella washed herself with a pink bar of soap that smelled almost as good as the water. She then washed her hair in shampoo that was also pink with a lovely scent. She noted that there was other soap and shampoo available on a nearby shelf, and it was evident Lisette had provided the fine and more feminine products for Ella. It wasn't difficult to see that Lisette Moreau was a woman who appreciated the value of some simple self-pampering. Ella's mother had been like that. It was the first time Ella had allowed herself to think about her mother in a very long time, but she forced that thought into the same cavern as her thoughts of Irene and everything and everyone else that seemed to be begging to be acknowledged. But Ella knew she didn't have the strength. She simply had to get from one day to the next.

Ella dried off with a soft towel and put on the clothes Lisette had left. The underclothing was finer and more soft than she might have expected from a woman whose family ran a simple bistro, but perhaps it was something important to Lisette, a part of her entire feminine charm. The dress was cream-colored and simple in design, but soft and comfortable. Once dressed, Ella brushed out her hair and pinned it up. She rinsed out the tub and made certain everything was tidy. She took the money that she'd had tucked in her clothing back to the room where she was staying, and slipped it into the back of a drawer that held some folded bed linens.

Ella went downstairs to find that her timing was perfect. Supper was just being put on the table. Jonathan was there and introduced her to his sister Sally, and to Sally's husband, Frank. They had been gone earlier on some errands and to a doctor appointment, since Sally was pregnant. Ella was told—mostly by Lisette and Violet—that Sally hadn't been feeling well with the pregnancy, and that Frank was working in the bistro, although he mostly did cleaning since he was not much of a cook, and was even worse at baking. This was discussed with good-natured laughter, and Ella could see that Frank fit comfortably into the family. They were all seated, and Ella was glad to have Jonathan sitting next to her, especially when she felt his hand take hers beneath the table. She recalled the tender things he'd said to her earlier, and her heart responded with a quickened delight. She pushed away the temptation to talk herself out of enjoying the possibility that something good might come of it. For now, she wanted to believe that it would.

A prayer was said over the meal before a hearty beef vegetable soup was ladled out, and thick slices of bread were passed around. Ella looked at the people surrounding the table and the lovely meal spread out there. *The best of France,* she thought. How could she be so blessed?

Ella enjoyed supper very much, and she felt surprisingly comfortable, but she noticed that the topic of the *Titanic* didn't come up at all. She knew that it had to be on everyone's mind. Jonathan had been among the rescuers, and it was in all of the newspapers. She knew the subject was being avoided for her benefit, and she felt grateful, given the fact that she didn't want to talk about it; but she couldn't help wondering what they were all thinking about what she'd experienced. Did they pity her? Would they be speculating and talking about it when she wasn't in the room? She felt certain both questions could be answered in the affirmative, but she tried not to think about it.

When supper was over, Lisette commented that Ella looked very tired and suggested that she should hurry along to bed. Ella didn't argue. She *was* tired, but she also dreaded trying to sleep when she knew that lying in the dark or closing her eyes lured the memories far too close. Still, she had to at least try to sleep.

Jonathan walked her to the door of her room and asked, "Do you have everything you need?"

"I do, yes. Your mother has been very generous."

"She loves you. They all do. I think that bringing you home is the best thing I've ever done."

Ella wondered what to say in response to such a comment, then she decided to just admit to the truth. "I'm not sure what to say . . . or do . . . when you tell me such things."

"You don't have to say or do anything, Ella. I just . . . think you should know how I feel. But perhaps I should give the matter more time and keep my feelings to myself."

Ella considered whether or not she would prefer having him be a little less candid with her. Coming to a firm conclusion, she said, "I . . . I'm glad to know how you feel. I just . . . well, be patient with me. I . . . can hardly think, and . . ."

"I understand, Ella. I do. I just think that you should know you're not alone in the world."

"I'm very glad to know that," she said. "And . . . your family is wonderful. I think that your bringing me home with you is the best thing that's ever happened to me."

Jonathan smiled, then he kissed each of her cheeks. It was a gesture that she had seen many times this day as being common among members of his family, except that he did it slowly, pausing a moment between his kisses to meet her eyes with his. Ella's heart quickened and her stomach fluttered.

"Good night," he said and crossed the hall, glancing at her over his shoulder before he went into the other bedroom.

Ella closed the door and leaned against it, wishing that such feelings could completely banish the thoughts she had to face when she was alone. She was surprised to see a lovely nightgown spread out on the bed. Lisette thought of everything. Ella changed into it and crawled into bed, resisting the temptation to leave the light on. She hated the darkness. When the lights of the *Titanic* had finally gone out, the worst of the horror had begun. The sounds from the darkness that had followed that moment were still resounding in her head, and lying there in the dark, all alone, she couldn't will them to stay away. She hummed a silly song, surprised that it actually helped her relax, and she soon slept. She woke up four times during the night, gasping for breath as if she were drowning and shivering as if she might freeze to death. When she knew that dawn was not far off, she opened the curtains and stood at the window, waiting for the light of day to rescue her from the darkness, the same way that the *Carpathia* had appeared just before dawn to offer refuge to the survivors.

Ella went downstairs as soon as she heard evidence that people were awake and moving about. When Jonathan appeared a few minutes later, she was in the kitchen helping Lisette and Marie—or, more accurately, she was watching Lisette and Marie and trying to find a way to be useful.

"Good morning," he said, his glance passing over all of them, but resting firmly on Ella.

"Good morning," all of the women said. Lisette and Marie pretended not to notice the way Jonathan was staring at Ella, but Ella knew they were just being polite. Since she couldn't keep herself from staring back at Jonathan, she was especially grateful for their discretion.

Breakfast proved to be a more simple event than supper had been, but it was still overflowing with laughter and conversation. Ella mostly just listened and took it all in, but she felt comfortable—and safe— and she couldn't help being grateful. She wondered—not for the first time—how a tragedy like the one she'd experienced could have led her to such a situation as this. It just didn't seem right that something so horrible could precede something so fine and good. She didn't have any answers on that account and put it away with all the other things she couldn't bring herself to think about.

After breakfast Jonathan went to the bistro with his father and left his younger siblings to work on their lessons until the lunch rush began. Frank went to work with the men. Sally would be resting in the parlor where she was available to supervise the lessons. And Lisette escorted Ella into a taxicab that would take them to a place in the city where they could find some suitable clothes for Ella that wouldn't be too expensive. When Ella told Lisette that she had her own money, some of which she'd brought in the pocket of her coat, Lisette sounded pleased but surprised.

"Surely you didn't intend to buy new clothes for me," Ella said.

"I surely did, and I will if you need me to do so."

"But surely you can't afford to—"

"Oh, *ma chéri*," Lisette said, putting a hand over Ella's. "The bistro provides well for our family. The house and business are paid for, and we have much money put away for Bastien to retire when he no longer feels up to working. The children who want to do their father's work will be able to make their own living from the bistro. I *can* afford to buy some clothes for you, and I would consider it a privilege to do so. I just might do so anyway," she concluded with a smile. She then furrowed her brow and asked, "How do you have money when all of your things—"

"My friend—Irene . . . Did Jonathan tell you about Irene?"

"He did, yes," Lisette said. "I am so sad to know that you lost your dear friend."

"Yes, well . . ." Ella cleared her throat. "She . . . uh . . . she said that I should get my money, and tuck it inside my dress. I did. Otherwise, I would be utterly alone *and* utterly penniless."

"Oh, *ma chéri*," Lisette said and put a motherly hand on Ella's face. "You are not alone."

Ella wanted to cry, but the taxicab stopped and Lisette declared, "We are here!"

She paid the fare and the two of them wandered about for a long while, perusing many things. Ella thought about how she'd been helped by Irene and Brother and Sister Pack following the birth—and death—of her baby. She wondered if this was meant to be a continuing pattern in her life, to be dependent on the charity and kindness of others. For the moment, she could only be grateful for such kindness. She was again grateful for Irene's admonition, even if she couldn't think about it without replaying those final minutes with Irene in ways that always made her wonder what they might have done differently.

As Ella thought of Brother and Sister Pack for the first time since the tragedy had taken place, it occurred to her that she should write them a letter. They had surely heard of the sinking of the *Titanic*, but they had to be wondering about the outcome in regard to her and Irene—and even Mr. Stead. She didn't *want* to write such a letter, but knew that it was important. She concluded that she would ask Jonathan to help her.

Ella bought some lovely things for herself, liking Lisette's suggestions on things that would make her feel more feminine, and she seemed an expert on what colors a woman should wear or not wear according to her hair color and complexion. Lisette insisted on purchasing a particular dress for Ella, and said that she could wear it to church on Sundays.

"You go to church, then?" Ella asked, not surprised considering Jonathan's previous declaration to her that he'd been raised with Christian principles.

"We do, yes. Is it good for you to come with us?"

"I would like that, yes," Ella said, wondering what it might have been like to go to Utah with Irene and attend church there. She wondered if the church that the Moreau family attended might be anything like those few meetings she'd attended with the Mormons in London.

Lisette took Ella to a little Italian restaurant for lunch. "A change of pace from always French is good, no?" she said after a waiter had guided them to a little table near the window.

Ella loved the way that Lisette chattered through lunch. Not only was she a completely delightful person, but it was also easier not to think about the traumas swirling in her mind when she was absorbed in such enjoyable conversation. Lisette talked about her life in France, and she told the story of how she and Bastien had fallen in love as if it were the most romantic tale in history. She was still deeply in love with her husband, and often mentioned how good her life had turned out to this point. Ella couldn't deny that. She'd been with the family only twenty-four hours and she felt almost as if she'd landed in a tiny spot of heaven that had been carefully hidden away in the busyness and chaos of New York City. She felt completely comfortable in the security—emotional and physical—that she was able to glean from this family.

They returned to the house and took the packages upstairs, where Lisette helped Ella put her new things away. She insisted that Ella put on one of her new dresses and go down to say hello to Jonathan. Since Ella's heart quickened at the very mention of his name, she didn't have to be talked into it. She entered the bistro to find the lunch crowd had diminished to just a few stragglers. Marie and Violet were clearing and cleaning tables. They were excited to see her and made a fuss over the new dress as if it were a grand event to have something new to wear.

"Jonathan and Papa are in the back," Marie said. "You must—"

"Perhaps you shouldn't disturb them," Ella said.

"You can come with me," Marie said, taking her arm. "It won't disturb them."

"Look who's back!" Marie declared as they went through the swinging door. Bastien, Frank, and Jonathan all turned from their work to look at her.

"Oh, hello," Frank said and went back to his work.

Bastien put his hands on his hips and gave her that wide smile. "*Tres jolie, mademoiselle,*" he said.

"Indeed!" Jonathan said, smiling much like his father.

Ella didn't know what it meant, but it must have been good. She was more caught up in the sight of Jonathan Moreau with a white apron tied around his waist, his hands covered in flour.

"Did you have a good time?" Bastien asked.

"Oh, yes," Ella said. "Very much so, thank you."

"*Tres bien,*" he said and went back to his work.

"What did he say?" Ella asked as Jonathan moved closer.

"He just said *very good,*" he explained, his eyes displaying unmasked adoration.

"And before that?" she asked, looking away.

"*Very pretty,*" he said. "And I agree." He glanced down. "The dress is lovely, but even better than that, *you* look better."

"Better?" She looked at him then.

He spoke quietly so as not to be overheard by the other men. "Do you want me to explain what I mean . . . honestly?"

"I do," Ella said, gathering the courage to hear what he might have to say.

"I mean that the traumatized look in your eyes is less evident today, and I'm glad for that."

Ella looked down. "Your mother is very charming. She makes it easy to forget."

"Good. I'm glad," he said. "And yes, she *is* very charming."

Ella looked up at him, compelled to admit to her next thought. He'd been very candid with her about his feelings; surely she could be the same. "You also make it easy to forget."

"I hope that's a good thing," he said with that wide Moreau smile.

"I hope so too," she said, then cleared her throat. "I shouldn't keep you from your work."

"Come, I'll teach you," he said, and a minute later she was wearing a long apron that covered almost the full length of her new dress. Jonathan rolled out pastry dough, then had Ella brush melted butter over it before he folded it and rolled it again. They did it over and over while he explained that when it baked, every thin layer would puff up and flake apart from the butter in between, and it would be heavenly. "That's why we call it puff pastry," he said, and she helped him cut it in small pieces and put it into one of the large ovens.

When that was done, Bastien had Ella help him chop up ingredients for a chicken filling that would go inside of crepes. He talked and laughed while they worked, and Ella felt as comfortable with him as she did with his wife.

Jonathan observed Ella with his father and wanted to drop to his knees at that very moment and beg her to never leave. But he instinctively knew that for all of her managing to put a smile on her face and participate in the life going on around her, she was deeply troubled and he would be a fool to think that her turmoil would be easily solved. He wanted to ask his mother how their outing had gone, wondering if she might have a different opinion about how Ella was doing. While Ella was busy with his father, he said to them, "I need to go upstairs for a few minutes. I'll be back soon."

"I'm fine," Ella said.

"I will take very good care of her," Bastien assured him.

Jonathan washed the flour and butter from his hands but didn't remove his apron before he went upstairs. It occurred to him that his mother might be napping, as she did on occasion in the afternoons, so he entered the house quietly, not wanting to disturb her. He found her in the kitchen, and she obviously hadn't heard him come in. What little noise he'd made had likely been muffled by her unrestrained sobbing.

"Whatever is wrong?" he asked, startling her.

"Oh," she muttered and stood abruptly, turning her back to him, as if that might conceal the evidence of her tears. She reached for a clean dish towel and wiped at her face.

Jonathan put his hands on his mother's shoulders. "What is it, Mama?"

"I tried to be happy with her. I tried to keep her from thinking about this horrible thing that has happened, but . . ." she sobbed again, "I see the pain in her eyes. She is very noble in trying to keep it to herself, no? But I can see it, and I know she is hurting so very much."

"I know it too," Jonathan said, tempted to cry along with her.

"I want to help her, Johnny," she said, "but I do not know how."

"I don't know how, either," he admitted. "All we can do is . . . give her a safe place to live, and just to . . . be. And you're very good at that, Mama. She's comfortable here. She likes you and Papa very much. I *do* know that."

Lisette turned to look at him, holding a fist to her chest. "Oh, do you think she does feel safe here?"

"I do," he said.

"I think that she feels safe with *you*, no?"

"I hope so," he admitted.

"You are her rescuer," she said. "It is very romantic, no?"

"Mama," he said with a sigh, "I'm very glad I was there . . . that I was the one to lift her up out of that lifeboat, but I don't know that we could say it was romantic. How can there be anything romantic among so much death and ruin?"

"Life tests us, Johnny, to see if we can find the good that comes from the tragedy. No one can change what has happened, but we must find a way to go on and be happy."

"There's your answer, Mama."

"My answer?"

"You said that you don't know how to help her. If you can teach her that, you will have helped her a great deal, I think."

Lisette sighed. "I do hope so. She is very dear."

"She is, yes."

"You love her," Lisette stated. It wasn't a question.

Jonathan looked down and cleared his throat, but he couldn't make a fool of himself by lying to her. "I can't deny what I feel," he said, "but I'm certain it's far too soon to know whether or not I could make her happy for a lifetime."

"Or perhaps you *do* know," she said, and he looked at her. "We must be cautious in the decisions of life, my son, but we must trust the truest feelings of our hearts. It seems destiny that you have saved her." Her eyes grew distant. "You have saved her in body, at least. I fear her heart is shipwrecked at the bottom of the ocean."

"Do you think it's possible for me to rescue her heart?" he asked, more grateful than he ever had been for the keen insight and wisdom of his mother.

"Only God can do that," she said. "But you can guide her to such a place." She put a hand over the center of his chest and looked hard into his eyes. "Has God healed your heart, my son?"

He took a deep breath when he realized what she meant. They hadn't talked about it for months. She was one of the few people who knew how deeply he'd been hurt. Until earlier this week, he had believed that nothing worse could happen to a person. But the tragedy of the *Titanic* had given him—and a lot of other people—an entirely new perspective on life and death. Without getting into a topic he preferred to avoid, he said, "It's getting better."

"Perhaps Ella can heal your heart as you heal hers."

"You just said that only God can do that." He smiled at her.

"We can all work together toward that end, no?"

"I believe we can," he said and hugged her before he went back downstairs, weighed down with the thought of Ella's shipwrecked heart. But she smiled at him when he came again into the kitchen, and he had to believe that simply giving the matter some time would be the best remedy for now. He wanted to believe that each day she felt safe and secure here with his family would take her a day further away from the tragedy, and hopefully make her continually stronger. He was glad for the way he felt about her, but he knew he needed to be patient and allow time to lead them to whatever might become of this. While he couldn't imagine ever being without her, they barely knew each other and they had met under circumstances that no human mind could have conceived of being possible prior to April 15.

Late in the afternoon while Jonathan and Ella were sharing tea and a pastry, he was surprised when she asked him, "Will you help me with something?"

"Anything!" he said eagerly.

She smiled slightly at his enthusiasm, then glanced down, and he could tell her request was something difficult for her to express. "I need to write a letter . . . to some friends in London; people I stayed with there for a while. They also knew Irene very well." She looked back up at him. "I know it has to be done . . . they deserve to know what's happened, but . . . I can't do it alone. Will you help me write the letter?"

"I'd be happy to," he said. "Let's do it now and get it over with."

"I'd like that, thank you."

Jonathan gathered paper and pen and they sat together in the parlor. "What exactly do you want me to do?" he asked, handing her the pen.

"Just . . . be with me," she said. "Help me know if I'm being tactful and appropriate."

"I can do that."

Ella took a deep breath and set the pen to paper to write the date at the top, but her hand began to shake so badly that it was barely legible. She wadded up the piece of paper and picked up a clean sheet. She took another deep breath, but her hand was still shaking and she abruptly handed the pen back to Jonathan. "You write it!"

He sighed and tried to think of the best way to handle this. "Do you want to dictate to me, or do you want *me* to write it?"

"Just write it, please," she insisted and stood up, pacing back and forth in front of the couch where he was sitting.

"Let me give it a try and if you don't like it, you can say so and we'll start over."

"Excellent idea," she said and planted her hands firmly on her hips in an effort to stop their shaking.

Jonathan asked who he was writing to and she said, "Brother and Sister Pack."

"Brother and sister?" he asked.

"They belonged to the same church that Irene attended. That was how they addressed each other."

"I see," he said and wrote: *Dear Brother and Sister Pack, I am writing on behalf of Ella Brown. She wishes to let you know that she has arrived safely in New York City. Since you have surely heard of the fate of the* Titanic, *she wanted to let you know the outcome in regard to her and your mutual friend, Irene. She is heartbroken to have to inform you that Irene did not survive the disaster. The entire event was extremely difficult for Ella, but she is doing as well as could be expected and she is in the care of my family.*

He went on to briefly explain who he was and how he had met Ella, and a little bit about the situation here with his family and the bistro where Ella would be welcome to stay for as long as she needed.

"May I read you what I have so far?" he asked. "If you don't like any of it, I'll change it and copy it again."

"Go ahead," she said, and he did. He noticed that Ella became visibly agitated as he read it, and she wrung her trembling hands while she continued to pace, but when he was finished she said, "It's perfect. Thank you."

"Anything else?"

"Yes," she said. "Please write that Mr. Stead also perished. Say it . . . gracefully, as I know you will."

"Who is Mr. Stead?"

Ella explained who he was and how Irene had met him. She told Jonathan that she'd made his acquaintance only a couple of times, omitting any details on how Mr. Stead had shown an interest in her because of the trauma in her life. She spelled his name, and Jonathan wrote some more, then read the rest to her, which met with her approval.

"That should be sufficient," she said. "Please include your address in case they want to write back."

"Of course," Jonathan said and read the letter once more silently to make certain there were no errors. He sealed it up and they walked together to post it immediately. Once it was sent off, Ella admitted feeling some relief in having it done, and she declared there was no one else who needed to be informed. He distracted her with a walk through the neighborhood in which he'd grown up, telling her stories from his childhood, which helped her relax.

The evening went well and Ella seemed relaxed, but Jonathan could see what his mother had described. There was pain in her eyes. She was very noble at trying to keep it disguised. She likely didn't want to be a burden to anyone, or cause any kind of upset. He did his best to make certain she was comfortable and had all that she needed. But he felt it was best to avoid the subject of the *Titanic* for now, hoping that a time would come when she would be willing and able to talk about it, and that doing so might help heal her shipwrecked heart.

The following day was Sunday, and since the bistro remained closed, the family was together most of the day. They all attended church service, and Jonathan enjoyed having Ella beside him as they went into the church, and he enjoyed even more having her sit next to him during the meeting. He took her hand soon after they sat down, pleased to see her smile at the gesture. He threaded his fingers between hers, wishing it could begin to express how he felt about her, feelings that he was trying to rein in until they'd known each other longer.

Ella was thoroughly enjoying the church service, and having Jonathan there at her side, until her mind wandered to how it had been to attend church with Irene. The thought of Irene being dead jolted her heart as if she had just newly learned about it—or perhaps a part of herself had finally come to accept it. Being in the midst of a congregation, she fought especially hard to keep her composure. She tried to force her mind away from Irene, but the service reminded her of what she had been doing *last* Sunday. She'd attended a church service on the ship with the Blackhurst family. The children had been horrible, and by the end of the day she'd been fired. And then that night . . .

"You're trembling," Jonathan whispered.

Ella looked down at her hand in his, then met his eyes. "Am I?" she asked, pretending she hadn't noticed.

Jonathan looked at her more intently, as if he could see bold evidence in her eyes of the thoughts spinning in her head. She wouldn't be surprised if he could hear the pounding of her heart. The irony of the depth of her feelings for him in so short a time felt shocking, and memories of the moment they'd met came back to her in the same whirlpool with thoughts of Irene and memories of the massive destructive capabilities of an iceberg.

Ella heard her own breathing becoming shallow, and felt sure that Jonathan heard it too. Her trembling increased, and they both looked down at their clasped hands at the same moment. She looked up and beyond his shoulder, glad to note that he was the only person between her and the aisle. "I need to go," she whispered and stood, easing past him and rushing toward the doors at the back of the chapel as quickly as she could manage without making an utter spectacle of herself.

CHAPTER ELEVEN
The Weight of Water

ELLA GASPED FOR BREATH AS she came into the open air and hurried down the steps and around the side of the building where there was a narrow alley between the church building and the house next to it. She pressed her back against the brick wall of the church and flattened her palms over the same wall, as if doing so might hold her upright and keep her from falling. A quick glance in both directions reassured her that she was alone enough to vent just a little bit of the pressure building in her chest and taking a route across the top of her head before it escaped through her lips in heaving breaths.

Jonathan only wondered for a moment if he should follow Ella out. He momentarily wondered what people might think of her leaving so abruptly, especially if he went out right after her. Then he realized he didn't care. He hurried out of the church, and it only took a few seconds to find her.

"Ella," he said. She gasped and looked toward him, then looked away in shame. "It's all right," he said and stood beside her. "You don't have to hide the way you're feeling from me." Instinctively believing that he needed to convince her she could truly confide in him, and that he would understand, he took hold of her shoulders and said with gentle firmness, "Ella, I can't imagine what it was like for you out there, but I know what it was like for me. Coming upon that cold, black ocean where a floating city should have been made me so sick I could barely keep myself from throwing up. It *haunts* me, Ella. I can't sleep; I have trouble eating. I wonder why them and not me. I don't know *why*, Ella. But I know that we *are* here. And we're together. You don't have to hold this inside. You don't have to face this alone. Do you hear what I'm saying?"

Ella nodded and hung in his hands, almost like a rag doll. Steaming tears fell down her face as she muttered with a quivering voice, "A week ago they were all alive. They were singing in church and eating meals and talking and laughing and breathing and living, and they had no idea that their lives were about to be swallowed up. There was so much fear and panic. People were crying and screaming. Now they're gone! They're all gone! Hundreds of them! And Irene is gone too! Why her? Why her, Jonathan? Why not me? No one would have missed me! No one would have noticed!"

"*I* would have missed you!"

"That's ludicrous!"

"Maybe it is, but I wonder if somehow I would have felt some kind of emptiness that I never would have been able to understand. I can't tell you *why*, Ella. But I *can* tell you how grateful I am that you're here, that I found you. And I can tell you that we're going to get through this together. Do you hear me?"

Ella nodded again, then pressed her face to his chest and sobbed like she hadn't allowed herself to do before now. She held to him tightly, knowing she would crumble in a heap on the alley floor if not for the way he held her. She lost track of time while she wept. In fact, she wept so hard that she became conscious of her crying in a way that felt as if she'd cried herself into unconsciousness and had just awakened again. A minute later she heard organ music from the other side of the wall, and Jonathan whispered, "The service will be over soon. Let's start walking."

"Won't your parents wonder where we are?"

"They know we both left. We're adults. I'm sure they'll understand." He eased her arm around his waist and put his arm around her shoulders. She leaned into him as they walked briskly out of the alley and away from the church, toward home.

"Forgive me," Ella said, her tone expressing her embarrassment.

"For what?" he asked, surprised.

"For . . . breaking down like that. For walking out of the service, and—"

"There's nothing to forgive, Ella. Truthfully, I expected you to break down like that long before now. Many people *were* breaking down like that on the *Carpathia*, and I wondered how you could hold it all inside."

"I've been afraid to cry," she admitted. "Afraid to feel it. What if I can't stop?" Her quavering voice was evidence of more grief bubbling out.

"Better that than trying to hold it all inside."

They continued walking in silence, but they moved quickly, as if doing so might keep them ahead of the pain they were talking about. Ella found it easier to keep from crying while she held both her arms tightly around his waist. She felt compelled to ask, "Did you really feel that sick, when . . ."

"I really did," he said, hoping that his willingness to talk about it might help all of this open up for her. "I think we were all wondering the same thing. We expected to find a sinking ship; expected to take luggage and passengers on board. It was incomprehensible that a ship as large as the *Titanic* could have completely disappeared in so few hours."

"Two and half hours," she said.

"What?" he asked and stopped walking to look at her.

Ella spoke with a surprisingly even voice, as if the emotion had gone back to sleep. But at least she was talking. "I noticed the time soon after we felt the engines stop, which was apparently only a few minutes after we struck the iceberg. Someone in the lifeboat commented on the time right after the ship disappeared. It was barely over two and a half hours."

Jonathan shook his head. "I cannot even imagine . . . how it happened; *why* it happened. And I can't imagine how you survived."

"I can't imagine why I survived, either," she murmured.

"I didn't say *why* you survived. I said *how*. There must be *many* good reasons *why* you survived. And I don't mean how you survived physically. You were blessed enough to be in a lifeboat, but I wonder how you've coped emotionally with what's happened."

"I'm not sure that I *am* coping," she said and began to walk again, not letting go of him. She loved the way he felt so strong at her side. She wondered for a moment how she might be handling all of this if she'd gone home with Mrs. Olsen—or if she were working for the Blackhursts. She wanted to get down on her knees and thank Jonathan for rescuing her from all of *that* as well as everything else he'd done.

They arrived at the house before anyone else, and Jonathan asked, "Are you tired? Would you like to get some rest?"

"I *am* tired," she admitted, "but I can't close my eyes without . . ." She stopped herself, cleared her throat and concluded, "No, I don't want to rest."

"Would you like to be alone, then?" he asked.

Ella met his eyes and wanted to say, *Don't ever leave me alone again! I'm terrified of being alone with my thoughts!* She said in a toneless voice, "I would prefer not to be alone right now, but if there's something you need to be doing or—"

"There's nowhere I would rather be than with you, Ella," he said, and she felt somewhat validated in her own desire to have him near.

"But how will you explain to your family why I left the service like that?"

"They all know you've been through something difficult. They don't need any other explanation. We were all taught to respect the privacy of others. I think they're all concerned about you, but you don't need to wonder if you embarrassed them or anything. You didn't."

"How do you know?"

"I know them," he said.

"And how do you know how to always say the right thing . . . the thing I need to hear just when I need to hear it? You hardly know me at all."

"I have no idea," he said, "but it feels like I've *always* known you. How is that possible?"

Ella wanted to say that it *wasn't* possible, but she felt the same way. She felt it but she also felt afraid to admit it. She wanted to fall into his arms and just soak in the strength he gave to her, but they heard noises at the bottom of the stairs and Jonathan announced, "Sounds like they're back."

"I'm just going to . . ." She motioned toward the stairs, wanting to say that she wanted a few minutes in the bathroom before everyone else was competing for time in there. He nodded as if he understood. She hurried up the stairs before anyone came into the parlor where he stood.

Jonathan turned around to face his family as they came up the stairs and through the door one at a time or in pairs, each one asking if Ella was all right. He simply told them she was and let it drop.

The family worked together to put on a lovely Sunday dinner that was finer than any other meal of the week. Ella came to the kitchen and offered to help, as if nothing in the world was wrong. Jonathan was glad to see her smiling and chatting, and he loved the way she was fitting in so comfortably, but he knew for a fact that some volatile emotions were brewing just below the surface. He prayed in his heart that she would survive what they might do to her, and that he might be able to help her when they finally fully exploded. He'd been through intense grief, and he knew how ugly it could be. But what he'd felt couldn't hold a candle to this.

The remainder of the day went well. Jonathan felt tired due to the lack of sleep he'd been getting, but he knew Ella was suffering from fatigue as well. He enjoyed being with his family, especially when he considered that there were many families of people who had gone to sea recently who were grieving today, most of them likely planning memorial services that would be conducted without a body to bury. He knew that at least one ship had gone out to the coordinates of the wreckage to search for bodies, but he suspected the majority of them wouldn't be found. He could be glad he wasn't working on *that* ship.

He forced his thoughts back to the present moment, enjoying the antics of his siblings as they all played some silly games, then they read together from the Bible. The activities were typical of the Moreau family and provided a stark contrast to his sad thoughts. But Ella seemed comfortable, as if she could take it all in like a starving child in a candy shop. Watching her countenance in that regard he began to consider the reasons. It was a comforting distraction from thinking about shipwrecks and body recovery. She'd told him she had no family, but she'd never expounded on that statement or shared any details with him. He wondered now how that had happened, and why her being engaged in such simple activities with *his* family seemed like a great extravagance to her. He wanted to ask her, but the moment had to be right.

When Ella couldn't stop yawning—even though it was early evening—Jonathan suggested that perhaps she should try to get some sleep. She insisted that she was all right, but then Lisette took her hand and walked with her up the stairs, as if she would fully honor the role of mother that she'd taken on and see that Ella went to bed. Lisette came back a few minutes later and said, "I do not think she is sleeping well. I hope she can get some rest."

"So do I," Jonathan said.

With Ella absent, his siblings took the opportunity to ask Jonathan some questions about what had happened. He couldn't blame them for their curiosity, and they'd been very polite about avoiding the topic whenever Ella was around. He told the story again, wishing he could do it without always feeling sick to his stomach. He finally said that he'd answered enough questions related to the disaster for one day. Feeling utterly exhausted himself, he told the family good night and went up to his own room, hoping to get some decent sleep. Even though he hadn't actually *seen* what Ella had seen, he'd heard it described, and he'd seen enough that his mind's imagination seemed eager to fill in the gaps. He too found it difficult to close his eyes without seeing a scene in his mind that was severely disturbing.

He was still awake when Lucas came in to go to bed. He thought about Ella in the room across the hall and liked to imagine her sleeping peacefully. He hoped that she was. When he realized that Lucas was sound asleep, he knew that he was losing enough sleep for both himself and Ella, and again he imagined her in a pleasant slumber. The very picture of that in his mind was relaxing to him.

Jonathan was glad to still be awake when he heard a distinct cry from across the hall. He didn't hesitate for even a second before he pulled on pants and shirt and dashed across the hall, pausing for only a moment outside of Ella's door, just long enough to hear her cry out again. He went in without knocking, flipped the light switch, and knew his suspicions were correct. She was lost in a nightmare, oblivious to the lights coming on or anything else around her. She was writhing in her bed as if she were plagued by some hallucinatory fever, crying out in fear. Jonathan felt a tightening in his chest as he considered the reasons for her terror. How well he recalled that hollow stare he'd seen on her face the first time he'd seen her.

"Ella," he said, putting one knee on the bed. "Ella, wake up." He nudged her gently without any success, hoping he could wake her before she woke anyone else. "Ella, it's all right," he said close to her ear, nudging her with more strength. She gasped, and her crying stopped abruptly. The long moment of silence was followed by a single sharp cry as she sat up and clutched on to Jonathan as if she were drowning and only he could save her. Oh, how he wanted to!

"It's all right now," he said. "You were having a bad dream."

"I'm sorry I disturbed you," she said, holding to him in a way that contradicted her apology.

"No need for that," he said.

"Don't leave me alone," she muttered with a surprising lack of pride. Except for her brief breakdown outside the church today, he'd seen little evidence from her of anything but a stoic façade and a determination to be completely independent in coping with the tragedy in her life. She was either still half asleep or so utterly terrified that pride had no power.

"It's all right now," he said again, knowing he couldn't stay here with her and maintain any propriety.

He was just considering how to leave her alone long enough to get his sister when he looked up to see Lucas standing in the doorway. "Is everything okay?" he asked.

"She's had a nightmare and shouldn't be alone," Jonathan said. Ella turned her face more against Jonathan's shoulder but made no attempt to let go of him or move away, which deepened his theory that she was utterly terrified. "Will you get Marie? And try not to wake anyone else?"

"I will," Lucas said, and Jonathan heard his brother's bare feet pattering down the stairs.

He felt Ella tighten her hold on his arms and heard her mutter, "Jonathan . . . tell me it was all a dream. Tell me it was just a bad dream. Tell me it didn't really happen." She sobbed and buried her face more tightly against his shoulder. "How could something like that happen?"

"I wish I had an answer, *ma chéri*," he said, gently stroking the back of her head. "I wish I could tell you it hadn't been real." He felt a twinge of guilt whenever he considered that if it hadn't happened, he never would have met her. It was a thought he needed to keep to himself—at least for now.

He heard his brother pattering back up the stairs and looked up to see Lucas wearing an apologetic scowl. "Sorry. Mama was already awake and met me in the hall. She wouldn't let me wake Marie. She's coming."

"Thank you," Jonathan said, relieved in part, but not entirely.

"I'm going to back to bed," Lucas said and disappeared, but a moment later his mother appeared in the doorway.

"What has happened?" she asked, tying a lacy robe around her waist.

"I heard her crying out," he said quickly, wanting to make it clear that he'd been in his own room. "I came in and found her asleep . . . having a nightmare."

"The poor, sweet child," Lisette said and eased onto the bed, on the opposite side from where Jonathan was sitting.

"Clearly it's improper for me to be alone with her," Jonathan said, "but she's obviously terrified, and—"

"I'm sorry to be causing such a fuss," Ella said, turning to look at Lisette without letting go of Jonathan. "I . . . I don't know what's wrong with me." Lisette pushed Ella's hair back from her face and put a hand over her cheek that was wet with tears. "It haunts my mind every minute I'm awake . . . and when I sleep . . . it's worse."

"There is nothing wrong with you, *ma chéri*," Lisette said in earnest. "You must have time to be at peace with such a horrible thing."

"I don't want to be alone," Ella cried.

"We will not leave you alone, *ma chéri*," Lisette promised.

"I should go," Jonathan said, "and leave you to—"

"You should stay," Lisette said with a motherly command in her voice and a nod toward the evidence that Ella was clinging to him. "I will stay with you and it will be all right."

Lisette turned on a lamp on the bedside table and turned off the glaring overhead light. She put a pillow behind Jonathan, and he leaned back against the headboard of the bed without letting go of Ella. His mother then curled up on the bed next to Ella and stroked her hair while she sang a quiet lullaby in French as Ella wept. Jonathan noted the glisten of tears in his mother's eyes, and he felt the sting of them in his own. Ella's question haunted him. *How could something like this happen?* More than twice as many people had died than had survived. It was too horrifically astronomical to even comprehend! But it seemed the entire trauma of the sunken the *Titanic* had been wrapped up in the heart of this young woman. Jonathan felt certain that every survivor was now experiencing his or her own brand of shock and grief. But he wondered if any of them were as alone in the world as Ella. And he wondered—not for the first time—what other burdens were locked away in Ella's heart, swimming around in there with this new, incomprehensible horror.

While Jonathan's mind wandered, he remained aware of Ella's every breath and whimper. She gradually stopped crying, then her breathing became soft and even. "She is asleep," Lisette whispered. "You should go to bed and I will stay with her."

Jonathan eased Ella carefully from his arms and watched her nuzzle down into her pillow in what appeared to be a peaceful sleep. He kissed her brow, then leaned over her to kiss his mother's. As he stood up straight, Lisette whispered, "You really are in love with her."

They'd talked about this before, but apparently the truth of this fact was becoming more obvious. He tried not to act too surprised, and had to admit, "I haven't been trying to hide it . . . from you *or* her."

"But she does not see it because she is too traumatized to see love right now."

Jonathan swallowed and took the opportunity to express his deepest fear, grateful for a mother he could trust with such feelings. "Or perhaps she will never feel for me the way I feel for her."

"Time will put everything right, *ma chéri*," she said as if she knew beyond any doubt that in the end, everything would work out for the best.

Jonathan looked at Ella, her expression unusually serene. "I do hope so," he said and left the room, closing the door quietly behind him. He leaned his back against the wall in the hallway, staying there for enough minutes to let his mind catch up to his heartache on Ella's behalf and the love for her that he felt growing inside him. He finally returned to his own room to find Lucas fast asleep. He climbed into his own bed but stared toward the ceiling a long while before sleep overtook him. He woke up to find Lucas gone and his bed made, and he wondered how he could have slept so long. Mostly he felt grateful to have actually gotten some decent sleep for the first time in many days. But he wondered how Ella was doing. He hurried to get dressed and make his bed so that he could find out.

The door to Ella's room was closed, but Jonathan didn't know if that meant she was still in there, or if she'd just closed it when she'd left. On the chance that she might be sleeping, he didn't want to disturb her. He found his mother in the kitchen, enjoying a cup of tea while she looked at a magazine. The electric washing machine in the corner of the kitchen was noisily busy, which meant that Lisette would soon be out behind the house hanging laundry to dry. The house appeared to be quiet and empty otherwise.

"Good morning," he said.

She looked up and smiled. "Did you sleep?"

"Better than I have since . . ." He sat down across from her. "And Ella?"

"She woke up many times," Lisette said, a weighted sigh laced through her words. "But when she knew she was not alone, she went back to sleep."

"Did *you* get any sleep?" he asked.

"I got plenty of sleep for what little I need to do today, and if I can give up a little sleep so that Ella can get any sleep at all, I will be happy to do it."

"You are a treasure, Mama."

"I am glad you think so. It will help you feel better while you are hanging the laundry for me."

"I would be happy to," Jonathan said, and she smiled.

"You really *must* love her. I have never asked you to hang laundry without getting complaints. It is not manly. It is too tedious. Is this Ella's influence?"

"Perhaps," he said. "Or gratitude. Or perspective."

"All three maybe, no?"

"Maybe," he said.

He waited a short while before he ate a late breakfast, hoping Ella would come down and they could eat together. He went downstairs to see if his father needed help, but Sally was feeling well today and working with Frank. Bastien insisted that Jonathan should watch out for Ella today. His parents had obviously been talking, but, of course, he would know why his wife had spent most of the night in another room of the house. Jonathan went back upstairs to find that Ella still hadn't come out of her room. He finished hanging the laundry, and when Ella was still absent, he began to feel worried and asked his mother if she would check on Ella. She agreed and went quietly up the stairs while he paced the hallway outside the bathroom, one flight below where he hoped that Ella was just getting caught up on some sleep.

"Jonathan!" he heard his mother call, and he took the stairs three at a time. He came into the doorway of Ella's room to see that she was curled up in the bed beneath the covers, her back to him. "Perhaps you should sit with her," Lisette said, but her expression seemed to be telling him something else, something she didn't want to say aloud. "I will get her something to eat."

She walked out of the room and left the door open. Jonathan walked around the bed, guided by the small amount of daylight that was reaching through the closed curtains. He tried not to gasp when he saw her face. That hollow look he'd seen in her eyes when they'd first met had magnified and deepened. She stared at nothing, her hands clutched so tightly to a pillow she held against her chest that her knuckles were white. He considered the possibilities of what might be going on in her head—and in her heart—and hot tears stung his eyes. He blinked them back and moved the chair close to the bed. He sat down directly in the path of her vision, but there was no indication that she saw him.

"Ella," he said, putting a hand over hers. He rubbed her fingers. "Ella," he repeated, and she started as if she'd been asleep and he'd awakened her.

"Jonathan," she said, her voice mildly slurred. She leaned up on her elbow and looked around. "What time is it?" She glanced at the clock. "Good heavens! I've missed breakfast and should have been helping in the—"

"Don't worry about that," he said. "Mama's bringing something up for you."

"There's no need for her to wait on me," Ella said and sat up. Jonathan put a hand on her shoulder to urge her to stay put.

"I think you need your rest," he said.

She looked mildly embarrassed as she said, "I just . . . lost track of the time. I suppose I was . . . daydreaming."

"Daydreaming?" he echoed as if she'd said that she intended to move to Africa. "I don't know where your mind was when I came in the room, Ella, but there is no exaggeration that could define it as *daydreaming*."

"I'm sorry," she said, squeezing her eyes closed.

"Sorry?" he repeated. "You have nothing to apologize for. I just want to understand what you're feeling." He took hold of her hand, and she gripped it with a tightness that implied her need for him to save her just as surely as when he'd lifted her up out of that lifeboat.

"I'll be fine," she said with a forced smile and eyes that completely contradicted the statement.

"You know what?" he said with gentle firmness. "I believe that you will. I really do. You *will* be fine, Ella. But the road we might have to take to get there might not be easy."

"We?" she countered. "The road *we* might have to take?" She pulled her hand from his. "You've been so kind and generous with me, Jonathan, but this is not *your* problem. Just because you brought me home with you and let me use your room and share your family does not mean that you are responsible for me or this—"

"Listen to me, Ella," he said, less gentle and more firm in spite of the quietness of his voice. "I was *there*! I didn't see the *Titanic* go down, but I was a part of this drama. I was *supposed* to be there. You're not the only one who needs to walk this path. Whatever the future may or may not hold for us, Ella, we are in this together. We have been since the moment we laid eyes on each other in that lifeboat. Until we can both move beyond this with some kind of peace, we will remain in this together. Do you understand what I'm saying?"

Ella nodded, and tears pooled in her eyes. She reached again for his hand. "Be patient with me, Jonathan. I need you. I do! I just . . ."

"Just what?" he pressed when she hesitated.

"I just . . . feel like such a burden. I mean . . . look at me. I'm . . . a mess." The tears spilled down her face and she dropped her head.

Jonathan lifted her chin and leaned toward her. "I think you're beautiful; always beautiful." Their eyes connected firmly and he seriously considered kissing her. He certainly wanted to, and it was far from the first time he'd thought about it. Then he heard his mother's footsteps on the stairs and drew back, certain it was better to wait. This was far from the ideal moment for a first kiss.

"Ah, you look better already," Lisette said with a smile when she came into the room with a tray. Ella looked mildly embarrassed again, and Jonathan knew she had some awareness of having been caught in such a dazed state. But since both he and his mother had been privy to the impact of her nightmares, he felt sure it was good for her to know that she wasn't in this alone, and that she had no reason to feel ashamed.

Lisette set the tray on the bed near Ella and said that Jonathan would make certain she ate enough to stay strong. She then put both her hands on Ella's face and said with gentle warmth, "You must not be afraid to share your burden with us, *ma chéri*. We will help you through. Now, I will leave it up to you, but I think that you should just rest today. We will check on you and not leave you alone for long, if that is what you would like."

"Thank you," Ella said. "I think I *would* like that."

Lisette smiled and left the room. Jonathan *did* make certain she ate a fair amount, then he asked, "Do you want to rest? Would you like me to go?" She hesitated and he added, "Give me an honest answer, please."

Her voice trembled as she admitted, "I *do* want to rest. I've been tired ever since it happened, but . . ." She closed her eyes and her chin quivered. "I don't want to be alone. Maybe . . . if I'm not alone, I'll be able to sleep."

"I'll stay right here," he said, leaning back in the chair. "If you wake up and I'm gone, I'll be back in just a minute or two. I promise."

"You're very good to me," she said, and Jonathan wished he could tell her what it meant to him that he could make a difference in her life. He felt as if her need for him was offering him some kind of opportunity for redemption. He knew that only God could offer true redemption, but he believed more than he ever had that God sent people into each other's lives to help facilitate such things. And he believed in his heart of hearts that Ella was the best thing that had ever happened to him.

Jonathan hardly left Ella's room the rest of the day. His mother brought meals there for both of them, reporting that she would tell the rest of the family that Ella was not feeling well and Jonathan was watching out for her—which she declared with a wink to be entirely true. Ella *did* get some rest, but it came in spurts as she came in and out of nightmares. Her exhaustion always lured her back to sleep after Jonathan did his best to help soothe her fears and reassure her that all was well.

That night, Lisette stayed with Ella again, and Jonathan got some sleep as well. The following day, Ella came down for breakfast and appeared to be doing well. Lisette had privately told Jonathan that she believed Ella needed to keep busy and have routine and normalcy in her life. "As long as she can get some sleep," she said, "I believe that time will make her strong enough to face these things."

Jonathan wanted to believe that was true, and he felt grateful beyond words for the love and support of his mother. A week later Ella had worked herself into the rhythm of the family so perfectly that he couldn't imagine her not ever being there. She helped his mother with cooking and laundry, and she spent time in the bistro each day it was open. She became comfortable with his siblings, and he saw a side of her coming out that he'd only gotten glimpses of before. She was a genuinely kind woman with a deep desire to be a good person. He fell in love with her more every day, but also found himself growing to love her in proportion to his growing admiration and respect. They spent very little time alone together, but he did manage to lure her away now and then to go on a walk with him, and one evening he hired a taxicab and took her to Central Park. She was delightfully amazed at this enormous oasis in the middle of the city. They walked and talked for most of the evening, and by all outward appearances she seemed to be happy and doing well. But he knew that look in her eyes, and he knew what it meant. He knew there was much healing yet to do—for himself as well as for her—and he prayed that they would be able to find that path of healing together.

More than a month after Jonathan had lifted Ella onto the *Carpathia*, he knew that his mother was still spending most of her nighttime hours in Ella's room, helping her get through the nights. Lisette had reported that most of Ella's dreams were of freezing to death or drowning—or both. It was as if she felt the entire weight of the Atlantic Ocean bearing down on her, and the immense power of that weight left her terrified, even though she'd not even set eyes on the ocean since their arrival in the city. And Lisette also told him that she frequently cried out Irene's name. When Jonathan thought of Ella losing her dear friend, it was hard sometimes to keep his composure. He knew what it was like to lose someone who loved you, someone who had had a profound impact on your life.

During the days, Ella seemed fine, but Jonathan knew she really wasn't. He'd managed to support her in avoiding the topic altogether, but he began to feel like enough time had passed that the habit of *not* talking about it could cause a bigger problem. He discussed it privately with his mother, and she agreed that it would be good for him to at least try to get Ella to talk about what she was feeling. With any luck, the conversation would not be a complete disaster.

CHAPTER TWELVE
Lingering Shock

JONATHAN MADE ARRANGEMENTS WITH HIS family for him and Ella to be gone for the afternoon, and perhaps longer. After breakfast he said to Ella, "I'd like to take you out to lunch, and then maybe we could just . . . go for a long walk or something. It's a beautiful day."

"That sounds lovely," she said. "Could we go to Central Park?"

"If you'd like," he said, thinking that might be a nice place to have a private conversation. There was plenty of space to keep their distance from anyone else who might be enjoying the afternoon there.

"Where would you like to eat?" he asked once they'd set out.

"How about that Italian restaurant where your mother took me? I liked it very much."

"Excellent idea," he said with a smile and told the driver.

They enjoyed a nice lunch, and it was easy to sit there and pretend that they had not been participants in the greatest disaster of their time. After they'd eaten, they went to the park and strolled at a leisurely pace for quite a while before Jonathan asked, "How are you doing, Ella?"

"I'm fine," she said.

"I mean . . . how are you really doing?"

"I'm fine," she repeated, almost sounding defensive.

"Ella," he said and stopped walking to turn and face her. He took her shoulders into his hands, and for a moment his thoughts went to his growing love for her. He'd felt it was best to put his romantic feelings on hold until she'd had more time to make peace with all that had happened, but there were moments when he felt impatient to explore their relationship more deeply, and to get on with their lives in every respect. He forced himself to focus on the most pressing issue and said gently, "I know you're still having nightmares, because my mother is there with you most of the time and—"

She looked away. "I've told her she doesn't need to stay with me every night. It's ridiculous for her to have to—"

"Ella, that's not the point. She's glad to help. *I* am glad to help. I just . . . don't know what to do."

She continued to look away from him, and he felt sure she would have walked off if he'd not been holding to her shoulders. "You can't fix this, Jonathan."

"I'm not saying I can, but I think we should at least talk about it, as opposed to trying to pretend it didn't happen." He sighed and added, "It's been weeks, Ella."

"What are you saying? That I should just be able to put the entire episode behind me because it's been *weeks*? Should I just be able to . . . move on . . . get on with my life?"

"I'm not saying that at all. But perhaps enough time has passed that you should start talking about it."

"Talk about it?" she countered. "I can't even *think* about it without shaking. What makes you think I should be able to *talk* about it?"

"Maybe if you started *talking* about it, you might stop shaking." He felt her start to shake, as if she'd been cued. "Ella, listen to me. What happened to you—to us—will always be with us. It will always be a part of our lives, of who we are and who we will become. But we can't let it destroy us. You *survived*, Ella. There must be a reason. I know it's painful. I know it's hard, but . . . what happened that night has become completely taboo as a topic of conversation when you are present. It shouldn't be that way. I'm no doctor and I don't know how the mind works, but I've got enough common sense to know that *not* talking about it is *not* going to make it easier. I would think that holding so much inside could make you sick if you let it; *really* sick." She finally looked up at him again. He pleaded gently, "Please, Ella. Just . . . talk to me. Let's . . . talk about what happened that night—for both of us. Let's talk about those days on the *Carpathia*. And . . ."

He hesitated and she demanded, "What? And what?"

"Tell me about Irene. Tell me everything about her. Talk about her. Cry if you need to. Scream if you want. But please . . . talk about these things. Let me share your burdens."

Ella thought about what he was saying and wondered how she could tell him everything about her relationship with Irene and not have him regret ever having brought her into his life and into his home. But her reasons for meeting Irene were not the most important issue at the moment, and had nothing to do with what he was trying to achieve. She admired his ongoing commitment to her happiness, and perhaps she'd been wondering if he would actually remain committed to it this long. The fact that he'd not lost patience with her made her wonder if he was right. Perhaps enough time had passed that she should be able to talk about all of this—especially with him. He *had* been there. And she trusted him, likely more than she'd ever trusted anyone in her adult life, with the exception of Irene.

"Very well," she said and motioned to a nearby bench in the shade of a large tree. It was away from the common paths through the park, and would afford them a certain amount of privacy. "Let's talk."

"Let's," he said, and they sat down.

"You first," she said and turned on the bench to face him.

"All right," he said, even though Ella could tell he would have preferred to not have to lead the conversation with his own experiences. But he began with what it had been like that night after the distress signal had come in from the sinking *Titanic*. He became mildly emotional as he talked about how it had felt to be standing at the rail of the *Carpathia* and arrive at the coordinates to find the great ship gone. He told her how he'd felt while he'd helped one person after another up out of the boats, working together with other members of the crew to see that survivors were warmed up and given medical attention where needed.

"I think I was in shock," he said. "Absolute shock. I look back and it feels like a dream, like I was functioning by some power outside myself. And everyone had that same look in their eyes. Whether they were crying, or begging for information, or saying nothing at all, they all had the same look in their eyes."

Ella couldn't keep from shedding tears as he spoke, recalling all of it from her own perspective. The conversation naturally flowed into her sharing her viewpoint of all that had happened, telling him things she'd never allowed to pass through her lips before. Her emotion increased, but his shoulder was there to absorb her tears, and his arms were there around her to give her strength.

They descended into silence while Ella kept her head on his shoulder and he kept his arm around her shoulders. Ella didn't know if all they'd talked about would help her feel better in the future, but right now she felt relaxed, safe, and secure. When she admitted that she was getting hungry again, they walked arm in arm to a little café at the edge of the park. While they were eating, Ella said, "You're very good to me, Jonathan."

He smiled, and she wondered for the thousandth time if she might be blessed enough to have his smile with her for the rest of her life. He reached across the table to put his hand over her cheek. "I've very glad to have you in my life, Ella."

They shared dessert that they both declared fell short of the pastries Jonathan's father produced in his kitchen—things they were both learning to make; but neither of them could master Bastien's finesse. Jonathan took her hand across the table and said, "I would like to propose an idea. I don't think you'll like it much, but I want you to keep an open mind. So, just . . . hear me out."

"All right," she said.

"I've thought many times that it's too bad you can't talk to others who have been through what you've been through, then I realized that you can."

It only took her a moment to perceive his implication. "If you mean that I should go and visit Mrs. Olsen, I do *not* need to listen to her dramatize it over and over and—"

"You said you would hear me out. I know she can be overly dramatic, and she talks up a storm. But one visit is not unendurable for either of us. I'll go with you, of course. And I really do believe that it would be good for you to be able to talk with someone who feels the way you feel—even if she'll likely do most of the talking. When you last saw Mrs. Olsen, everyone was mostly in shock and hardly knew what to think or how to feel. Now some time has passed, and I think it would be good for you. That's all. If nothing else, she will probably be thrilled to see you, and your visit will make her very happy."

Ella sighed, unable to argue with his reasoning. "I suppose this means we'll be meeting Baxter and Dexter as well," she said, with just the tiniest hint of a smile.

"I suppose so," Jonathan said and smiled, pleased that she was willing to go. He'd thought he'd have to do a lot more talking to convince her.

Perhaps deep down she *did* want to talk to someone who had simultaneously experienced the tragedy. Perhaps the fact that they'd spent most of the afternoon talking about it had helped her believe that she could *keep* talking about it. He hoped that once she got started, she could talk and talk about it until she got it all out of her system so that it would stop festering and erupting in her dreams.

Two days later they went together to visit Mrs. Olsen. Jonathan had told Ella that was enough time for her to feel prepared, but not sufficient time to dread it too terribly much, or to talk herself into backing out.

Ella felt utterly nervous as they stood in front of a large, beautiful home that reminded her a bit of the Blackhursts' home in London. She thought of Mrs. Olsen's constant, drama-laced chattering, and she felt a little nauseous, but Jonathan took her hand, smiled at her, and said, "I'll be with you every moment. If it becomes unbearable, we'll leave."

"All right, then," she said. "Let's get this over with."

Jonathan rang the bell and kept a tight hold on Ella's hand. A maid answered the door; she was a stern-looking, middle-aged woman with prematurely gray hair that was cut into a short bob.

"May I help you?" she asked.

"We've come to call on Mrs. Olsen," Jonathan said.

"Oh, I'm afraid she's not well," the maid said.

Ella didn't want to leave now that she'd gathered her courage enough to be here, and she didn't want all of their trouble to be for nothing. "Perhaps she would like some company, then?" she suggested with hope.

"Oh, I don't know if . . ." The maid didn't finish her sentence, but there was something about her tone that implied she might actually believe that Mrs. Olsen *would* like some company.

"Is she ill?" Jonathan asked. "Has she seen a doctor? Is there something we can do?"

"Oh, you're very kind," the maid said, "but . . ." She stopped as if her temptation for candor had been cut off by her desire to be appropriately discreet. "Might I ask how you know Mrs. Olsen?"

Jonathan glanced at Ella, then back to the maid. "I met Mrs. Olsen when she came on board the *Carpathia* after the . . . disaster. Ella here met her when—"

"You're Ella?" the maid said with high-pitched enthusiasm and took Ella's hands into hers with what some might consider complete impropriety for a maid greeting guests at the door. "Oh, my goodness me. Come in. Come in. Oh, bless me. The good Lord *does* answer prayers. He does! He does!"

Ella glanced over her shoulder at Jonathan as she was practically hauled into the house and through the door of a finely decorated parlor. Jonathan closed the front door and followed them.

"Oh, my goodness me," the maid said again as she sat on the sofa and urged Ella to sit beside her. Jonathan took a chair across the room. "Ella. Dear, sweet, Ella. I've heard so much about you. It's just me and Mrs. Olsen here. I'm Bertha, by the way."

"Hello, Bertha," Ella said.

"Mrs. Olsen's always treated me real good, almost like family. It's just me and her here most of the time. Most of the house is shut up and she doesn't require much help—most of the time. But I've just been beside myself these last few weeks, worried sick to death about her. The first week or so after she came back, all we could do was talk about how glad we were that she'd survived, and she told me the story over and over." Ella and Jonathan exchanged a discreet glance that went unnoticed by Bertha. "And then . . ." Bertha hesitated and seemed to be struggling with her emotions. "Then she just . . . stopped talking about it at all. And then she stopped talking about *anything*. If you know Mrs. Olsen, then you know that this is *highly* unusual."

"Yes, it certainly is," Ella said, comprehending Bertha's concern, and at the same time completely compassionate to Mrs. Olsen's ailment.

"She's haunted by it, I tell you," Bertha said. "But I just don't know what to do. It's nothing any doctor can do anything about. I've taken to praying that she could find some peace, that we could get some answers, some help. *Something.* And here you are, showing up on the doorstep like that. I'm certain that you'll cheer her spirits. I mean, look at you. Dear, sweet, Ella. You survived that *horrible* . . . event . . . and you look as right as rain."

"I suppose looks can be deceiving," Ella said, surprised at her own admission. But Bertha was so thoroughly forthcoming that Ella couldn't help but want to offer her some reassurance, and she was already very glad that they'd come.

"It's been difficult for you too?" Bertha asked.

"Yes, Bertha," Ella said. "Very difficult. If Mrs. Olsen is willing to see us, perhaps we could all talk about it and maybe we'll all feel better."

"Oh, I do hope so," Bertha said and sprang to her feet, rushing out of the room without another word.

"Well, well," Jonathan said. "How remarkable."

"Remarkable?" Ella asked.

"That you might be the answer to Bertha's prayers."

"It was your idea," Ella said. "I would think that *you* are more the answer to her prayers."

"Mrs. Olsen is *your* friend," Jonathan said.

"I don't know that I would call her a friend, exactly, but . . . she certainly was there when I needed her."

"And now it seems she needs you," Jonathan said. "I agree with you completely."

"About what?"

"That perhaps we can all talk about it and maybe we'll all feel better."

"I do hope so," Ella said.

Bertha rushed back into the room with two small dogs at her heels. The dogs were full of energy and apparently excited by company, but no more so than Bertha. "Oh, she's coming down," Bertha said. "It's a miracle. She nearly jumped right out of the bed when I said you were here. She'll just need a moment to make herself presentable, she said."

"I'm so glad she's willing to see us," Ella said while the dogs put their paws up on her knees and begged for attention. "Baxter and Dexter, I presume," she said, laughing softly at their playfulness.

"You must forgive them. They're quite starved for attention."

"It's not a problem," Ella said. "They really are adorable. Mrs. Olsen talked a great deal about them."

"I imagine she did," Bertha said with a little laugh. She seemed in much better spirits than she had just a few minutes earlier. "Oh, goodness me. I should make some tea." She rushed out of the room, and Baxter and Dexter followed her, as if they sensed they might find more excitement by investigating her reason for leaving the room.

Just a couple of minutes later Mrs. Olsen entered the room, looking a bit rumpled, as if she'd not done much with her hair after spending the day in bed. Ella stood up to greet her and was surprised at how good it felt to see her.

"Oh, my dear, sweet Ella," she said, as if her name was always spoken along with the same two adjectives in this house. They hugged each other tightly and Mrs. Olsen added, "I couldn't believe it when Bertha said you had come to visit. I've so wanted to see you, my dear, but I had no idea of where to find you. I didn't even know if you were still in the city, and . . ." She stopped when she realized they weren't alone. She turned to see Jonathan standing there. "Oh my!" she said. "Jonathan, isn't it?"

"That's right," Jonathan said, holding out a hand. "How good to see you again."

Mrs. Olsen ignored the hand and hugged him as well. "How good to see *you*, young man. I see you've been taking very good care of our dear, sweet Ella."

"I've been trying," he said.

"He *has* been taking *very good* care of me," Ella said, and they were all seated, with Mrs. Olsen taking Ella's hand into hers and holding it tightly. "I've been staying with his family, and helping some in the French bistro that the family runs. They're wonderful people and have made me feel very welcome. And the food they make there is sublime!"

"You'll have to come and try it some time," Jonathan said. "My parents would love to meet you, I'm certain."

"We'll have to do that. Bertha and I could use an outing." By the way she said it—and the way that Bertha had been behaving—it was evident that the two were more like friends than any typical relationship shared by a woman and her maid.

Ella jumped into the conversation they needed to have by saying, "Bertha said that you've not been feeling well."

Mrs. Olsen nodded, tears brimmed in her eyes, and she said with a tremor in her voice, "It's been very hard. But you would know about that, I'm sure."

"Yes," Ella said, tightening her hold on Mrs. Olsen's hand, "it's been very hard."

"I cannot even believe that it happened at all. It seems like a dream. A very bad dream. But how can a person conjure up such a thing in her dreams, when it's completely unimaginable?"

"I've had the very same thought," Ella said.

"Have you?" Mrs. Olsen said, and Jonathan watched the two women as their eyes met and connected with perfect empathy for each other. Ella nodded and they began to talk about what they'd felt and experienced on that horrible April night. Bertha came in carrying a tray laden with tea and cake, and she sat to join them as a friend, sitting on the other side of Mrs. Olsen on the sofa. Jonathan said very little, but he felt deeply gratified to see what was unfolding. They stayed nearly three hours, and were only allowed to leave once they'd arranged to see each other again soon. Bertha showed them out and tearfully thanked them for their visit, saying that Mrs. Olsen had not been so much herself in weeks.

"You did a good thing, Ella," Jonathan told her on the ride back to the bistro.

"As I already said, it was your idea."

"But you said some amazing things to her. It took a lot of courage to talk about it like that. I know how hard it's been for you."

"I think Mrs. Olsen makes it easy to talk about it."

"Maybe," Jonathan said. "But she gained a great deal of strength from you. I could see it."

"Do you think so?"

"Absolutely," he said. "And how do you feel?"

"A little better, I think." She took his hand. "Thank you."

He just smiled and kissed her hand. Once they were dropped off in front of the bistro, he kept hold of her hand and said, "Let's walk. It's a lovely evening and the house will be crowded."

"I would love to," she said, and they ambled up the street.

After they'd walked in silence for several minutes, Jonathan said, "There's something I want to say, Ella."

"All right," she said, and they stopped walking in order to face each other. "I've hinted at it, and I haven't tried to hide it, but . . ." Ella took a sharp breath as she guessed what was coming. "I just need to say it. I don't want you to have any doubts about where I stand." He sighed and took hold of both her hands. "I love you, Ella. I think I fell in love with you that very first day, but now I've known you long enough to know that you are a woman worth loving." He sighed as if he were nervous, then went on. "I don't know if you could ever feel the same way for me, Ella. I hope you can; I want you to. But . . . I know that the circumstances under which we met are so tangled up with so many different things to feel and think about that . . . I understand if you need time, or—"

"I love you too, Jonathan," she said, putting a stop to his stammering.

In the glow of a nearby streetlight he searched her eyes as if to reassure himself that she meant it. He smiled and said breathlessly, "You really mean that."

"I really do," she said and squeezed his hands. He squeezed them in return, and she added, "But . . . there's so much you don't know about me, Jonathan, and . . . I don't know if—"

"It doesn't matter, Ella," he said. "Whatever your past might be, it doesn't matter. I have a past too, and maybe one day we'll be ready to talk about those things, but . . . that doesn't mean we can't make a good life together. We can start over from this day forward. As long as I know that you love me, and that you'll give me a chance . . . that's all I need right now."

Ella took in his reassurances with a warm sigh. She believed deep inside that if he knew the whole truth he would feel differently. But she liked the idea of starting over, and wanted to believe that it was a possibility. For right now, she chose to bask in the joy of this moment, and it became all the more joyful when he eased closer and bent to kiss her. She'd never been kissed before, but she'd convinced herself that such a thing as being kissed by a handsome man who actually loved her would simply never happen in her life. But it *was* happening, and it was truly the sweetest moment of her life. With his kiss she could almost believe that she *could* start over, that she could put the *Titanic* and every horror that had preceded it away forever. He let go of her hands so that he could take hold of her face as he kissed her again. She took hold of his arms and wanted the moment to last forever.

"I've wanted to do that for so long," he whispered, his lips almost touching hers still.

"How long?" she asked, opening her eyes to look up into his.

"Since I brought you home with me," he said, and kissed her again. "Maybe before that."

Ella felt tears burn into her eyes, but they came on so unexpectedly that she didn't have time to blink them back or turn away before Jonathan noticed. It wasn't as if he'd never seen her cry.

"What is it?" he asked, still keeping his face close to hers.

"I'm so . . . grateful to be here . . . now . . . with you. So grateful for the place I've found in your family . . . and for the way we feel about each other, but . . ." She closed her eyes and the tears fell. She bit her lip and her voiced trembled. "How is it possible to feel so grateful for *this* and to *know* that it wouldn't have happened if not for the *Titanic* sinking? All those people who lost their lives . . . all the suffering and destruction . . . and Irene—sweet Irene . . ." She sniffled and put her head to his shoulder, loving the way he so naturally encircled her in his arms. "How can I be this glad to be where I am and have what I have, when I'm so horrified and haunted by how it happened?"

"I can't answer that, Ella," he said and pressed a kiss into her hair while he stroked the back of her head with his hand. "But I do know that these events are out of our control. What happened was horrible beyond belief, and it will forever be a part of us, but we cannot go back, and we cannot change it. I just think that we have to decide we'll live our lives with gratitude for having survived it, and never take for granted how we've been blessed in a way that might help compensate for it. I wonder how many of the survivors could say the same."

Ella lifted her head to look up at him. "You're a very wise man, Jonathan Moreau."

"Am I?" He laughed softly. "I never considered myself wise. Truthfully, until that day, I think I was rather a fool. Seeing such stark evidence of how vulnerable mankind can be made me realize how I'd wasted most of my life up to that point. I'm determined not to squander another day."

Ella sighed, taking in a tangible sense of hope—a feeling she'd not felt to this degree since long before her parents had died. She refused to think too far ahead and wondered how they might cross the remaining bridges between the present and the possibility of them sharing a permanent relationship in the future. For the moment she just basked in the hope and had no qualms about saying, "I really do love you."

He laughed and his eyes sparkled, which made her laugh as well. "Oh, I really love you too," he said and took her hand. "Come on, let's go home."

Ella put her head on his shoulder and loved the way he put his arm around her as they walked. And she loved the way he referred to his home as *her* home. She prayed that it might last, even while she knew she lacked faith in her prayers, certain that the past would catch up with her eventually, and she would go back to wishing that she'd died on the *Titanic*.

That night Ella told Lisette that she didn't need her to sleep in the same room. Lisette assured her that it was all right, but Ella said—while Jonathan stood nearby, "I've had a very good day, and I'm hoping that it might make a difference. Just let me stay on my own tonight, and . . . if I have a bad night, I'll ask you to stay with me tomorrow."

"Such a brave girl," Lisette said and hugged Ella. "If you change your mind, you know where to find me."

"Thank you," Ella said, and Lisette went up the stairs to go to bed.

Jonathan walked Ella to the door of her room and kissed her good night before he backed across the hall to his own room, not taking his eyes off of her. They gazed at each other for a lengthy minute before he finally turned away and went into his room, closing the door behind him.

Ella *did* sleep better that night, even though she did wake up a few times, and she did have some difficult dreams. Still, it was *not* as bad as it had been, and she had to credit Jonathan's insistence on getting her to talk about it as being greatly responsible for that. Their visit with Mrs. Olsen had also been good, and she was grateful for his insight on that. But she was most grateful for his confessions of love, and the sweet kisses he'd given her beneath the glow of the streetlight.

The following week, Ella received a very kind letter from Brother and Sister Pack, which included a personal note to Jonathan, expressing their gratitude for his taking care of their *precious Ella*, and also for his writing to them. The letter to Ella was both difficult to read and comforting. She was able to write back to them without any help from Jonathan, telling them more about what had happened while sparing them any unsavory details. She wrote instead about Irene's remarkable example and strength, and she expressed gratitude once again for all that Brother and Sister Pack had done for her. Jonathan went with her to mail the letter, and she felt one step closer to healing.

Throughout the summer, Ella felt changes taking place within her. The love blossoming between her and Jonathan seemed the greatest source of those changes. She began to believe that she truly could put her past behind and begin a new life with this man and his loving family. But she could only believe it when she could manage to entirely avoid thinking about the ugliness of her past that she felt sure would be utterly repulsive to Jonathan—*and* to his family. She was determined to keep her past a secret, and perhaps with time she would be able to completely forget about it and put it behind her for good.

Ella felt certain that Jonathan wanted to marry her. He'd not come right out and used the word *marriage*, but he continually implied that they would share a future. He talked about how well the bistro was doing, and that with time his father would be able to retire and Jonathan and his brother-in-law would be able to work together to run the family business and bring in sufficient income for both of them to get homes of their own and support their families. Imagining such a future with Jonathan warmed Ella to the core. Only the occasional intrusion of repulsive memories would make her hope grow cold, but she was getting better and better at not thinking about them at all.

Ella and Jonathan made a habit of weekly visits to Mrs. Olsen's home, and Bertha would usually join them in their chats. They talked of many things, but the disaster of the *Titanic* was always the main topic. Ella couldn't deny—and neither could the others—that the conversations were helping them heal. They all heartily agreed that *not* being able to talk about it had a way of holding the pain too tightly inside. It was an event that had permanently altered all of their lives. It was woven into their hearts and minds as surely as the threads of a tapestry that could never be pulled out without unraveling the entire piece.

Ella still cried to think about Irene's untimely end, and she wondered how her friend's family was coping with such an immense loss. She still felt horrified to think of what had happened to all of those people. She still saw it unfold in her mind when she closed her eyes to go to sleep, and she could still hear the cries of the dying at the strangest times. She talked to Jonathan about her feelings, and she was even able to share them with his parents and occasionally with his siblings. They were all compassionate and kind, and they all assured her that it would surely take a very long time to heal from the trauma of such an event. Ella was glad to have come to a place with her new family where she didn't have to avoid expressing her thoughts and feelings on the matter, and it seemed good that they all knew they could express their thoughts and feelings as well. Even though none of them had witnessed it personally, Ella realized that the sinking of the *Titanic* had affected every person who had any connection to it whatsoever. Citizens of New York who had no actual connection to it were still aghast and overcome with what had happened. Months after the fact, it was still a common topic of conversation in the bistro, at church, and on the streets. Everyone seemed to be trying to cope with this event that had brought mankind to its knees. Once Ella got over not feeling traumatized whenever she heard the topic discussed, she began to feel a strange kind of comfort to know that she was not alone in her feelings of horror over what had happened. And as long as she had Jonathan at her side, she believed that she would be able to go on and make a decent life for herself. She sometimes wondered about the other seven hunred and four survivors. With the exception of Mrs. Olsen, she had no idea how *they* were coping—or not coping—with the impact of the event on their lives. She felt especially blessed to have people around her who were willing to talk about it. If Jonathan and his family were telling her to just forget about it and move on because it was too uncomfortable, she felt certain she would go insane.

As summer reached toward autumn, Ella felt confident that she had adequately and permanently put away her past regarding the sinking of the *Titanic*, and that with time she would be able to see that April night as nothing more than a bad memory that was best avoided. Then, as if the trauma of the *Titanic* had been addressed just enough to allow room for older pain and trauma to demand to be heard, she was assaulted by memories that made it difficult to breathe, memories so horrible that she wondered how she could ever find her way past them. It started with a nightmare, a dream entirely different from those that had plagued her in regard to the *Titanic*. She woke up gasping and shaking and wondering how she could have believed that putting her past behind her could ever be possible. By the time she had managed to get herself to the kitchen for breakfast, fighting to keep a pleasant expression on her face, she had convinced herself that the best thing for everyone would be for her to find a way to leave here and move on. The thought of even trying to tell Jonathan the truth made her sick to her stomach. Leaving would be easier. She just had to gather the courage to do it.

CHAPTER THIRTEEN
Sinking

JONATHAN FELT THERE WAS SOMETHING different about Ella the moment he saw her. He kissed her on the cheek in a greeting that was typical between them when others were present. She returned a similar kiss and smiled up at him, but it was a *forced* smile, and he knew something wasn't right. She hurried to busy herself with helping get breakfast on the table, and he wondered when they might get the chance to talk.

The day went on as usual, with both of them working in the bistro and keeping busy. But Ella skillfully avoided being alone with him for even a moment, and he wondered why. She'd been doing remarkably well, all things considered, and he'd become more hopeful each day that they were nearing a point when he could confidently propose marriage, knowing that time had confirmed the feelings he'd been confronted with the first time he'd looked into her eyes. Now, something was terribly wrong. He felt literally nauseous more than once as he considered what his instincts were telling him. During the ticking away of busy hours while Ella managed to steer clear of him, his mind began putting together pieces of information he'd accumulated through the months he'd known Ella. They'd become so thoroughly focused on coping with the drama of the *Titanic* that he'd forgotten about the evidence he'd seen right from the start that she'd always been very evasive about her past, and he'd suspected there were other, underlying layers of trauma in her life separate from what had happened that April night. He wondered what to do now, and knew the answer was the same as it had been for confronting her adamant resistance to talking about the *Titanic*. She hadn't wanted to face it or talk about it, and she'd resisted it, but in the end, doing so was helping her heal. He simply needed to be forthright about whatever else might be going on, and do everything in his power to get her to confront that as well—whatever it might be.

After supper he asked her if she would go for a walk with him. He purposely asked her in front of everyone else so that she couldn't get out of it without making a fool of herself. His mother and sisters insisted that she should go while they took care of putting the kitchen in order.

"Are you not feeling well?" Lisette asked, as if she too had sensed the tension throughout the day and Ella's current dilemma in trying to avoid being alone with Jonathan.

"I'm fine," Ella insisted with another of those convincing smiles.

"Just a short walk," Jonathan said, "and then you can go to bed early, if you prefer."

Ella tentatively put her hand into his as if it had not spent countless hours there, as if he were a stranger and she had some kind of fear in trusting him. He couldn't begin to imagine why, but it almost made him angry. What had he ever done to earn such distrust?

They walked out to the street, then ambled slowly along a route that had become familiar. A pleasant coolness in the air whispered the promise of autumn offering some relief from summer's relentless heat. They walked in silence while Jonathan continued to ponder all he knew of this woman he'd come to love so dearly. He felt as if a very big piece of a puzzle was missing; there was something he didn't know, didn't understand. But he could never understand if she didn't share her heart with him. He even prayed silently that he would be able to find that missing piece and help her move beyond it so that they could both enjoy a good future together. He knew she deserved it, and he wanted to believe that he deserved it too.

Jonathan stopped beneath the streetlight where he had first kissed her. He turned to look at her, then he leaned down to kiss her, certain the moment would be magical. But she turned away so abruptly that it startled him. It was the first time she'd avoided his kiss, and he wondered why. As he considered her unhappy expression, he stopped long enough to ponder the reasons behind her aloofness for an idea to occur to him—an idea that made his heart quicken with dread and his stomach tighten into knots.

"Ella," he said, and she turned her back to him. For reasons he could never explain, the gesture only strengthened his theory that he was on the right course. He took a deep breath and chose his words carefully. "Is there a reason you don't want me to kiss you?"

"It's not that," she said, and he believed her, but she still kept her back to him.

"Then what is it?" he asked and put his hands to her shoulders. Initially she seemed startled by his touch and tried to retract, but he kept a gentle grasp, and she softened but didn't completely relax. He took another deep breath and hoped he wouldn't regret saying this, but now that the idea had come to him, he had to know the truth. He could never ignore it and find any peace in pursuing this relationship. "Ella," he said again, more softly, "has someone hurt you?"

He heard her gasp, then became aware of her breathing becoming shallow by the way her shoulders moved up and down. "I have no idea what you mean," she lied in a convincingly even tone of voice and bolted out of his grasp, turning to face him with a vivid, defensive fear in her eyes that boldly contradicted the words that came out of her mouth. "I don't know what you're talking about."

Now that he'd opened this door, Jonathan refused to close it again. At the risk of alienating her completely, he had to confront this—once and for all. He allowed all of his tiny nagging suspicions to conglomerate in his brain for a long moment while she stared him down as if he might retract his question and dismiss the conversation. She attempted to leave, but he grabbed her arm. She looked at his hand on her arm, then at his face. He couldn't be sure if she was angry or afraid, or if one emotion was trying to disguise the other. Everything came together so clearly in his mind that he had to believe his prayer had been heard. He kept a firm hold on her and asked in a gentle voice, "What were you running from, Ella, when you boarded the *Titanic*?" She gasped again, and he saw hot tears of truth brim in her eyes. "Tell me, Ella," he pleaded with tender compassion. "Tell me and you can stop running."

Once again she tried to bolt, but he took hold of her other arm as well, looking directly into her eyes while he spoke close to her face. "Tell me, Ella," he implored.

"I can't," she muttered, shaking her head as tears spilled down her face. She broke free and started to run, but at least she was running toward home. He sighed and followed, catching up with her just as she came through the door into the enclosed stairwell.

Jonathan grabbed her arm again, determined to finish this conversation. At least she had as good as admitted that there *was* something she'd kept from him. "There is *nothing* you could tell me," he insisted, "that would make me feel any differently about you. *Nothing!* Do you understand?"

"How can you say that," she cried, trying to break free, "when you have no idea what you're talking about?"

"Oh, I think I have a pretty good idea," he said with a certain amount of confidence. "You're not a very good liar, Ella. Your eyes tell the truth."

She looked down abruptly, as if she refused to let her eyes betray her any further. Jonathan leaned a little closer and said near her ear, "I love you, Ella. Please talk to me." He felt her slump beneath his hands, but she wouldn't look at him.

Ella wanted to slink away somewhere and just die as opposed to having this conversation. A part of her had known it would come to this. Maybe she should have left here long before now, long before he'd figured out she was hiding a part of herself from him. She knew now there was no avoiding it, but she wasn't sure she could allow the words to come out of her mouth. She knew he *did* love her, but she felt certain his opinion of her would change once the full truth came to light. But it was too late to turn back now. She would likely lose him either way. At least they could part with honesty between them, and he would realize that he would be better off without her. She finally drew courage enough to look up at him and spoke what she considered the most important truth of all. "You deserve better, Jonathan; so much better."

"Better than what?" he rumbled and tightened his grip slightly, pulling her closer. "Better than *you*? There is *nothing* better than you."

"You don't know what you're saying," she insisted. "You have no idea what I'm really like."

"Oh, I think I do," he insisted just as firmly.

"I was such a fool," she said, overtaken by more tears and an inability to hold her head up. She dropped it forward, avoiding his gaze while she sobbed once, then again. "I was so stupid, so naive and gullible."

"We all make mistakes," he said gently.

"Not like this!" she said, making another attempt to squirm out of his grasp. "There are a thousand women out there, Jonathan, who are more deserving of what you have to offer."

"Why don't you tell me what you're avoiding and let me decide that for myself."

"Why don't you—"

"What on earth is this?" Lisette said, appearing at the top of the stairs.

Ella took advantage of the distraction to break free. She ran past Lisette, through the parlor, and up the stairs to her room, thinking even as she did that it would have been better instead to have gone the other direction instead of coming back here. She should have just left and never returned.

Jonathan watched Ella leave and tried not to feel frustrated with his mother for the untimely interruption. "What are you doing to that poor girl?" Lisette demanded, putting her hands on her hips.

"Do you really think I would hurt her?"

"No, I do *not* think you would hurt her; not intentionally, at least. But she looked awfully upset to me. Now, talk to your mother."

Jonathan sighed, hoping that perhaps his mother's intervention might work to his advantage. If not his, then Ella's. "Something happened to her, Mama—before she left England. I'm certain of it. She's been trying to hide it from me. But she's running from something she'll never be able to outrun, something inside of her that's tearing her apart. She's convinced that it would change how I feel about her if I knew the truth, but it wouldn't."

"How can you be sure when you do not know what she is hiding?"

"I know you're asking me that to test me, and I'm telling you that I love her, Mama. I love her for who she is now. *You* talk to her. If she won't tell *me* what happened, maybe she'll tell *you*. Maybe you can convince her that I really do love her, and I'm not going to think less of her . . . no matter *what's* happened." He took a step toward his mother and added with fervor, "I'm afraid she'll try to run away, and I'll never be able to find her. Please try to talk some sense into her. Please."

Lisette looked at him long and hard, as if she might be able to gauge his sincerity by doing so. She finally sighed and said, "Very well. I will try my best to talk to her. You be patient and mind your manners."

* * * * *

Ella frantically paced her room, wondering how she could get out of the house unnoticed, wishing she had some kind of bag or suitcase in which to pack her minimal belongings. She fought back her temptation to curl up on the bed and sob. She thought of the moment she'd realized her baby was dead, and the temptation to break down completely increased dramatically. She knew that if she started to cry like that, she'd not be able to stop for hours. And she had to keep control of her senses. Leaving was the best option; the *only* option now. She wished now that she had left weeks ago. She didn't think about where she might go or how she might manage; she simply had to go!

A knock at the bedroom door startled her, and she stopped pacing abruptly, frozen there in fear and dread as if a wild animal might break the door off its hinges and attack her. "I need to be alone," she called, unable to face Jonathan right now. With any luck she would never have to face him again. She just had to wait until everyone was asleep, then she could sneak out of the house and never look back.

"It is me," Lisette said and took Ella by surprise. "Please let me come in, *ma chéri*."

"I'm very . . . tired," Ella said. "We can talk . . . tomorrow." She regretted the lie even as it came out of her mouth, knowing that she fully intended to be gone before the sun came up.

"Please let me come in," Lisette repeated. "I think we need to talk tonight."

Ella could almost believe Lisette had predicted her plans. Or perhaps Jonathan had told her enough that she had figured it out. Ella heard his words again in her mind and felt chilled. *What were you running from, Ella, when you boarded the* Titanic? She took a deep breath and opened the door. Lisette looked concerned but pleased that Ella was willing to talk to her. Ella hoped she wouldn't regret it as she motioned Lisette into her room and closed the door, not wanting Jonathan or anyone else to overhear their conversation, even though Jonathan had already heard everything she intended to say.

Lisette turned to face her, offering an expression of compassion that very much reminded Ella of Irene. She suddenly missed Irene so badly that the grief of losing her rushed in to smother her irrational thinking.

"What is it that troubles you so?" Lisette asked, and in her mind and heart, Ella could almost feel Irene urging her to be trusting. Ella had no reason to believe that Lisette's motives were not pure, and she certainly had no reason to mistrust Jonathan. She sat down on the edge of the bed, and Lisette sat beside her. She thought of how Irene had urged her to tell her story to Mr. Stead. His kindness had made it easier to talk about than she'd expected at the time. But then, that had been an entirely different situation than this mess she'd gotten herself into now. It broke her heart to think of losing Jonathan, but perhaps it was best to just get this over with and move on. Nearly an hour after Lisette had come into the room, Ella found the courage to tell her what she had once shared with her trusted friends who had died on the *Titanic*. Lisette was completely kind and compassionate, and not nearly as surprised as Ella might have suspected. She wept as she wrapped Ella in her arms and gave her all of the love that she would have wished to receive from her own mother.

Lisette allowed Ella to just cry there in her arms for a long while. When Ella had settled into a silence weighed down with both fear and regret, Lisette said gently, "Jonathan must know the truth, *ma chéri*. He assures me that he will love you no matter what might have happened in your past. I believe you must at least give him the chance to decide that for himself. If he decides that he cannot live with your past, then you can go forward with your life and know that you tried your best, and we will do everything we can to help you make a fresh start. You must not run away with so many words unspoken. You must at least give him a chance, no?"

"I'm sure you're right," Ella said, wishing she was capable of more rational thinking. She couldn't deny the truth in what Lisette was saying, but the thought of having that conversation with Jonathan made her want to throw up. She looked at Lisette and said, "I agree that he should know, but I don't want to tell him. Will *you* tell him?"

Lisette hesitated a long moment but said, "If that is what you want, I will tell him. But you must promise to give him some time and allow him a fair chance to consider his feelings. That is only fair, no? If he tells you that he cannot marry you, then you will know, but you must be patient and give him a chance."

"Very well," Ella said. "I promise."

Lisette assured Ella that everything would be all right, but Ella felt hesitant to believe her. She did feel some relief, however, to no longer feel like she had to hide her past. Now she could face it and move on. She reminded herself that she was a capable woman. She could accept life without marriage and children, and she could work to provide for herself. She would be fine. And with time she would come to terms with the way she felt her heart breaking. But she had survived a great deal, and she would survive this.

When Lisette opened the door to leave the room, Ella saw Jonathan sitting on the floor in the hallway, his back against the wall. He sprang to his feet and asked in a hushed voice, "Is everything all right?"

"I suppose that remains to be seen," Ella said, still not certain that Jonathan would be as accepting of her past as his mother had been.

"I will let the two of you talk," Lisette said and went down the stairs to go to bed.

Ella found it difficult to look at Jonathan until she realized he was standing in the doorway, watching her intently. He leaned his shoulder against the doorframe and sighed.

"Ella," he said softly, "you don't have to tell me whatever you may have told my mother, but . . . please don't leave. There's no need to run away from your past, whatever it may be. It's only the future that matters now. And I want you to spend your future with me." He let out a sharp breath, and she realized he was nervous. "I'm asking you to stay . . . permanently. I'm asking you to marry me, Ella."

Ella could hardly breathe. She couldn't imagine anything more wonderful ever happening to her, but she also couldn't imagine that he would stand by his proposal if he knew the whole truth. "How can you ask me that," she said, "when you don't know what—"

"It doesn't matter, Ella. Whatever it is, it doesn't matter."

"It matters, Jonathan." She stepped forward and took his hand. "It's very late, and . . . we're both tired. Talk to your mother. I told her that she should tell you. I believe you should know, but I don't want to have to say it to you. Talk to her, and then . . . give it some time . . . and see how you feel."

"It won't change how I feel," he said.

Ella appreciated his being so noble, but she found it difficult to believe him.

"Please, just . . . give it some time."

"Promise you won't leave. If you're asking me to give this some time, you must promise me that you'll still be here when I've come to my decision."

"I promise," she said, "but only if you promise to be completely honest with me. You cannot patronize me for the sake of being kind, Jonathan. You must . . . love me as I am, or I cannot stay."

"I promise," he said and stepped toward her, leaning forward to press a kiss to her brow. "Sleep well." He took her shoulders and looked into her eyes. "I love you, Ella. I'll see you at breakfast."

Ella cried more than slept, certain that nothing would ever be the same with Jonathan once he'd had a chance to speak to his mother. For the first time in months she found herself sincerely wishing that *she* had died on the *Titanic* instead of Irene. Jonathan would have never known the difference, because he never would have met her. Everything would have been better for everyone: for Irene, for her family, for Jonathan. And especially for herself.

* * * * *

Jonathan doubted very much that he could sleep, and he hoped that his mother might be willing to talk to him tonight. He wanted all of this in the open and cleared up—once and for all. He wanted to get on with his life, and he wanted Ella to be happy and free of the burdens she'd been carrying. He'd spent a great deal of time thinking about the horrors she had witnessed the night the *Titanic* went down; but to fully take in the reality that she had brought a great deal of pain with her onto the ship made him wonder how she could manage to hold herself together with so much grace and courage. The answer was that no person could put forward that much strength indefinitely. She was crumbling inside and he knew it. Surely it would only have been a matter of time before all of this would have come to the surface. He was glad that it had, and he hoped and prayed that they could move forward together, with no secrets between them.

The house was quiet and he knew that everyone had gone to bed. For a minute he feared that his mother had done the same, but he found her in the kitchen, looking out the window to the dark street below, a tear sliding down the cheek that was within his view.

"Are you all right?" he asked, leaning his shoulder against the doorjamb.

Without turning to look at him, Lisette said, "Oh, what that girl has been through!" She then turned and gave him a piercing gaze. "I am so grateful, my Johnny, that you brought her home to us. Whether you choose to marry her or not, she will always be a daughter to me. I will insist upon it!"

"I don't have a problem with that, Mama," he said. "But I think I would rather have her be my wife than some kind of adopted sister."

"I would prefer that too," she said, turning back to the window.

"She said that I should talk to you. I don't think I'll be able to sleep while wondering what she told you."

"I am certain it will be easier for a mother to tell her son such things than it would be for a woman to tell the man she loves."

"But you still don't want to have this conversation," he stated matter-of-factly.

"It is necessary," she said and sat down. "I am glad to have no more secrets. I think we have both known all along there was more that was troubling her than the shipwreck."

"Yes, I think so," Jonathan said and sat across the little table from her. His heart was pounding so hard he feared she might hear it.

Lisette mostly looked at her hands on the table in front of her as she told him Ella's tale. The financial destitution of her family and the deaths of her parents would have been enough to break his heart on her behalf; but her struggle to survive on her own, her poverty and hunger, life in the dirtiest parts of London, seemed too much to bear. Then came the despicable situation that Ella had been lured deceitfully into; a situation that had left her pregnant with a child who had died. And carrying all of that in her heart, she had boarded the *Titanic* with the hope of putting the past behind and making a new life for herself in a new land—with a true friend who had tragically died that night in a cold ocean. Jonathan shamelessly let tears roll down his face while his mother talked, and he made no effort to wipe them away. He could understand why Ella had not wanted to tell him, but he *couldn't* understand how she might have believed that it would change his opinion of her.

He talked the matter through with his mother, and let her know how much he appreciated her candor as well as her kindness toward Ella.

"She is easy to love," Lisette said as he stood to leave, needing some time alone to let all of this sink in.

"Yes, she is," he said, kissing his mother's brow. "And so are you."

For much of the night Jonathan lay in his bed in the darkness, gazing toward the ceiling, or perhaps toward the sky that he knew existed above it. Tears leaked from the corners of his eyes into his hair while he wondered how one young woman could be called upon to endure so much in a lifetime. And he wondered if he was capable of giving her a life good enough from this moment forward to compensate for all that she had suffered. Well, he was certainly going to try!

* * * * *

The following day was Sunday, but Jonathan didn't feel at all like going to church. He was tired and overwhelmed and afraid that Ella might leave here in spite of anything he could do to convince her to stay. She didn't come down to breakfast, and he paced the kitchen while his mother took a tray up to her room. She came back to report that Ella had said she didn't feel up to attending church.

"Perhaps I should stay here with her," Jonathan said.

"That is exactly my thought," Lisette said and put a hand on his arm. "Perhaps you can take advantage of a quiet house to talk to her. You *must* talk to her. Do not let time keep passing with this between the two of you."

"I'll do my best," he said.

After the family had left the house, Jonathan went quietly up the stairs, took a deep breath, and knocked quietly on Ella's door.

"Come in," she called, and he peered inside to see her standing by the window, waiting to see who was there.

"You didn't go to church?" she asked, but her voice sounded more hopeful than surprised. Perhaps she wanted to get this conversation over with as much as he did.

"I was thinking that we could talk," he said.

"Of course," Ella said, but he didn't miss the brief flash of panic that passed through her eyes. "Give me . . . a few minutes. I'll . . . come to the parlor."

"I'll be there," he said, thinking that she couldn't get out of the house without passing by him. She'd promised she wouldn't run away, but he would still feel a lot better when she had been convinced of his love for her.

About twenty minutes later she came down the stairs, looking so beautiful that it took his breath away. He felt some inner satisfaction to realize that he'd not been fooling himself over his convictions. He *did* still love her every bit as much as before—perhaps more. She offered him a faint smile, then sat on the sofa across from him. Wanting to face her directly, he picked up a lightweight chair and set it right in front of her. He sat down and met her eyes for only a moment before she looked away and cleared her throat tensely.

"You spoke to your mother?" she asked with obvious fear in her voice.

"I did," he said. "She said that she told me everything you told her. Unless there's something you omitted last night, I know everything."

"You know everything," she said, but she wouldn't look at him.

Ella felt herself trembling in a way that reminded her of those first weeks following the disaster at sea. She couldn't bring herself to look at him, certain she would see some sign of disgust or embarrassment. But he took hold of her chin with his fingers and tilted her face toward his. She closed her eyes, but he said softly, "Please look at me, Ella." She drew courage and opened her eyes, surprised to see the same warmth in his eyes that had always been there. "I love you, Ella," he said. "I will always love you. Nothing has changed except my relief in finally knowing what's been weighing you down."

"But . . . how can . . ." She couldn't form her stammering words into a sentence. She cleared her throat again as if that might help, and she managed to say, "How can you want me in your life when I've done such a horrible thing?"

"You were a victim, Ella. How could any half-decent, Christian man hold you accountable for such a thing?"

Ella could hardly believe what she was hearing. She felt sure that his mother must have left something out when she'd repeated the story. Not wanting there to be anything left to misunderstanding, she said with surprising force, "I had a baby, Jonathan."

"Yes," he said, as if he were confused over why that would be a problem. "That's how you met Irene. I've wondered, you know. You never told me how the two of you met, and yet she had such an impact on your life. Now I know. She helped you through a terribly difficult time. I can't even imagine how you survived all of that, Ella. But I'm grateful that you did."

Ella wondered why his easy acceptance of all this had made her limbs feel weak and her breathing shallow. He held her gaze firmly, as if he might be expecting her to say something. When she couldn't imagine *what* that could be, she said, "I don't understand."

"What don't you understand?" he asked.

"How . . . you can . . . learn what you've learned about me and . . . so easily just . . ."

"It's not easy, Ella," he said. "My heart breaks to think of what you've been through." Tears glistened in his eyes as if to bear a second witness to his words. "But it does not remotely change how I feel about you, and I do not see how it changes anything between us. If anything, it only makes me love you more now that I understand what your life has been like. The more I learn about you, the more I admire you."

Ella tried to comprehend what he was saying, feeling as if his words were being forced through a dense fog that made it difficult for her mind to absorb and understand them. After a couple of minutes of silence, he asked, "You act as if you don't believe me." Ella couldn't answer, and he added, "Do you really think so little of me that you believe I would be that shallow and unfeeling? Do you think I'm the kind of man who would blame *you* for such a thing?"

Ella had never thought of it that way before. She had to admit what she'd believed all along. "I was so foolish." Tears finally came as she allowed herself to feel the memories. "I was stupid and gullible. I should have . . ." She sobbed. "I should have been . . . stronger, and . . ."

"Ella," he scooted his chair closer and took her hands, "you were deceived and manipulated."

Irene had told her the same thing, and so had Mr. Stead, but something deep inside Ella had found it difficult to believe that she couldn't have done something to prevent such a horrible thing from happening. She was wondering how to express such a thought when he said, "But you know what, Ella? Even if you *had* made a mistake . . . even if it *was* your fault—which it was *not*—I would still be able to let it go and love you just the same."

"Why?" she cried. "How?"

"Oh, Ella," he said, putting a hand to her face, wiping her tears with his thumb. "It's the Christian thing to do. It's the *right* thing to do. Who am I to carry the burden of judgment? We're all human. We make mistakes. We stumble and fall. We must forgive and accept if we expect to be forgiven and accepted. I love you, Ella. Nothing else matters. Nothing! Do you understand?"

Ella inhaled deeply in an attempt to take in his words—and the full depth of their meaning—and she began to sob so hard that she could hardly breathe. He eased closer still and urged her head to his shoulder, wrapping her fully in his arms while she wept without control. The tears carried her fears and memories into the open, while her heaving breaths seemed to take in, little by little, the real possibility that Jonathan Moreau really was the kind of man who could love her in spite of her defiled and appalling past.

CHAPTER FOURTEEN
Choosing Life

MANY MINUTES PASSED, AND ELLA continued to cry, finding it difficult to calm herself down, even though she made a concerted effort. Jonathan seemed to sense a problem when he took her shoulders into his hands and asked with sincerity, "What is it, Ella? Is there something else you need to say?"

"I don't know," she managed, then sobbed. Logically she knew that having the truth laid out between her and Jonathan, and knowing that he loved her still, was a miracle and a blessing. She felt relieved and grateful. But the conversation seemed to have sprung a leak in the dam that had been holding back all of her troublesome past and its associated pain. Now that it was flooding forth, she couldn't stop it.

"Ella?" Jonathan asked, growing in concern.

"I'm just . . . I . . . I . . . it's just so . . ." She sprang to her feet and began pacing, as if doing so might help her think more clearly, or at least allow her to connect more than three words together. "It's just all been so . . . difficult . . . so awful."

"I understand," he said and leaned back but kept his eyes keenly on her. He sensed her need to unburden herself, and he felt certain that this eruption was good for her. He just wasn't certain if he knew how to handle such volatile emotion, and prayed that he might know what to do and say. "Just . . . talk to me, Ella," he said. "Surely whatever is troubling you will—"

"Don't you understand?" she cried, as if his urging had suddenly given her permission to fully let go of all she had carried for so long. "I wanted to *die!* I wanted so badly to die that I seriously considered taking the matter into my own hands and putting myself out of my misery."

Jonathan was startled by the way his heart raced even before his brain fully perceived her implication. He felt so brutally affected by her confession that he feared saying something he might regret. He reminded himself to keep perspective, but his own buried pain suddenly reared its head with an ugliness and power that took him utterly off guard.

Ella was apparently oblivious to his reaction as she went on. "When the *Titanic* went down, all I could think about was how it should have been *me* that died that night. Not Irene! Not all those women who would actually be missed . . . who could have done something with their lives that—"

"Don't you *ever* say anything like that again!" Jonathan jumped to his feet and bellowed in a voice so harsh that Ella gasped and took a step back. "Don't you even *think* something like that again! Not *ever*! Do you hear me?"

"I hear you," she said in a voice so quiet and timid that it seemed to snap him out of some kind of enraged daze. Ella wondered what had upset him so much. She'd never seen him so angry; in fact, she'd never seen him angry *at all*. He'd graciously accepted all of the horrors of her past that she had wrongly believed would have angered him or provoked him to banish her from his life. Why would he be so upset *now*?

Jonathan saw Ella's terrified expression and wondered what had incited him to speak to her like that. He turned his back to her, ashamed of his outburst. But he only had to think about it a moment to know what had triggered his worst self to the surface. He squeezed his eyes closed as painful memories haunted him and tore at places in his heart he had wanted to believe were healed.

"I'm sorry," he said, keeping his back to her. "I shouldn't have spoken to you like that. Forgive me."

Ella breathed in his soft tone that was more like himself, but she wondered what had caused such a reaction in him. He'd been so perfectly kind and accepting of all of her bad behavior and frenzied emotions. She could never give him anything less than he had given to her.

"What is it, Jonathan?" she asked, still a little shaken but not at all afraid. She knew he would never hurt her, and she had enough sense to understand that his anger was not directed at her so much as at something she didn't understand. When he said nothing she asked, "Am I not the only one with painful secrets?"

He still said nothing, but she saw his shoulders slump and heard him sigh. She forgot all about her own struggles and emotional dilemmas. For as long as they'd known each other, everything had seemed to revolve around his efforts to help her come to terms with the drama in her life. She had selfishly assumed that *his* life had been only good, and that beyond the impact the *Titanic* had had on *him*, there was nothing in his past that might have caused him pain. She stepped closer and put her hands on his upper arms, leaning the side of her face against his back.

"What is it, my love?" she asked and felt him sigh again. "After all the effort you have put into making me talk about the things in my heart, you can't make a hypocrite of yourself now." She hesitated to allow him time to speak, but still he didn't. "Please talk to me," she said and wrapped her arms around him from behind.

He turned slowly and took her into his arms, holding to her fiercely, as if he feared that he might lose her otherwise. "I could not bear to lose you, Ella. Not for any reason. Not ever!"

"The feeling is entirely mutual, Jonathan, but—"

"What you said about wanting to die . . ." He kept a tight hold on her but pulled back to look into her eyes. "Promise me that you will never think like that again. Promise me."

Ella took in the severity of the expression in his eyes and felt suspicious of what this might be about, although she could only guess. "That was in the past, Jonathan. I have a reason to live now. And the thing is . . . even though I *felt* those things, I never could have done it. And I'm glad that I survived the *Titanic*. I am! It's just that . . . the ironies are sometimes difficult to think about."

He nodded, then pressed her head to his chest, holding her impossibly tight. "Please talk to me," she said again.

"I loved a woman once," he said in a husky voice. "Her name was Edith. We met at church when she moved here with her father and sister, and we knew each other for a couple of years before we fell in love. We talked about getting married. We became very attached to each other." He sighed deeply and held her tighter. She knew something awful was coming. "Her sister died of cancer. It was a slow and painful death, and very difficult to observe. But . . . after the death . . . Edith . . . never got over it. She became reclusive and depressed, and there was nothing that I could say or do to get through to her. She . . ." He took a sharp breath, and Ella tightened her arms around him in silent support. "She took her own life," he said, and Ella gasped but kept her face against his chest, sensing that he preferred to avoid having her see his face right then. "I'm the one who found her," he added, and she gasped again.

Jonathan let out a long, slow breath as if he felt some relief in having it out in the open. "I had trouble getting over it, but I was determined not to do what she had done . . . not to get depressed and cut myself off from the world. But still . . . it was close to my heart and a very heavy burden. When I made the decision to find work at sea, I had this instinctive feeling that . . . going away like that could somehow purge the pain from me." He finally drew back to look at her. "In a way, it did. I found you, and you have healed me in ways that I could never tell you, but . . . I cannot bear to lose you, Ella. It's one thing to lose someone to . . . an accident . . . or a tragedy . . . or illness. But when someone you love makes a choice like that . . ." He didn't seem to want to finish.

"I understand, Jonathan. I do. I'm not certain I've ever fully recovered from my father leaving us like that. Obviously my mother didn't. When there was no one to miss me, it was easier to think such thoughts, but you need to know that I would *never* do to you what my father did to me. Never! Do you understand?"

He nodded, and she saw his chin quiver slightly before he pressed her face to his chest again. Whether it was simply to hold her closer, or to prevent her from seeing his emotion, she didn't know. But she held tightly to him, more grateful than she'd ever been that they'd found each other. She found it strange that his confessions had soothed the very matter she'd been so emotional about at the beginning of the conversation. She had ample incentive to live, and to live a good life. And she would!

* * * * *

For a couple of days Ella felt drained of strength—emotionally and physically—and a little bit dazed and disoriented. She couldn't deny feeling better, now that she'd shared her burdens and she no longer had to fear the secrets she'd been keeping from Jonathan. But her mind seemed to have a need to assimilate the changes that had taken place inside her and between her and Jonathan. She couldn't help noticing that he seemed to be in a similar state of mind. He was more quiet than usual, and even when they had the opportunity to be alone together, neither of them had much to say. But she saw love and acceptance in his eyes, and she felt no need to fear that he might change his mind about his feelings for her.

At supper Jonathan leaned toward Ella and whispered in her ear, "After everyone goes to bed, will you meet me in the parlor?" She looked at him, surprised, wondering over the seeming formality of his request. He smiled and added in a quiet voice that only she could hear, "I'd take you for a walk, but it's raining."

"I'll be there," she said, and throughout the remainder of the evening she anticipated their time together. Because they hadn't shared much conversation since all of the drama had erupted between them, she hoped that they could just sit and visit and feel some normalcy between them.

When the house was finally quiet after everyone had gone off to their separate bedrooms to rest up for another busy day, Ella found Jonathan sitting in the center of the sofa, his legs stretched out in front of him and crossed at the ankles, his arms spread out over the back so that when she sat down it was easy for him to wrap one of them around her shoulders.

"I think you look especially beautiful today," he said and pressed a kiss to her temple.

"You're very sweet," she said, shivering slightly from the tingling sensation created by his lips touching her skin.

Ella took a sharp breath when Jonathan went abruptly to his knees and took hold of both of her hands. She didn't even have time to wonder if this was what it seemed before he blurted the words, "Marry me, Ella; marry me soon."

"What?"

"What do you mean . . . what?"

"I don't . . . understand."

"What's to understand?" He let out a nervous chuckle. "I love you. I want to spend my life with you. I'm asking you to marry me. What I have to offer is simple, but it comes from my heart, and I pledge to do everything in my power to care for you well, and to make you happy."

"But . . ." She found it difficult to actually form the question in her head into a comprehensible sentence.

"If it's your past you're concerned about," he said, and she was glad to not have to say it, "I know everything, and it hasn't changed how I feel about you, nor will it ever."

"How can you be sure?" she asked.

"Sure?" he echoed and shook his head. "Ella, I love you. Life may change, but the way I feel about you won't. Sooner or later you're going to have to learn to trust again, Ella. I'm asking you to trust *me*. Trust me when I tell you that I consider it a privilege to do whatever it takes to help you through this life. If it takes a lifetime to recover from what happened to you when the *Titanic* went down, so be it. If you *never* recover, I can live with that, too. And the same goes for whatever happened to you *before* you sailed for America." He tightened his grip on her hands and eased closer. "Ella, let me be there in the night to hold you when you have nightmares. Let me be there beside you whenever you're frightened or plagued with the memories. I'll be there for you, Ella; I swear it!"

Ella couldn't think of a single reason to decline such an offer. Or rather, every reason she could think of had already been countered, as if he'd predicted her every possible protest. He was right: he *did* know everything, and he still loved her and was willing to stand by her. He was willing to provide for her and see her through this life. How could she ever ask for more than that? In truth, the life he offered her was far more than she'd ever expected or hoped for when she'd found herself destitute and on the streets. She loved Jonathan, and she loved his family. She loved helping in the bistro and being a part of such a simple and beautiful way of life. She felt suddenly more happy than she'd imagined possible. Even in her secluded and ignorant youth, she couldn't recall ever being this happy. She laughed and threw her arms around his neck, landing on her knees, facing him.

"Does that mean yes?" he asked, taking her shoulders in his hands. He forced her to look at him, as if he needed to know immediately what her eyes might tell him.

"Yes," she said. "Yes, it means yes."

Jonathan let out a joyful laugh and held her close. She'd never been so happy! And amazingly, she knew that Jonathan felt the same. It was a miracle!

* * * * *

Jonathan and Ella were married in the lovely little chapel where they had been attending church with his family every Sunday since she'd come to New York City. She wore white and felt beautiful—especially with the way that Jonathan looked at her. The church was filled with the aroma of the flowers that hung at the end of each pew and over the windows. It was also filled with the kind faces and beaming love of family, friends, neighbors, and churchgoers who had come to wish them well. But Ella knew that these people—with the exception perhaps of Jonathan's parents—could have no idea of the enormity of the miracle taking place that day. Never in her wildest dreams, while she'd been wallowing in the dirty streets of London, could she have imagined such a day as this. She was not naive enough to believe that being Mrs. Jonathan Moreau would magically erase the lingering heartache inside of her. But having him by her side—and knowing that their being together was permanent—would surely make facing her challenges easier, and she knew that he would always love her, no matter what.

Following the wedding, a glorious celebration was held at the bistro. There was food and drink that magnificently matched the abundance of the dancing and laughter. Ella had never been the center of attention as she was that day in being the bride, the newest member of the Moreau family, but given the reason for the festivities, she enjoyed every minute.

Ella's only thoughts of sadness came in a moment of missing her parents and wishing that they might have been present, and even more than that, she missed Irene. But if what Irene had taught her about angels was true, then perhaps they were all present in spirit. Mrs. Olsen and Bertha were there, and had a wonderful time. Mrs. Olsen was always a reminder of the dreadful events on that ill-fated April night, but Ella chose not to think about that. Not today. Today was the best day of her life.

Jonathan took her on a beautiful honeymoon—all the way to New York City. He told her more than once, "Why waste time and money traveling when there's so much to see and do right here in the city; things we've never seen or done before?" She had to agree with him, and quickly found that it was easy to hide from friends and family in a city so huge. They had a lovely hotel room that was comfortable without being lavish, and it was within walking distance of many forms of entertainment and good food. But they rarely left the room and simply enjoyed their honeymoon for its intended purpose, to get to know each other as husband and wife in ways they never had before, and to become comfortable with this new season of life that they were embarking on together.

When they returned home to the Moreau house above the bistro, every member of the family was as excited to see them as if they'd been gone for months. Little changed except that Jonathan moved his things across the hall to share a room with Ella. In time they would be able to afford their own home. For now, before children came, they would save their money and enjoy the opportunity to be surrounded by family. Eventually they would likely be glad for some distance, but in the meantime they would make the most of the little room they were able to share where they were perfectly comfortable together. And Ella was continually amazed at what a wonderful man she'd been blessed to find. His kind nature and tender attitude proved themselves more true every day. He was every bit as decent and gentlemanly a husband as he had been a suitor.

Winter came and went, and a new year began while Ella couldn't help thinking about where she had been a year earlier, and what she had been doing. She was grateful for Jonathan's patience in allowing her to talk through her memories over and over while she attempted to come to terms with all she had gained—and all she had lost. They both found the dilemma ironic as they considered more deeply than ever before that they would not be sharing the life they had found together if the *Titanic* had not met with disaster and taken more than fifteen hundred lives with her.

Ella still occasionally struggled with nightmares, or sometimes she just had an especially difficult day. But Jonathan was patient and compassionate, and he'd been just close enough to the *Titanic* experience to have some empathy.

With the hint of spring in the air, it was impossible to not consider how, last year at this time, Irene had been getting ready to return home, and Ella had been working for the Blackhursts, who were planning a holiday to America. Irene and Ella—and everyone else involved—had been utterly oblivious to the fact that death was on the horizon, and those who had survived in body would be forever scarred in spirit.

Ella often wondered if she would *ever* be able to be completely at peace over the tragedy. Would she ever be able to think about it without feeling sick—or starting to shake? Would she ever be able to sleep at night without some trepidation in wondering if the experience would invade her sleep? She felt certain that if Irene had survived, she would have had the answers for finding such peace. She'd just been the kind of woman that seemed to have the answers—especially to the most important aspects of life. Like every thought that Ella entertained for more than a moment, she discussed it with Jonathan, sharing with him some of the spiritual beliefs that Irene had shared with her. He was intrigued with the things that Ella had learned from Irene, which led them into discussing the principles of Christianity in ways that neither of them had ever considered before. They talked about life after death and the ironies of living in a world that was filled with evil and disaster. They both agreed that their conversations seemed to provoke more questions than answers, but they also agreed that they enjoyed their stimulating conversations, and it was one of the highlights of the life they shared.

On the anniversary of the day that the *Titanic* left port in Southampton, Ella felt especially emotional and was relieved when Jonathan suggested she get some rest. He brought her a breakfast tray and assured her that they would manage in the bistro without her. She spent the morning shedding a ridiculous amount of tears and wondering once again if she would ever be able to make peace over the devastation and horror she had witnessed that April night.

Ella heard Jonathan coming and hurried to wipe away her tears and appear composed, but he entered the room and immediately said, "You want to talk about it?"

"It's . . . complicated," she said and moved to the window, but she didn't bother to open the curtain and therefore couldn't see anything but a close-up view of the tiny flowers printed on the fabric.

"I think we've established that we can deal with *complicated*," he said and crossed the room to put his hands on her shoulders. "Talk to me, Ella. Tell me why you've been crying."

Ella attempted to find the most obvious point of her thoughts. "I just . . . can't stop thinking about Irene. And I can't think about Irene without thinking of the hundreds like her who lost their lives that night." She sniffled and let out a humorous chuckle. "I don't know how you're not sick to death of me talking about it. Or maybe you are and you're just too polite to say so."

"I think it's far better for you to talk about it than it would be for you to hold it inside. What you witnessed was the kind of thing that changes people's lives. If you need to talk about it every day for the rest of your life, I'm willing to listen. I don't have any answers, Ella, but I'll surely listen." Ella said nothing, and he added, "Now what is it that you're thinking about Irene?"

"I keep thinking about her family . . . her children, her parents, her husband. How are they managing without her? What is their grief like? Forgive me for sharing such thoughts, but . . . you know there was a time when I wished that I had died instead of her. No one would have missed me; no one would have noticed. She had so much to live for." She turned to look at him. "Now . . . I'm starting to really believe that I can have a good life . . . be happy . . . make others happy . . . do good things."

He smiled and lightly touched her hair. "I'm glad to hear it."

"But . . . given the way I've been feeling all this time, now I feel . . . confused. I want to believe that I can make you happy, Jonathan, and that we can make a good life together. But if I had died that night, you never would have known the difference. And Irene's family is . . ." She bit her lip and looked down.

"Come sit down," he said and took her hand, urging her to sit on the edge of the bed beside him. "I know that your original plan in coming to America was to eventually go to Utah, where Irene lived. Going to Utah for a visit isn't a practical option for us right now, although it might be someday. However, there's no reason you can't write a letter to her family. Perhaps contacting her parents would be best, from what you've told me. I'm certain they would love to hear from you."

"What would I say?" Ella asked, not certain they *would* love to hear from her. She wasn't sure *why* she felt that way; she just did.

"Tell them that you became friends with Irene in London. Tell them how much you admired her, and what a fine example she was to you. Tell them how brave and strong she was. Whether or not you ever hear back from them, I believe writing such a letter would be very good for *you*."

"Perhaps it would," Ella said thoughtfully.

"And perhaps they might be able to answer some questions for you."

"Questions?"

"About Irene's religious beliefs. Perhaps they can shed some light on some of the things we've discussed. I know that you've wished you knew more . . . that you understood what it was about her that made her so strong. Perhaps her parents can tell you."

"Perhaps they can," she said, feeling some enthusiasm settle into her as the idea took hold.

Over the next few days, Ella spent most of her spare time working on a letter to Irene's parents. She wasn't certain if it was helping her not think about those oblivious days on the *Titanic* prior to the tragedy, or if it made her think of them more, but she did feel that writing the letter was a good exercise for her in coming to terms with the loss of her dear friend. She wondered more than once why she'd never thought to write such a letter before, but perhaps it just hadn't been the right time—for her *or* Irene's parents.

Ironically, she posted the letter on April 15. The papers were spread with fresh observations about the *Titanic* disaster, given that it had been exactly a year. Inquiries had taken place; fingers of blame were being pointed in many directions but couldn't seem to come to rest in any one place. Ella didn't care whose fault it was; she felt sure that it was simply the result of several factors that came together all wrong. And given the things that Irene had taught her, she had to believe that, for all its horror, it had somehow been a part of God's plan.

Ella sent the letter to Bishop and Mrs. Colvin in Provo, Utah. The day after she mailed it, she began to imagine how Irene's parents might respond upon its receipt. Would they be pleased to hear from a friend of Irene's? Or would it only be a painful reminder of their daughter's absence? She tried not to think about it, knowing it would be weeks before she might get a reply—if she ever got one at all. After a few days it became easier not to think about it, but a day never passed without remembering Irene and the things that she had learned from this remarkable woman.

Ella woke up one morning with a strangely familiar sensation. For a minute it brought back memories so horrible that the sickness smoldering inside of her was heightened, but she breathed deeply and reminded herself that she was living a good life and nothing was the same now as it had been then. She reached to the other side of the bed and found Jonathan's arm, which she stroked gently, making it easier to hold to the present. He sighed and rolled over, easing her into his arms, completely eradicating the ugliness of her life in London. The sensation inside of her heightened unexpectedly and she hurried out of the room and down the stairs to the bathroom, glad it wasn't occupied. While she was throwing up, it occurred to her that she would have to be better prepared in the future. The trek to the bathroom was just too far! She rinsed out her mouth with mouthwash and dampened her face with cool water, then was startled to hear a light knock at the door. She pulled it open to see her husband looking bleary-eyed and concerned.

"Are you all right?" he asked.

"I'm fine," she said and took his hand, leading him back to their room.

Ella closed the door but immediately knew from the expression on her husband's face, made visible by the faint light of dawn in the room, that Jonathan was not convinced by her answer. She sighed and figured he might as well know, although she might have hoped for a more romantically atmospheric moment to share such news. She was glad to note that she could smile as she formulated the words, and she considered that to be a great triumph.

"I think I'm pregnant," she said. "In fact, I'm relatively certain."

He gasped, then laughed softly, then sat on the edge of the bed. "How can you know for sure?" he asked.

"I've been pregnant before, Jonathan. I know." She took his hand and sat beside him, loving the way she could say such a thing to him and not feel the least bit judged or uncomfortable.

"A baby!" he said, as if the words were magical and they'd filled the air around them with fairy dust.

"Let's not tell anyone else yet," she said. "It can be our secret—at least for a little while."

"What a delightful secret!" he said and pressed a kiss into her hair.

"Although," she added with chagrin, "if you're going to sleep in the same room, you'll have to endure my throwing up every morning, and if it's like last time, I'm not sure I can make it all the way to the bathroom."

"I shall take very good care of you," he said. "Both of you."

"Oh, I'm not worried about that," she said and settled her head on his shoulder.

Later that day, soon after lunch, Ella felt so sleepy that she was glad to be able to go upstairs and rest for a while. She felt doubtful that they would be able to keep their secret for long when her symptoms would surely give her away. She drifted off quickly then woke up to see Jonathan sitting on the bed beside her, leaning against the headboard, a dreamy expression on his face.

"What are you thinking about?" she asked, alerting him that she was awake.

"Did you get some rest?" he asked.

"I did, thank you."

"How are you feeling?"

"As long as I don't let my stomach get empty, I'm fine." She yawned. "I'm tired."

"Well, I have something that might perk you up."

"Really?" she said and sat up.

He reached down to the floor beside the bed and lifted up a small package. "Ta-dah!"

Ella gasped and took it from him, noting the return address was Provo, Utah. She started to tear away the brown paper, then stopped and looked at her husband. "I'm a little scared."

"Why?"

"Whatever this might be . . . it will surely bring back memories of Irene, and . . ." She got choked up, and Jonathan put his arm around her.

"So, have a good cry if you need to. Open it. I can't stand the suspense."

Ella did so and gasped again to see a familiar book appear in her hands. "Oh, my goodness!" she said as memories flooded over her, and with them came a warm peace that boldly enhanced the memories. It was as if the spirit that had radiated from Irene was somehow radiating from this book.

"What is it?" Jonathan asked.

"This is a copy of Irene's favorite book. It's some kind of scripture. She read to me from it, and told me stories. She gave me a copy, but I never had time to read much, and now it's at the bottom of the ocean." She laughed softly and held it to her heart. "Oh, it's a miracle!" she muttered, closing her eyes as if that might help her feel closer to Irene, and somehow it did. Warm and comforting tears slid down her cheeks, as if to tell her that Irene was close, and that this book had been a gift from her. She could almost imagine Irene telling her, from somewhere inside her own mind, that this book would be the key to everything she could ever need or want in her life. From it she would find the peace she was looking for, a peace that surpassed understanding, a peace that was capable of healing every heartache and assuaging all suffering— whether it was disaster at sea or the personal pain of the human heart.

Ella held tightly to the book until the feeling gently subsided, leaving behind an imprint on her spirit that she instinctively believed was eternal. Jonathan asked to look at the book, and while he thumbed through it with great interest, Ella took a deep breath and opened the letter that had been enclosed with it.

The majority of the letter was from Irene's mother, although her father had also written a couple of paragraphs. Ella wept with mixed emotions as she read words of gratitude for the letter Ella had written to them, for it had been a great boon to them in their grief, and had reminded them of what an amazing daughter they had, and that her life had not been given in vain. Ella read about Irene's three children and how they were doing, and there was news of other family members that Ella had heard Irene talk about. Each of Irene's parents expressed their personal and abiding gratitude for the atoning power of Jesus Christ, and how it was through this—and only this—that they had found the strength to endure such a great loss in their lives. They both wished Ella well and expressed gratitude on Irene's behalf, and she was surprised that they both wrote of how Irene had mentioned Ella in her letters home while she'd been living in England. Irene's mother asked that Ella keep in touch, and she offered the book as a gift that she felt sure Irene would have wanted her to have. *May you find the peace you are seeking from within its pages,* she wrote.

Ella felt a fresh sensation of warmth that let her know beyond any doubt that what Irene's mother had said was true. She was more glad in that moment than she ever had been that she had survived the streets of London and that she had survived the *Titanic.* She was determined to take the gift of life she'd been given and do with it what Irene would have wanted her to. She would find a way to make a difference in this world: as a wife and mother, and as a woman. *She would!*

EPILOGUE

ELLA GAVE BIRTH TO A healthy baby girl on a winter morning with beautiful snow coming down outside the windows. She felt Irene close to her in a way that she hadn't since the day she'd received that precious book in the mail. She couldn't help but think a great deal about the last time she'd given birth, when her life had been a bundle of tragedy and despair. But in her darkest hour, Irene had been there, like an angel sent from heaven even while she'd been alive and well. Now Ella fully believed in angels—both mortal and immortal—and Irene had been both to her. If not for Irene, Ella would likely have died on the streets of London, or perhaps on the *Titanic*. Now Ella had a life before her; a *real* life, a *full* life—with joy and peace at the heart of it in ways that Ella had never imagined possible.

It was Jonathan's idea to name the baby Irene Lisette, but Ella felt warmed by the suggestion, since it was exactly what she had been thinking. Being named after two such amazing women, their daughter would surely grow up to be great.

As soon as Ella and the baby were up to going out, Jonathan took his new little family to church, and everyone there was thrilled to see them. About six months earlier they'd begun attending this branch of the same church that Irene had belonged to in Utah. Some of Jonathan's family had not been pleased with their choice to change family traditions in regard to religion, but it hadn't taken long for them to see that Jonathan and Ella were very happy, and their religious choices were not marring their family relationships in any way. Since Jonathan and Ella had moved into their own home a couple of months before the baby was born, their attending a different church had been less of an issue. They still ate together as a family on Sundays, and they still all worked together at the bistro and helped watch out for each other the way that families should.

On a pleasant April afternoon, two years beyond the *Titanic*, Jonathan and Ella took a pleasant stroll with little Irene sleeping contentedly in the red baby buggy that Jonathan's parents had given their new granddaughter when she'd arrived. They talked about the events that had changed the way that mankind viewed their abilities in light of the power of ocean and ice. They reminisced casually, as if it had not shaken the world and left them both reeling emotionally for unmeasured weeks and months afterward. Its mark would forever be branded in their spirits, but they readily acknowledged that they were the lucky ones. They had walked away with each other, and they prayed every day for the survivors and rescuers who had walked away with nothing but a reason to have nightmares for the rest of their lives. It was that day they made a mutual agreement to pray for these people every day for the rest of their own lives. And they prayed for the families and loved ones of those who had perished. Those who had died suffered greatly that night, but their suffering was brief. Those who remained behind had heavy burdens to bear, and they prayed that those burdens might be lightened.

In an effort to lighten the burden of the only person affected by it that they actually knew, Jonathan and Ella went to visit Mrs. Olsen, who made such a delighted fuss over little Irene. Bertha too was smitten with the baby, and they had a wonderful visit. They couldn't get together without the subject of the *Titanic* coming up, and they all knew it would probably always be that way. But they were able to talk about it with reverence and gratitude, and move on in a spirit of making the most of the lives they had left to live.

That very night Ella woke abruptly from a dream, gasping and clutching at her chest, where her heart was pounding. While she was trying to catch her breath, the memory of the dream flashed through her mind in vivid detail. And just a moment later the meaning of it settled into her mind with perfect clarity, letting her know that this was no ordinary dream, and she'd been meant to learn from its message. Whether what she saw was the representation of something that had been literal, or whether it was simply symbolic in a way that she could understand, she knew that it was a gift, given to her as an offering of peace and understanding.

Ella felt Jonathan's hand on her shoulder just before he whispered, "Are you all right?"

"I think so," she said and sat up, leaning back against the headboard in an attempt to breathe more easily. "I'm sorry I woke you."

"I'm not," he said, sitting up as well. "A nightmare?"

"No, actually. It was . . . a dream. A beautiful dream." Her voice broke. "Beautiful, but . . . tragic. Like . . . a story with a sad ending, but . . . at least the ending has . . . meaning."

Jonathan reached over to turn on the lamp on the bedside table before he sat up to face her directly, taking her hand. "Do you want to tell me about it?"

"I do," she said. "Just . . . give me a minute."

He nodded, and she closed her eyes, breathing the vision into herself more deeply. "It was rather simple, actually," she said, keeping her eyes closed. "I saw myself getting into the lifeboat, and the boat being lowered into the water, but . . . it was as if I could see myself through Irene's eyes. Then . . . it came in quick flashes, but . . . it was as if I could see what she saw after that . . . and feel what she felt."

"How very horrible!" Jonathan muttered, unable to imagine how it must have been for those stranded on the *Titanic* at the very end.

"It *was* horrible," Ella said with surprising composure. "But it wasn't. She was . . . calm, at peace, too busy to be afraid while thinking about how she might help those around her. There was . . . a moment of fear, but then . . . she was too busy. It was as if . . . she had taken everything she'd learned about bringing lives into this world as a midwife . . . and she was applying it in doing everything she could to help usher lives out of this world . . . as calmly and painlessly as possible."

Jonathan felt tears gather in his eyes, then fall, but Ella kept her eyes closed and didn't notice. He just let his tears fall rather than wipe them away and bring attention to them. He felt completely overcome with what she was saying, and with the serenity in her expression that seemed oddly out of place. He just held her hand and listened.

"Many people were panicked and afraid, but others were calm . . . as if they quickly made peace with facing the end once they had known it was inevitable. Irene was reassuring and kind to many, and . . ."

Jonathan saw Ella's brow furrow as if she were trying to understand something from her dream. Her eyes came open abruptly in response to an idea that lit up her face with enlightenment, but her eyes showed deep poignancy. She turned to look at him and caught him crying. His tears distracted her from her thoughts, and she put a hand to his face. "Are you all right?" she asked.

"I'm fine," he said. "Tell me the rest."

"Ether," she said.

"What about it?" he asked.

"They used it when I had the baby . . . at the end . . . so that I would sleep through the worst of the pain."

"Yes, I remember," he said.

"But . . . they used it before . . . Irene used it . . . when I gave birth . . . in London." Her brow furrowed again, and her eyes took on a distant expression, as if she could see something in her mind that was far away and long ago. "Would she have had ether with her?"

"I don't know," he said, "but it's possible. Why?"

Tears finally crested in Ella's eyes and fell. She looked again at Jonathan. "She was helping the children, Jonathan. She was helping them sleep so they wouldn't be afraid . . . so they wouldn't suffer."

"Merciful heaven!" he muttered breathlessly, immediately struck with a harsh horror and an unfathomable comfort at precisely the same moment, in exactly equal proportions.

"Do you think that what I dreamt could be true?" Ella asked, as if he should know the answer.

"I don't know," he said. "How could we possibly know for certain? But . . . if this dream has given you some added peace . . . if it's helped answer your questions, then . . . it is surely a gift."

"It *is* a gift," Ella said. "I *do* feel more peace." She wrapped her arms around him. "She was amazing to the last, Jonathan. She made a tremendous difference, the way she always wanted to." She drew back to look at him. "It was her time to go. Her death had meaning. I don't know exactly why or how, but she was where she needed to be. I can't explain it; I just know it's true."

"That's good enough for me," Jonathan said. "She made a difference in *your* life, and she made certain you got on that lifeboat. I will forever be grateful to her for that."

"She was a remarkable woman," Ella said, resting her head on his shoulder. "She *is* a remarkable woman. I know in my heart that she lives on, and that she's still making a difference. And I was privileged enough to know her . . . to be a beneficiary of her grace and generosity."

She wrapped her arms tightly around him and sighed from deep down, as if she had just been relieved of a great burden. "Everything's going to be all right, Jonathan. It's hard to explain, but . . . I believe we have everything we need to make the best possible life for ourselves—now and in the world to come." She sighed again. "Everything's going to be all right."

"Yes," he said, pressing a hand gently over the back of her head, "I believe it will be."

ABOUT THE AUTHOR

Anita Stansfield began writing at the age of sixteen, and her first novel was published sixteen years later. Her novels range from historical to contemporary and cover a wide gamut of social and emotional issues that explore the human experience through memorable characters and unpredictable plots. She has received many awards, including a special award for pioneering new ground in LDS fiction, and the Lifetime Achievement Award from the Whitney Academy for LDS Literature. Anita is the mother of five and has two adorable grandsons. Her husband, Vince, is her greatest hero.

To receive regular updates from Anita, go to anitastansfield.com and subscribe.